CREEK SONGS

Other Books

All Ways A Woman

a celebration of women
their thoughts, their loves, their lives
their dreams and desires

A Collaboration:
Words by Carol Mann
Watercolors by Lynn Centeno

CREEK SONGS

Collected Short Stories

CAROL MANN

Carol Mann

The characters, incidents and dialogue in this collection of short stories are fictional, drawn from the author's imagination. Readers familiar with the various locales will recognize that the author has taken liberties. This was done intentionally to provide a backdrop of authenticity.

Mann, Carol
Creek Songs

1st edition

Library of Congress Control Number: 2021914060

ISBN 978-1-7324567-8-5 (paperback)

Published by
AquaZebra™
Book Publishing
Cathedral City, California
www.aquazebra.com

Editor
Lynn Jones Green

Cover/interior design
Mark E. Anderson
AquaZebra™
Web, Book & Print Design
www.aquazebra.com

Printed in the United States of America

For my dear Tony

CONTENTS

"If it weren't for the rocks in its bed,
the stream would have no song."

—Carl Perkins
American singer-songwriter

ACKNOWLEDGMENTS

The following stories have appeared previously in literary journals, anthologies, and magazines, or have earned contest recognition:

- "The First of the Season" (under the title "First Snow") in *RiverSedge*
- "Helios" in *Atlantic/Pacific Press*
- An excerpt from "The Rule of L. Pennington Chalmers" (under the title "A Little French Pastry") in *Dual Coast Magazine*
- "Not Even Gloria" in *The Sun Runner Magazine*
- "Funny Man" in *The Sun Runner Magazine*
- "The Waiting Room" (under the title "Baggage") in the anthology *The Road Taken*
- "Mrs. Kaminsky's Note" (under the title "The Long-Playing Record") in *The RavensPerch*
- "Walking with Harvey" (under the title "Parallel Worlds") in *Cantaraville*
- "Creek Songs" in *Bloodroot Literary Magazine*

"Hannon's Folly" and "Bingo and the Gown" earned contest recognition with the Palm Springs Writers Guild; "The Phone Call" (under "Shaken for a Moment") earned contest recognition with the National League of American Pen Women.

The personal essay "Exploring the Inner Canyons" appeared in the anthology *Coachella Calling* and in the essay magazine *Six Hens.* The personal essay "The Modeling Period" received contest recognition in the Palm Springs Writers Guild Memoir Contest.

I thank these stalwart writers in my critique group for their comments and suggestions: Danielle Cook, Larry Lauritzen, B. Channing Hillway, Linda Carlson and Toni Hafey.

Three organizations in which I have longstanding memberships (the Palm Springs Writers Guild, the National League of American Pen Women-Palm Springs Branch, and the Literary Society of the Desert) have been the source of many opportunities and much learning.

I appreciate and thank writing teacher Cindy Muscatel, editor Lynn Jones Green, publisher AquaZebra Book Publishing, book designer Mark E. Anderson at AquaZebra Web, Book and Print Design, photographer Mitchell Kmetz at Unsplash for the cover photo and photographer Kathy Rappaport for the author photo.

Thank you to Kim Kressaty for sharing an idea from sociologist Morris Massey, to author Lynne Spreen who introduced me to the world of blogging that kept me writing, and to Briana Zamora who gave me the gift of time.

I am grateful.

—Carol Mann

Summer of 2021

AUTHOR'S NOTE

In February of 2012, I attended a "Meet the Author" champagne reception for novelist Gail Tsukiyama held in Palm Desert, California, and hosted by Friends of the College of the Desert Library. I looked forward to the event, having read two of her previous novels, *The Samurai's Garden* and *Women of the Silk*.

Meeting Ms. Tsukiyama one on one was a delight. During a very pleasant exchange about her work, she graciously asked about me. I shared that I liked to write.

At the end of the evening, she signed her then most recent novel, *The Street of a Thousand Blossoms*. On the title page of my copy she inscribed a single sentence: "May my words inspire your words."

The inscription remains in my mind after the passage of years. Always, it recalls Ms. Tsukiyama's generosity and encouragement. And I thank her.

And now, as you read this collection, I hope my words about ordinary people sorting through their lives, buffeted by their wants, needs, and the whimsies of fate, give you pleasure and linger in your thoughts—as Ms. Tsukiyama's linger in mine.

—Carol Mann

La Quinta 2021

I

Despite the Cold Around Him

"The laden freight train rattling along the rails reminded him of his life, except he hauled a cargo of memories. Boxes of them. None of his containers was empty either, only life itself."

—David "Sims" Simpson, Jr.
"Behind the Triple K"

The First of the Season

Tommy Banks crouched behind the gnarled trunk of an apple tree, one hand under the barrel of his M1 rifle, the other hand on the trigger. He hid in an old orchard, waiting for a signal to move out. Leafless branches overhead seemed to reach into the sky like distorted fingers, adding to the eeriness around him. He pulled up the collar on his field jacket, pressed it close to his neck, then resecured the M1.

A cloak of gray had stolen over the countryside, bringing with it a stark drop in the late afternoon temperature. The weather worried him. Reconnaissance was hazardous enough in good conditions, worse in bad. Thoughts of what lay ahead made his palms sweat inside his army-issued wool gloves, despite the cold. Shifting his weight, he hunched forward, his shoulder against the tree trunk.

"See anything?" His raspy voice cut into the stillness.

A few yards in front of him, patrol partner Billy Lewis shook his head. He knelt on one knee behind a stacked stone fence, looking out across a barren farm field that lay between them and a small French village. He pointed at a gate in the fence. It stood open, dangling from rusted hinges.

"Go, go," came Billy's hoarse whisper.

Tommy dashed to the stone fence, sidestepped the gate, and

zigzagged across the fallow field toward a dirt lane with cottages and scattered outbuildings on either side of it. Once safely in the narrow roadway, he stayed near the corner of the first house, breathing hard, pressing his side into the rough fieldstone construction. Alert for German soldiers or snipers or any sudden movement, he listened. He looked. Nothing.

In the sinister silence, he signaled to Billy, who snaked his way across the field toward him. Tommy pushed his helmet up on his forehead, glancing again to the left, to the right. Nothing stirred in the waning daylight.

Billy ran up beside him, breathing hard while muttering about the cold. With his gloved hand, Billy pulled his pack up on his back, next checking a walkie-talkie strapped on his shoulder. His eyes scanned the lane, the field, the cottages. A muffler covered the lower part of his face like a mask.

The lieutenant's orders rang in Tommy's ears: "Reconnoiter the village. Maintain radio silence unless you observe enemy activity. Do not engage." He knew his platoon's mission: Secure the village in a push to the German border. Their company would follow.

Tommy whispered, "I'll check the cottage."

Billy stayed in position by the corner of the house as Tommy crept low beneath a mud-stained window toward a wooden door. He tried the iron latch. It wouldn't open. He waited. Hearing nothing, he jimmied the latch with his knife. Rifle set, his heart pounding, he nodded at Billy, pushed the door open and entered the cottage.

Tommy heard no sounds except his own breathing. He stood in a kitchen near the window he'd sneaked past. Nothing stirred. Slowly, he stole into the space, passing a metal sink, a cupboard and an iron cook stove. A scarred wooden table with mismatched chairs sat in the middle of the room. He crossed past them to a doorway that opened into a bedroom; in it, an iron bed with a sagging mattress and a small chest, its drawers open but empty.

Tommy returned to the kitchen, continuing under an arched doorway into what appeared to be a sitting room with two worn, overstuffed chairs on each side of a fireplace. He slipped in beside a solitary front window to peer through one of the soiled panes. Outside lay another untended field. It stretched down to a rail fence. Beyond the fence, a paved road. Beyond that, a thick wood. He checked an exterior door. It was latched.

With no inhabitants to be found, Tommy returned to the kitchen. From the doorway, he signaled Billy, who stole along the cottage wall, slipped in and latched the door.

"I'll take the kitchen," Tommy murmured. He pointed at the arched doorway. "There's a sitting room with a window in there." Billy nodded, disappearing beneath the arch.

Tommy looked from his vantage point out onto the lane. Seeing nothing unusual, he slipped off his pack, placing it on the table. It felt good to be rid of the weight. His M1 again in hand, he peeked out, becoming aware of a faint smell he knew well—onions. In his mind, he could see his mother at work, cutting large slices of her homegrown sweet onions and dropping them into a pot of venison stew simmering on the stove. The aroma would drift through the house out into the yard. When he came in from doing his chores, she'd hold out a wooden spoonful, inviting him to taste it.

He missed his people, his life before the infantry. But he knew memory lane was a road not to go down; not here, not now. He made himself concentrate. After another glance outside, he cracked open the back door. A whoosh of cold air hit him in the face. Images of home vanished, replaced by reality. He gave a low whistle to Billy who joined him.

"What's up?"

"I want to take a look outside," Tommy replied, removing his helmet. "Check the lane, the field, the paved road in front." He drew the hood of his field jacket over his head, putting his helmet back on.

With Billy stationed by the door, Tommy stepped into the lane and sidled to the corner of the cottage. Under a cloud-shrouded moon, he stared out into an early evening of unfamiliar, distorted shadows. He swallowed hard.

Slate gray clouds hung low on the nearby mountains as the first snow of winter slipped from the sky, casting white dust onto the countryside. Tommy stood motionless in the solemn, church-like stillness, feeling the calm, gentle peace of it all. But after a moment, he bit his lip. Bad weather was just that—bad. It hindered air support, made troops vulnerable and equipment hard to maneuver.

"Snow. Just what we don't need," Billy mumbled. "Come on back."

Tommy returned to the doorway. "Hope the road stays clear."

"Let's hope it'll be our guys usin' it." Billy spat in the snow-dusted dirt.

Their breaths hung in a hazy cloud of mist. Tommy glanced down the lane in the other direction at more cottages, each with chimneys standing like out-of-work sentinels, windows dark. Gone were any signs of vehicles or horse-drawn carts.

"Lane's clear," he said.

They slipped back inside. Allied and German troops fighting

nearby had driven villagers into the mountains or into hiding—or so it seemed. Tommy hoped if anyone remained, they were friends or members of the Resistance—not Vichy sympathizers, not German soldiers. A shiver slithered along his spine, making his lanky frame even more tense. So far, they'd seen no one.

"We better take turns grabbing some sleep." Tommy scratched his cheek. "We're gonna need it."

"I'm gonna eat some chow first," Billy said. "Nothin' like hot homemade stew in front of a blazin' fire." He made his way past the iron stove, through the archway, back into the sitting room.

With a nod to Billy's sarcasm, Tommy stayed in the kitchen. Moonlight filtered through clouds and snow into the cottage window, blending gray into black, light into shadow. He peeked out in time to see a large, long-eared dog—the size of his own hound, Lucky, back home—wander out from between two cottages across the lane. Short, patchy hair clung to its large but thin body. Tommy turned away, not wanting the dog to see him. Soon he heard sniffing at the door, followed by a soft whine. He stood still, fighting the impulse to bring the abandoned animal inside. Before long, the sniffing stopped.

Tommy waited for a short time before peering out again. The dog was gone. Picking up his backpack from the table, he returned to the front room. Billy sat on the arm of one of the chairs eating a K ration, his pack on the floor next to him, his rifle propped against it. Without speaking, Tommy settled on the arm of the other chair, parking his gear beside him. He took a meal of canned ham and eggs from his backpack. They ate for a while in silence until Tommy told Billy about the dog.

"You did what you had to." Billy shrugged. "He could've given us away."

"Yeah, but it didn't feel right to leave him out there." Tommy wiped his mouth with the back of his hand, growing quiet, putting any telltale signs of trash in his pack. Billy did the same. As if to change the mood, Tommy said, "I'll take the first watch."

"Okay," Billy answered as he took a ground sheet and blanket from his kit. Settling his sturdy body into the chair, he covered himself, leaned back, and crossed his legs. Soon he fell asleep, his snoring interrupted by his bouts of mumbling. Tommy roamed, weapon primed, checking through the windows for any signs of movement.

As the days became harder, he tried to avoid thoughts of home, but they wouldn't stay away. He kept seeing the same images. A warm fire, his girl nestled beside him. Tracking deer in the snow with Pops, with his brothers. His mother hanging up wash, the wind billowing through housedresses, overalls, long johns, denim shirts.

Come on, Tommy-Boy, he thought—"Tommy-Boy" being the nickname his big brother had given him. Tommy clenched his fists, forcing himself back to the moment. He listened for tanks, for aircraft. He stayed at the front window, watching for enemy activity. Anything. A glint of metal, a cigarette's glow, a careless flashlight.

The draft had hit hard in his rural West Virginia town. His father, watching the boys leave for training, had pounded his large fist into his callused palm, ranting about Hitler. Tommy hadn't known much about Nazis, Germany, or France. But he did now.

He hung his rifle sling on his shoulder, fumbling for the binoculars strung around his neck. He focused them into the cloudy night. Moonlight still peeked through gray clouds. Snow continued to fall. Turning his head like a slow-motion camera, he scanned the road and the periphery of the woods. A deer foraged along the edge of the trees. Near a fence post, a brown rabbit came to rest in the light snow. High in a roadside tree, an owl jerked its head, its large eyes alert for prey. The bird shook itself, motes of snow flying like dust from its plumage.

"Careful, Mr. Rabbit," Tommy whispered.

He lowered the binoculars, not sure if the platoon, followed by the rest of the company, would come through the apple orchard or along the road or up from the woods. It would depend on what they encountered. He also wasn't sure from where the enemy might come—if they came.

After another scan, Tommy let his binoculars rest against his chest. Fatigue drew at his eyes, his cheeks, the corners of his mouth, aging his young face. His tall, slender body yearned to rest on a soft bed. But he knew, bed or no bed, he wouldn't be able to sleep. Too much adrenalin.

To pass the time, he hummed mountain songs in his head, songs his grandmother had taught him. He kept checking at the windows in the two rooms, until he stood in the sitting room, his watch over.

Billy slept. His breathing rumbled softly. Before waking him, Tommy looked out with his binoculars once more. The same dog he'd seen earlier by the kitchen roamed like an out-of-control compass along the fence down by the road, then back among the cottages. No other signs of movement.

He shook his buddy by the shoulder. "Your turn."

Billy jerked awake. Disengaging himself from his covers, he heaved himself up from the chair, grabbed his gun and moved to the window. "Sweet dreams," he said, over his shoulder. "Everything's warmed up for you."

Tommy dropped into the same chair, leaning his rifle against its arm. He covered himself and, although he didn't think he would, fell asleep. It seemed like only moments before he felt Billy shake him, but hours had passed.

Tommy pulled himself onto his feet. He stretched, asking, "See anything?"

Billy shook his head. "No activity. Just snow. Gonna sit a minute before we start movin'." He sank into the chair.

Tommy liked the slivered hints of daylight beginning to slide into the room. A French newspaper on the table by the chair caught the light. He couldn't read the headline, but he understood the picture. A sober-faced officer in a Nazi uniform addressed an expressionless crowd.

Tommy stamped his feet to stir circulation, adjusted his gloves and worked his fingers. The fireplace, where a warm fire once burned, gaped at him with a cold stare. He picked up his M1, carrying it in his right hand. In the faint morning light, he peered through the window. Snow no longer fell.

"Hey, look at that," he murmured. He turned to Billy who'd fallen asleep. Tommy turned back. What once had been a light dusting of snow on dirt had become a thick virginal blanket of pure white.

He opened the door a crack, just enough to peer at the road and the woods beyond. He waited. His sharp eyes swept the stand of trees, their branches heavy with snow. Satisfied, he slipped outside into the transformed, untouched scene, leaving the door ajar.

A deep stillness layered with cool, clean air transported him to the foothills of his rural hometown. His thoughts made him smile. The snow reminded him of the thick white frosting on his eighteenth-birthday cake. Dropping onto one knee, he brushed the smooth snow with his free hand, the same gentle way he had caressed his grandmother's cheek for baking his favorite cake.

Like Midas savoring gold, Tommy scooped a handful of snow to his lips, felt the cold, gentle moisture. He closed his eyes, remembering Jenny's kiss, the night she slipped a silver ring on his little finger. "I'll be here, Tommy, waitin'." He'd hung the ring on his dog tags, by his heart.

He rose, savoring the beauty, the soundlessness of the snow-filled morning. Leaning toward the doorway, he rasped, "Hey, Billy, come take a look." He turned back to inhale the crisp air, walk a few steps in the untouched whiteness. A good steady snow, heavier than before, began to fall.

Billy snapped awake. Did Tommy just call him or was he dreaming? He glanced around the room for his friend. The door stood slightly open. Was something out there?

He hauled himself to his feet, rifle ready, and peered through the window. Tommy stood in the falling snow, holding his M1, his head tilted back, looking into the sky. Billy looked up, too, at nothing but snow. His eyes went to the woods, to the road. No activity, no troops. Nothing.

At the door, he cupped his hands around his mouth, his voice a gruff whisper. "Somethin' goin' on?"

"Snow," Tommy replied. "Just like back home."

"Yeah. Snow. Get your crazy ass in here."

Billy stepped back from the door. He folded his ground cloth and blanket back in his pack, feeling homesick, too. *Christ.* Tommy acted like he'd never seen snow. They had to continue reconnaissance and stay out of sight, not fool around. Billy returned to the window. He stared at the back of his buddy's head, murmuring, "Come on, Tommy, come back in here."

But Tommy slipped his rifle strap onto his shoulder and, bending down, filled both hands with snow. He tossed the clusters in the air, his arms thrust upward toward the sky.

Billy's face flushed. He looked right, then left, then straight ahead. What the hell was his buddy doing? All at once he saw it, a moving shape, coming through the falling snow, through the thick carpet of white toward Tommy. A villager? A German soldier?

Before Billy could yell a warning, Tommy must have seen it, too. He slammed his gun into position and aimed.

The sound of a shot exploded in the air, then another.

The shape coming through the whiteness leapt in the air, letting out a loud, high-pitched bark, followed by a muffled yip. The abandoned hound sprawled lifeless onto the snow at the same moment Tommy's knees crumpled, his body slumping forward, his blood darkening the whiteness like fine Cabernet. His hands slipped from his rifle; the scene once again quiet.

Billy froze, but only for a moment. He swallowed his panic as he jumped away from the window, scrambling backward, grabbing at his walkie-talkie. He wrenched up the antenna. "Rocky to Eddy Company, Rocky to Eddy Company! Man down! Enemy patrol, enemy patrol! Over!" He jammed his palm against the antenna, shoving it back into place.

Masked by shadow, feeling queasy and wishing he could help his buddy, Billy looked through his binoculars. Tommy hadn't moved, but a dark form at the edge of the woods had. A German soldier surveyed the clearing from the wood's edge with his binoculars. Raising his right hand, he pointed to the house as a nearby owl flew into the woods, a rabbit clutched in its talons.

Billy threw the backpack and radio onto his shoulders and ran into the kitchen. He skirted the wooden table, banging his hip against the iron cook stove. A grimace distorted his face as he headed to the back door, passing crocks, burlap sacks and field tools. His eyes were focused, a grenade on his belt. He whispered to himself, "You can make it. You can make it."

He dashed to a cottage across the lane, hopeful snow would soon cover his tracks. He rammed his shoulder against its front door and tumbled into a sitting room like the one he'd just left. Closing the door fast, he hustled through the house out into a dormant garden where withered cornstalks stood in the snow like weary villagers. Rushing by them to the neighboring cottage, he tried the door latch. It wouldn't open. He thrust his shoulder against the door. It wouldn't budge. A vise-like grip tightened in his belly. He had to find cover.

He cast a quick glance behind him and ran to the next structure. With every muscle he could muster, he thrust his shoulder against the back door—once, twice, three times—it flew open. He stumbled inside, closed the door, grabbed the radio.

"Rocky to Eddy Company. Rocky to Eddy Company. German patrol, German patrol. Over!"

A voice on the radio crackled: "Eddy Company to Rocky. Eddy Company to Rocky. Maintain. Maintain. Approaching your position, approaching your position."

Billy spotted a rope dangling from the ceiling. He pulled. A panel opened and a crude wooden stair dropped down. He scurried up, into a small attic. Binoculars in hand, he looked out through a dirt-spattered window, concentrating on the space between two cottages across the lane. Through it, he could see the shadowy form of a German scout, crouched low, crossing the road toward Tommy.

Sadness seeped into Billy like a trickling creek finding its way. He dropped onto one knee, wiping tears from his cheeks with his fist, knowing Tommy's memory would remain with him always. He bowed his head in sorrow for his best friend . . . lying in the snow . . . alone. The first of the season.

Behind the Triple K

A faded green tee shirt clung to his body, inkblots of sweat under his arms. Sims pulled the cloth away from his chest, flapping it to stir a breeze, making an image of tall pines with the words "Save the Trees" ripple in and out. Pine trees reminded him of snow, but not because he was playing some mind game, like "Think of a Cold Place and Cool Down." They made him think of freezing in Chicago and tramping through snow, trying to find a warm place to sleep. He'd left the Windy City behind, better to be hot and homeless in Palm Springs.

Sims picked up a dented soda can from the sand, flicked off a few ants, and tossed it in his "borrowed" shopping cart. Folks threw plenty of bottles and cans onto the busy roadside. Pickings had been good all day.

He leaned on his cart and yawned. He wished he could find peace at night, but sleep always brought the horror show. After forty years, he still saw men, women, children—burned and bloody—running through the village, their screams haunting him. He closed his eyes, breathed hard.

Shouts from the crowd at Chicago's Union Station when he and his buddies returned from Nam still echoed in his ears. "Losers! Baby killers!" Someone spat at them. Drops of saliva slid down his cheek onto the Silver Star hanging on his army uniform. He opened his eyes, rubbing the side of his face, trying to scour the memory away.

He stared out into the desert, pondering the early days of David Simpson, Jr., "Sims" for short. He was the best sprinter Chicago Tech High School had ever produced, star of the track team in '65 and '66. He'd married his high school sweetheart, Laurie Benson, right after graduation. He went to war. Afterwards, life had gone off the track.

A wisp of cloth interrupted his thoughts. It hung on the leafy branch of a nearby bougainvillea bush, white against the purplish-red flowers. He stepped closer. A small remnant of lace quivered in the afternoon air, sensuous, luring. On his first night home, Laurie had worn a filmy nightgown, its white lace caressing her breast. The lamp's soft glow made the moment feel gentle, quiet. He'd wept.

"Shhh," she'd murmured, holding him. "You're safe."

Wrapped in stolen moments of peace, he'd fallen asleep in her arms. But not for long. Images flashed in garish neon. Fouled rice paddies and burning huts, bullets kicking up geysers around him, Saigon's treacherous back alleys. He'd cried out. She'd helped him out of bed, poured him a shot of bourbon.

After his stint in the Military Police, he'd wanted to become a policeman in his hometown of Geneva, Illinois; to be a good husband and father, to buy a house. But he washed out of the city's police training. The psychological exam and polygraph test left some questions. Jobs came and went. He drank, heard the gossip, the slurs, felt the pity, and his anger grew. One day, he just walked away, leaving his wife and young son, Mattie. Three casualties not listed in the statistics.

He fingered the lace, its fragile beauty. *Laurie.*

Plop! A plastic water bottle landed beside him in the sand. He turned toward the street, felt the movement of air from passing cars and trucks on his face. Exhaust fumes made him cough. A driver waved from a UPS truck and Sims waved back, calling into the traffic, "Thanks, bro." Another five cents.

He wondered if humans, like bottles and cans, could be recycled. Someone should make a tee shirt and print "Save the People" on the front.

Sims stepped behind a Mexican bird of paradise to piss. He aimed the stream at an ant hill, watching the ants scurry, their lives messed up for a moment—not like his, messed up for a lifetime. Finished, he moved away from the bush, pulling the visor of his soiled baseball cap down over his forehead to shield him from the sun, from life.

He tamped down the dark recollections, looking at the lace again. He wanted it for his tin box. He needed to keep bits of tender moments close by, to remember. From a soiled backpack in his cart, he removed a dented candy tin, and opened it reverently to reveal a collection of postcards with pictures of pretty places, peaceful places. Under them lay a piece of water-smoothed blue glass Laurie had found in the Fox River, along with other memories of his past.

Tucked against the side of the tin nestled a miniature truck, once his son's favorite toy, its back wheel missing. He thought of Mattie, feeling proud he'd never raised a hand to the boy, unlike his own father who'd whipped him with a leather belt, its buckle cold and sharp, until he drew blood. Sims rubbed a scar on his upper arm.

Careful to avoid tearing the lace, he untangled it from the bougainvillea branch and laid it beside the toy truck. He'd call it "Laurie's lace." The tin closed with a soft click. He returned it to his backpack.

The sun moved toward the mountains, telling him it was time to buy a bottle of red at the Triple K Mart. Sims rubbed his belly, thinking of his new drinking buddy, Buck, a guy he met at the mission, a real talker after a few swigs. He sensed a mean streak in the guy—the way he poked a finger into your chest, talked in a loud voice or stood too close. But having company beat being alone. They met up about now.

Buck Olson made his way through the oleanders and scrub brush, looking for bottles and cans to toss into his old shopping cart. He stopped to pull a prescription bottle, an old one he'd found in the trash, from a pocket in his scruffy brown pants. The pills inside were his, bought and paid for. He twisted off the top, shook a pill into a dirty palm, slammed it into his mouth. His supply was getting low. He'd have enough money to make another buy soon.

Moving through the bushes silently—like in Nam—he looked for Sims. It was time to meet up as they did every day. The pill started to work. Buck felt himself grow stronger, craftier. He waited. *Come on, pill,* he thought, *come on. Make happy memories.*

He thought about that day in Nam. The old water buffalo stood in a rice paddy. He threw rocks, hit it in the ass, on the side. *Smack!* He landed one square on the animal's head. The water buffalo heaved itself out of the paddy and charged. His buddies cheered when he dropped the ugly sucker with a shot between the eyes. The CO chewed him out good, telling him, "The villagers need those animals." *Yeah, yeah. So what?*

His mind darted to Saigon, to a brothel. His favorite whore called herself Madeleine. She had smooth white skin and jet-black hair flowing to her waist. She'd push herself upward, moaning, as he plunged into her deeper, each thrust rougher than the last. Even now, he felt the sensation in his groin, felt her making him hard.

His face flushed at the thought of that last wild night in Saigon, of the guys filled with booze and drugs. Madeleine gave too much attention to a scrawny sailor while he waited. He grabbed her arm, hauled her behind the bead curtain. Before long, everyone's anger, liquor, and drugs erupted at once. A brawl broke out.

Buck lowered his head. For a moment, regret washed through him, trying to make him clean. But like water brought to a boil, he felt anger build in his gut. He didn't ask to be in Saigon, in Nam. He straightened his shoulders. Screw it, he thought.

He spotted Sims through the bushes, his back to him. The man had taken something from a bougainvillea bush. Buck stood quiet. Sims was always wired tight, ready to run. What the hell was the guy doing?

He watched Sims put a scrap of white cloth in a tin box. The guy always fussed about that box, never let anyone near it. He planned to look at it when the time was right.

"You ready to go to recyclin'?" Buck asked, stepping from between the bushes. "My cart's full." He eyed the tin.

Sims gave him a quick glance and buried the box in his dirty backpack. "Yeah, I'm done."

Walking ahead of Sims to the recycling hut by Farley Brothers Market, Buck relived the charging water buffalo, the scene vivid, the raging animal still making him laugh.

Sims called from behind, "Hey, Buck, what's so funny?"

"Just shootin'." He whirled around, aiming an imaginary rifle at Sims.

After the attendant weighed their bottles and cans, Buck waved his receipt. "Watch my cart. Gotta go in the store and get my money."

The cashier handed Buck fourteen dollars. He snapped a rubber band around his stash, running his tongue across dry lips, feeling the space where his front tooth used to be, before a bad fight on a pier up in Stockton. He had enough for a buy of happy pills.

While Sims took his turn in the market, Buck watched their carts. A well-dressed woman walked toward him, eyeing the faded red Coors tee shirt spanned across his belly, his dirty brown pants frayed on the bottom and dragging the ground. Buck sensed the vibes, felt his "feel good pill" work. With a gap-toothed grin, he bowed, sweeping his right arm out with a flourish. The woman stopped, her eyes wide, and redirected her path into Farley Brothers.

Buck laughed and leaned his elbows on the cart handle. His eyes narrowed. Sims always dawdled at the postcard rack. It was time to look in that tin box. He dug in Sims's backpack and pulled out a tin with Whitman's Chocolates printed on its lid. As he snapped it open, a hand landed on his shoulder.

"Get outta my stuff," Sims growled, his eyes slits, his lips tight.

Sims grabbed for the tin box. In the scuffle, it fell and bounced on the asphalt. Postcards tumbled out. A photo of a woman with a little boy floated into the air. A shard of blue glass, rounded and smooth, broke into sharp pieces. A key, a military medal, an old belt and a pocketknife clinked onto the ground. A piece of white lace drifted to the blacktop. Buck clapped, enjoying the show, while Sims scurried to gather his keepsakes back into the box.

Two men in a convertible drove over a toy truck, crushing it. Sims cried out, "Bastards! Dirty bastards!" He shook his fist at them as they drove away. A slight gust caught the white lace and whirled it in the air.

"Hey, Sims, don't forget this." Buck caught the lace, waving it above his head, his voice taunting. "Someone had a little nooky in the bushy."

Sims dropped the tin into his cart, snatched the lace and shoved it in his pocket. He clenched his fists.

Buck crouched, ape-like. "Come on, little man. I'll knock the crap outta ya."

A loud voice boomed, "Get away from here before I call the police." The store manager rushed across the parking lot toward them, followed by the well-dressed woman.

Sims unclenched his fists and nodded his head. "Don't want any trouble."

Buck straightened, put his hands up in an "I surrender" pose, and then saluted. "Okay, okay. We're goin'."

"Don't come back." The manager watched them leave, assuring the woman the parking lot was safe.

"Let's go eat." Buck laughed. "For chrissake, I'll get you a new toy truck."

Sims gritted his teeth. "Shut up."

"Oh, touchy, touchy. I'm shakin'." Buck banged his knees together, clownish. So, the guy was pissed. It'd blow over. Buck took another pill.

The Friendly Souls Mission in the next block was a good place to hang out and get a free meal, if a guy didn't mind listening to the Jesus stuff. Buck hated the way Sims prayed over his food, hearing that goddamn prayer he mumbled every night.

"Keep us safe. Amen."

Sims finished the last of his lemon meringue pie and watched Buck chew on the end of a toothpick. Men and women sat on either side of long tables eating, talking in low voices. Soon Buck nodded to a man at the next table. The two went out through a side exit.

Curious, Sims followed, hanging back, and saw Buck unroll a stash of bills. The other man held a baggie, shaking his head.

"That ain't enough," the man said.

"You lousy cheat!" Buck countered. "It was enough last time."

"Yeah? Prices went up."

The man turned to go back into the mission. Buck whirled him around by the shoulder, punched him hard in the stomach. The man dropped to his knees.

Sims ran up. "Hey, Buck, let's go. Don't want the cops. Come on."

Buck grabbed the bag of pills and threw money on the ground. "Yeah, let's get goin' before one of the holy rollers has somethin' to say."

The man called after him, "Last time you get anything from me!" He sat, catching his breath, eyeing the scattered money.

"You ain't the only snake in the sand!" Buck clutched the baggie.

They hustled back into the mission and, appearing nonchalant, took their carts that were parked along the wall and strolled out the front door. They quickened their pace once outside. The Triple K Mart was in the next block. Sims glanced at the clock on the Desert Valley Bank—8:32 p.m. It would be dark soon.

Buck went into the mart first to get his booze. Then Sims went in, taking his backpack with him. Buck sneered. When Sims returned, he cushioned his bottle in his belongings, then followed Buck as the man pushed his cart around the corner of the convenience store.

Once behind The Triple K, the two men rolled their belongings through sand and desert brush, heading toward a thick wind barricade of old tamarisk trees planted along busy Interstate 10. They ducked under one of the tree's gnarled limbs into their hideaway, pulling their carts in with them. Branches, thick with feathery leaves, formed a roof over a packed dirt floor; a surround of dense foliage kept the place hidden. Traffic thrummed close by.

Like every night, Sims spread a ground sheet, rolled out a sleeping bag, and wadded up an old shirt for a pillow. Also, like every night, before attempting sleep, he slumped down on a weathered milk crate scavenged from a dumpster at Farley Brothers and opened his bottle, ready for that first drink to take the edge off the night and his problems. The aroma hit his nostrils. He took a long, deep swallow, watching Buck settle in—until, seeming to study the dirt floor, his mind took him elsewhere.

At times he thought he might rejoin the human race. Then again, here under the trees, things were uncomplicated and simple. Living on the fringe, under the radar, suited him just fine.

He was hiding, not lost. He could come out whenever he wanted. But when? When would that be? He shook his head. *Shit.* The damn years kept pedaling by. He took another gulp.

The wine slid past his tongue and reached into his body, bringing a warm calm. "Twilight" he called it—the time before he passed out. Life softened, had a mellow glow about it. He apologized to Laurie and Mattie in his mind, something he did at least once a day. But what would either one want with him now? Sighing, he reached into his pocket and took out the lace.

"What the hell is with that fuckin' lace?" Buck asked, lounging against a tree trunk. He took a long pull from his own bottle, licking his lips as the cheap wine went down.

"Reminds me of my wife. She wore this beautiful nightgown to welcome me home. Must have been expensive."

"Lemme see it." Buck held out his palm, beckoning for the piece of lace.

"Yeah? You already saw it," Sims replied. "Remember?"

"You still sore? Come on. I'll give it back."

Sims hesitated, then extended the lace to Buck who spread it in his out-stretched palm.

"You know what this reminds me of?" Buck seemed to savor his next words. "A whore in Saigon. Madeleine was her name. Boy, could she fuck."

Sims grabbed at the lace. "Gimme that!"

Buck pulled his hand away, the lace in his fist. He kept on: "Her real name was Tuyet. You know what that means? White snow. Snow White, my ass." He rubbed the lace on his crotch. "We had a hell of a brawl that night at The Golden Dragon. Taught her not to jack me around, make me wait, play hard to get. Me and the guys wrecked the place. Made it out just before the MPs got there." He threw the lace at Sims.

Sims picked the lace from the dirt, brushed it off, and slipped it back into his pocket.

"I dragged the bitch into the alley. She didn't want me." Buck spit. "I fucked her anyway. Did some fancy knife work on her, too. MPs never found out who did it. What the hell. I was high on booze and dope. We all were."

Buck stopped talking, closed his eyes. Sims started to reply but didn't. MPs knew what booze and dope could do. They sat in silence until Buck crawled from the tree to his sleeping bag and soon passed out.

Sims scratched at his ear as he remembered a night he hadn't thought of in a long time; a night he and three other MPs had responded to a frantic madam's call. Her girls had been knocked around. Several had been raped. Shattered glass, broken furniture and booze bottles littered the place. They found the body of a young woman in the alley, lying in filth, her green silk dress pulled above her waist. Knife wounds, too many to count. Bruised legs spread at lewd angles. Long black hair stuck in dirt and blood. The madam had knelt beside her, crying, "Tuyet, Tuyet." He knew Madame Nguyen, owner of The Golden Dragon, and her girls. Tuyet—sold into prostitution by her brother.

Memories of that long-ago night rekindled Sims's sense of right and wrong. He sat up straight, images playing in his mind. He slipped over to his cart, dug in his backpack and removed an old leather belt. He wrapped it around his fist, letting its large metal buckle dangle free. Each wrap grew tighter, matching his growing anger. He walked toward Buck, intent on giving the man a beating he'd never forget or worse. Each blow would be for that young woman found dead in an alley so long ago.

Suddenly, Buck moaned. He thrashed his legs, jerking from side to side, calling out, "Get down, get down!" The man seemed sunk in his own horrors, haunted by his own ghosts.

Sims stopped, lowering his arm, watching. Buck kept crying out, his arms and legs flailing. It was the worst of Buck's outbursts Sims had seen, the horror becoming real in Sims's own mind. He felt the belt slip from his fingers and drop to the ground. He covered his face with his hands, shaking his head, wondering what he had become. Buck lived in his own purgatory, beating himself up. The man didn't need someone else to do it for him. Sims took a deep breath and stepped back.

He stood with his head lowered, knowing he had to get away for his own survival. He grabbed his backpack and gathered up his bedroll. With a final look at Buck, he slipped out of the tamarisk trees, bending low, trying to hide from the moonlight. Nearby, railroad tracks ran beside the Interstate. The overloaded freights often traveled west at night. Sims waited in the shadows.

Before long, he heard the rumble of a train, its forlorn whistle calling into the darkness on its westward crawl through the Coachella Valley toward Los Angeles—a trail of graffiti-covered boxcars, gondolas, and livestock carriers. The laden freight train rattling along the rails reminded him of his life, except he hauled a cargo of memories. Boxes of them. Growing up, his parents, high school, Laurie, Mattie, Nam, back home, Buck. None of his containers was empty either, only life itself.

As the slow-moving train rolled by, he watched for a cargo car with an open loading door, hoping the train hauled an empty car or two. He didn't want to wait or return to the tamarisk trees or join up with Buck again. A boxcar, its side door open, rolled into sight. He ran beside it, timing himself, tossing his gear through the opening. He scrambled inside and leaned against the metal siding, heaving a long sigh, one that said he was weary. One that said he needed rest. One that said he yearned for peace.

He looked to the City of Angels.

WALKING WITH HARVEY

Harvey sat in the sanctuary of an overstuffed recliner, its brown faux leather shaped to his angular torso. He brushed at scraggly gray hair, thin on top and in need of a trim. Creases between his eyes grew deeper. The story he was telling me seemed to need sorting before he spoke again. After a moment, his voice ended the short silence.

"You know, Ray, the sun blinded us, the way it bounced off the windows of city hall." He looked at me, eyes riddled with flecks of blue and white, the color of faded denim. "We waved signs. We shouted."

I sat on a worn couch, respectful, but half-listening to the man who started the Venice Beach Gym where my buddies and I trained. He founded the world-class bodybuilding competitions held nearby at Muscle Beach. We all loved and respected the guy.

I made myself refocus.

"It was the start of the Vietnam War." Harvey brushed at a small spray of spittle, his fingers lingering by the side of his mouth. "By then, my son, John, had been drafted." He fell silent again.

Nodding, I scratched my palm, glanced at my watch. After Harvey lost the gym in a bad business deal and retired, a few of us who worked out together took turns checking on him. Today, I noticed a sadness about him. Usually, the man had some good stories from his past, but this wasn't one of them. I knew where his words were going; I'd heard them before.

Harvey sighed, put his hands on his knees, rubbing them as if massaging away thoughts. "The crowd pushed toward the police barrier. A cop yelled, 'Stay back!' It was like a human tidal wave." He coughed; his shoulders hunched.

"How about some water?" I offered.

"Yeah, please."

I was glad to stand, to move away from the remorse and melancholy filling the room. Near the efficiency kitchen, I straightened a framed black and white photograph, one of the few pictures in his Venice Beach apartment. Harvey stood in a side-chest competition pose, muscles flexed, biceps bulging. In white letters at the bottom of the photo were the words "Mr. Muscle Beach, Venice, California, 1958."

I glanced at the man, still an icon at eighty-plus years. "Harv, you were one fine body-builder. Sure blazed a trail for all of us."

"You got that right." He massaged his upper arm. "Hell to see your muscles go south."

"You need to work out with me." I did a biceps flex. Harvey caught my eye and chortled.

"I could teach you young guys a thing or two." He leaned forward, pulled a wrinkled handkerchief from his shirt pocket, and wiped the side of his mouth. "Are you getting pumped for the upcoming Muscle Man competition? From what I hear, you got a good chance, Ray." He shoved the handkerchief back into his pocket.

"Working on it. I could use some pointers," I admitted.

Let's Make a Deal played on an outdated TV in the corner opposite the recliner, its volume muted. I picked up a water-spotted glass from the sink ledge, filled it from the tap, and took it to him, liking his change in mood.

"Thanks," Harvey said. He took several sips and wiped his mouth with the back of his hand. "From what I see, just keep training. Increase that muscle definition, refine the eight competition poses." He placed the glass on the table beside him.

I settled on the edge of the couch, ready to talk about my chances, pick his brain. But Harvey shook his head and said, "I just can't forget that damned police bullhorn. It kept squawking. Next thing, I was face-to-face with an LAPD helmet. Son of a bitch hit me with a baton." He pointed to a scar on his forehead. "Slammed me to the ground and cuffed me. I ended up in jail." He ran his tongue along his lips, as if to remove a bad taste.

"Ever show you this?" he asked. From the side table next to him, he pulled an old scrapbook hidden under newspapers. I hesitated. No, he hadn't. Maybe he'd sensed my restlessness, was looking for a way to keep me with him. "Go ahead," he said. "Take a look."

I opened the fake leather cover and idled through a few pages filled with yellowed clippings of the Vietnam War. I turned another page. Harvey pointed and said, "There. That one."

It was a *Los Angeles Times* story featuring a picture of Harvey being led away in handcuffs with the headline "Protestors Arrested After Melee."

"I paid my taxes, did my part," Harvey continued. "Never broke the law. You think I didn't have the right to protest?"

I had nothing to say. My war was Iraq. We sat in silence. I wanted to run away from his memories, away from the walls and words. I wondered if Harvey felt the same. What was it like to hang on to sadness, to anger, to regret? What was it like to watch your body slide away? More of Harvey's world seeped into me than I cared to feel. I closed the scrapbook and checked my watch again.

He sagged back in his chair, scratching an age spot on the back of his hand. His gaze drifted to a framed picture on a table next to the couch, a photo of his son in uniform. Harvey had told me about John, the nineteen-year-old who liked to play guitar and write songs, the son who never came home from Nam. I felt sadness circle the room, close around my chest.

As much as I wanted to escape his hurt and loneliness, I couldn't make myself leave. My own voice surprised me: "Hey, Harv, it's a nice day. How about getting some air? Let's go down to Hava-Java."

"Thanks, but you got something else you gotta do," Harvey responded, adding, "You've been checkin' your watch."

"There's time." A rush of guilt reddened my neck. "Coffee's on me. Let's get some air."

He shrugged. "Why not?"

With a tight grip on the chair's arms, he pulled himself to the edge of the seat and pushed up. I moved to steady him, but he waved me away. He took the cane leaning against the side of his chair and gripped it in his right hand.

"Let's go," he said.

We walked along the boardwalk, his steps careful and deliberate, mine slowing to match. Sightseers bustled in and out of the shops lining one side of the wide walk, lured by bead boutiques, a tattoo parlor, a taco stand, and windows packed with beach and surfing clothes. An old-fashioned barber's pole hung beside a window that displayed a sign: "Latest Cuts for Dudes." On the other side of the walk stretched a wide and sandy beach with picnic tables, palms, and an ocean rolling with low surf.

Gulls landed on the tables and on the sand. They soared out over the water. One swooped and dipped, playing a game of tag with small whitecaps, screaming as it escaped. I wondered if it was laughing—or maybe crying.

I glanced at Harvey. He seemed to enjoy the sights, the change of scenery. I inhaled the sea air, catching the bird's freedom—almost feeling like I could fly away. *Damn. That would be nice.*

A net of old memories settled over me, reminding me of a moment when, not far from here, I'd been happy and carefree. Some memories linger on instant replay, triggered by a touch, a smell, a word, a look, an object—a bird.

I was seven, at the Venice pier with my father. I liked to play while he fished. After all the years, a sharp image still remained in my mind.

I held a small piece of bait in my hand to throw to the gulls. I watched them swoop in and out as I timed the toss.

My father's voice broke the moment as he called to me. "I need the tackle box, Ray. It's there, by the bench." He extended his hand, waiting. "I don't want to leave my place at the rail. Saturday morning crowd."

I dropped the bait back into the pail. Rubbing my palms on my pants, I closed the metal box and grabbed the handle with two hands. I knew it was heavy.

I felt an elbow in my ribs. Harvey and I stopped walking.

"Ray," the old man said, "a gull just lifted a piece of bread off that picnic table over there, right off the woman's plate." He pointed, then folded his hands together on the cane's handle, giving an old man's chuckle of pleasure. "Sure surprised her."

"Those birds are crazy fast," I answered.

But on the pier that day with my father I wasn't fast enough, nor was he laughing. My father snapped his fingers. "Hurry up, Ray."

With my hands tight on the handle, I lifted the tackle box. Startled, I watched its contents clatter onto the pier. Knives, hooks, extra line, lures, an old reel, small tubes of sunblock, sinkers, weights. Some fell through the cracks to the water below. My father had just reorganized the box before we left our apartment. I'd forgotten to snap it shut as I'd been taught. I froze.

An angry scowl distorted my father's face. I took a giant gulp of air.

I heard Harvey laugh again. The lines on his face were continuous, from the corners of his eyes, around his cheeks, down to his chin. "When I was young and strong, I felt free and cocky like that gull."

"Yeah," I nodded, "it's a great way to feel."

I wasn't feeling free or cocky. My father leaned his fishing pole on the railing and said something to the man next to him about the day going to hell. "Damn it, Ray, can't you remember anything I tell you? Little weakling." He walked over, grabbed my arm and shook me.

In silence we gathered the fishing gear. "Stay by the box." My father returned to his fishing pole and reeled in the line. Another man filled his place as my father stepped away from the rail.

"Come on, we're going home."

He led the way, carrying the tackle box and pole, me trailing behind. I knew I was being punished. He'd promised, if I didn't bug him, I could hold the fishing pole and, if I were lucky, reel in a fish. I only wanted to please him and be his boy—his good boy.

My father's gruff, mercurial manner built a wall between us. When I was little, I tried to find a crack in that wall. As I grew older, I stopped. The past shouldn't matter anymore; the man was dead. But I wondered: *Will I be like Harvey someday, wanting to tell stories from my life, ones that were happy or sad or hurtful?*

I snapped out of my thoughts and glanced over at the old man. "Hey, Hava-Java isn't much farther."

"That's good," he said.

A homeless man sat on the sidewalk, leaning against an empty storefront. He held a cardboard sign: "Help a Vet." Harvey stopped to pull a leather change purse from his pocket and gave the veteran some folding money. I didn't need any encouragement; I did the same. We continued walking.

I thought about my return from Iraq, feeling anxious and unable to sleep. I thought of the men in my PTSD support group. The counselor had talked to us about finding an interest. He'd urged us to reach out to others. A few of us took his advice; started bodybuilding at the Venice Beach Gym, and met Harvey who encouraged us and cheered us on.

An inline skater in a red bikini glided by, the breeze billowing her California blond hair behind her. She smiled at me over her shoulder.

Harvey stopped again. "You got a girlfriend?"

"Nobody steady."

"There's one for you," he said.

I admitted I wouldn't mind meeting her.

After several more steps, Harvey's pace slowed until he stood leaning on his cane. "You know, Ray, when I was a kid, I never thought I'd ever be an old man. The one people rush by and forget about. But now I am—that old man. I feel life is passing me by."

"Hey, no one's passing you by," I replied. I put my hand under his elbow. "Let's have that coffee. We're almost there."

I wanted to say more, but words stuck in my throat. I did know we'd stop at the barbershop on the way back. I also discovered it didn't cost anything to listen, that it was the least I could do for Harvey and, I hoped, when it was my time—when I became that old man—someone would listen to me.

I opened the coffee shop door, aroma from the day's special, Kona Dark, greeting us. We found a small table without chairs.

Harvey looked at me. "Nothing to sit on." He braced himself with his cane.

"Hang on to the spot." I glanced around, ready to grab any empty chairs. I waited only a moment. A biker in a black leather vest pushed away from his table, said something to his three companions, and headed for the door. I hustled my way over.

"Mind if I take this chair?"

"Naw, man, you can take mine, too," said another man, shoving the last half of a bagel in his mouth. He stood, nodded to the men remaining and left.

I lifted the two chairs, one on each arm, and carried them to where Harvey waited. He eased onto the chair I steadied for him, placing his cane against the table. I sat on the other, about to ask him what he'd like. Before I could, he laid his hand on my forearm.

"Thanks, Ray," he said. "You're a good man."

Those were words I'd wanted to hear my father say. He never did.

II

A Door Left Ajar

"Oh, Jimmy, I wish I'd made my call the day I met you."

—Lori Anderson

"The Simian Society"

MRS. KAMINSKY'S NOTE

A black metal lunchbox in one hand, keys in the other, Stephen Bowles unlocked the door of his Los Angeles boarding house. He stepped into a once-elegant grand foyer, its floral wallpaper now faded and peeling, its hardwood floors and old oak stairway now scratched and worn. The room he rented on the third floor of the once stately Victorian home wasn't much to look at, but it suited his income and his acting ambitions quite well.

He hurried past manager Irene Kaminsky's apartment, the door ajar as usual, to check the contents of a bulletin board. On it hung a large, glossy calendar with photos of exotic, tropical birds. The April 1959 page featured a profile shot of an all-blue Brazilian parrot. Stephen didn't like the way it stared at him with one eye. He also didn't like Mrs. Kaminsky's dollar signs in the Friday squares, a weekly reminder rents were due, or the X marks on each day's square as it passed. Stephen didn't need reminding that his life slogged on, Friday to Friday.

Two folded notes tacked next to the calendar caught his attention: "K. Bishoff" written on one, "C. Lewand" on the other. None for S. Bowles, meaning the black payphone mounted on the wall next to the bulletin board hadn't rung for him yet again. He whacked the side of the phone with his palm, cursing at his only link to

Hollywood casting offices. He whacked it a second time, glancing at Mrs. Kaminsky's door, in hopes she wouldn't stir from her lair. He didn't need a confrontation about too much noise.

She didn't emerge.

He lingered in front of the bulletin board. Disappointment hit hardest on Fridays when he had to acknowledge another week gone without a call. Whenever he did find a note, he had hope, at least for a moment. He chewed on his lower lip, casually fingering the payphone's coin return for loose change, aware of noise droning in the background.

In a small alcove off the foyer, Mr. Ramirez from the second floor sat in one of two side chairs, watching a tabletop TV, its rabbit-ear antenna angled to catch the signal. Seven men in spacesuits appeared on the screen. Curious, Stephen joined him just as an NBC news commentator reported on the "Mercury Seven," America's first astronauts.

Mr. Ramirez glanced over at him. "Mark my words. We're soon gonna have a man on the moon."

Stephen nodded. He planned to shoot for the moon, too, so to speak, but his moon would be a successful acting career—if the damn phone would ever ring. For him.

"How come you're whackin' the phone?" Mr. Ramirez scratched his cheek.

Not in the mood for conversation, Stephen shrugged. "Just one of those days."

"You maybe should get a punching bag," Ramirez suggested.

"Yeah."

He checked his watch. Three-thirty. His acting lesson started at five. Friday afternoon traffic into downtown Hollywood would be heavy with everyone wanting to quick-start the weekend. He nodded to Mr. Ramirez and hustled up the stairs to the third floor, keys to the boarding house and his used '55 Ford Fairlane jangling against his lunchbox.

The third-floor hallway hummed with the sound of a communal refrigerator and, from behind closed doors, the low babble of radios and TVs. He swung open the fridge door, grabbed a brown paper bag with "Bowles" written on it, and removed a bottle of Bubble Up. Drinking it might settle the beef jerky indigestion gurgling in his stomach from a hasty lunch.

He walked down the hall, its dreary surroundings pulling on him, and unlocked the door to his room. Inside, he frowned at the all too familiar. Remnants of flowered wallpaper bled through beige paint. Scuffed, worn linoleum hinted at hardwood floors beneath. A single window let in daylight but not enough. The room's drabness did little to brighten his life or make it more than what it had become—a monotonous, long-playing record, minus an upbeat chorus or a new tune.

Sighing, he switched on the overhead light and placed his lunch box and bottle of Bubble Up on a painted kitchen table. It was flanked on one side by an unmade twin-sized bed and, on the other, by a Formica-topped counter with a chipped sink, coffee maker, and electric hotplate. Across the room stood a dark mahogany chest with a small TV on top. A cheap wardrobe mirror hung beside it. His deep-set brown eyes, dulled by assembly line work, stared back at him, reflecting an inner hollowness that threatened to drag him down. He hated this time of day, the room, the reality of it.

He sagged onto a wooden chair by the table to remove his work boots, aware of a curry smell seeping into the air from Mr. Singh's room two doors down. He shoved his boots under the bed. Every day, the place reminded him of his so-called "temporary plans"—temporary going on four years.

He pried the cap from the soda, chugged it down and tapped his fist below his sternum. Small burps rolled up from his belly. If the remedy worked, the afternoon's bellyache would be gone before his acting lesson began. For good measure, he took a few stale crackers from a Ritz box on the counter. A roach scrambled from under the container and dropped onto the floor. He chewed on a cracker, watching the insect run for cover.

His body cried for a quick nap, but he didn't have the time. He grabbed clean underwear and socks from the chest. From a curtained closet, he pulled out jeans, a sport shirt, and brown loafers. He took a large towel hanging on a wall hook and tossed it over his arm. Balancing his possessions, he hurried to the community bathroom down the hall. On the way he turned the shoes over and shook them to dislodge any animal life.

Fortunately, the bathroom was unoccupied. He charged in and locked the door. The clean clothes, he draped on a wooden chair, shoes underneath. The towel, he slung over a white porcelain bar. The oily, grease-stained clothes—the clothes he hated wearing—landed in a heap on the floor.

Pelting shower spray eased away the deafening assembly-line noise of the Pico Rivera Ford Plant along with the foreman's parting words: "Hey, actor, how's the movie business?" The foreman had laughed. Stephen hadn't. Water flowed over his body, washing away the day, a soothing feeling he wanted to last—but it wouldn't.

His nowhere acting career bothered him more than indigestion or a wise-ass foreman or his job as an on-call factory grunt filling in on the day or night shifts. Every free moment, he went to cattle calls, checked with casting agents. Sometimes he found work as an extra or he landed a small scene with a speaking part. So far, an agent hadn't spotted him.

He tilted his head upward into the shower flow.

Two buddies had just found acting work. Why not him? When would it be his turn? He was thirty years old. Would it ever be his turn?

Sighing, he turned off the water and stepped from the shower to towel down. A Kit-Cat Clock, its tail swinging and cat's eyes rolling, reminded him of the time. It also annoyed him, as did yet another calendar tacked by the mirror. He suspected Mr. Singh crossed off the days. Thoughts of passing time defined by passing years made him irritable, made him dress in a hurry, made him slam the bathroom door.

On the way to the Castle Argyle Apartments in Hollywood, he ran his lines, something he did daily with each new acting assignment. Tonight, with coach Milo Atherton, he'd do a scene from *On the Waterfront.* Milo sensed his impatience, his impulsiveness, his growing desperation, and he encouraged Stephen to study, to dig into the roles, to persist. Stephen thought of Milo's often-repeated mantra: "When luck and opportunity meet—and they will—you'll be prepared."

After he'd parked in the apartment's adjacent lot, Stephen removed a roll of antacids from the car's glove compartment. He chewed a tablet, waited a moment, then he chewed another, emerging from the Ford accompanied by a loud belch erupting from his gut.

"Real smooth sound, Stevie-boy, real smooth," said a man standing by the car next to his. It was Kevin Willis, also one of Milo's students. "You still wear your weekend uniform?"

The smug disdain in Kevin's voice angered Stephen. He waved, not answering. The urge to place a fist in Kevin's self-righteous face lessened as he walked toward the apartment entrance.

Looking into a lobby mirror, he finger-brushed his hair, then pushed the elevator button. Someone once commented on his resemblance to actor William Holden, who won an Oscar for the film *Stalag 17.* An Oscar. He wouldn't mind an Oscar. Stranger things had happened. He stepped into the elevator. The doors rumbled shut, opening again at the fifth floor. Stephen swallowed a small burp before he knocked on the coach's door.

Milo greeted him with, "Did you happen to see Kevin Willis? Exciting news. He's been cast in *Ben Hur.*"

"I did," Stephen said, his insides withering. "He didn't mention it. Big part?"

"It's a small scene, but another foot in the door of a big Hollywood production."

With Kevin's good fortune hovering around him like a malevolent ghost, Stephen forced himself to concentrate. He hoped his interpretation of the character Terry Malloy, a waterfront tough, wasn't an imitation of actor Marlon Brando who'd made the role famous. They ran the scene, Milo playing Terry's brother, Charlie Malloy. The scene ended with Stephen delivering the line, "I coulda been somebody, instead of a bum, which is what I am."

Milo prodded Stephen to explore his feelings, to reach deep into himself, to discover the pain of a character whose own brother used and betrayed him, nearly destroying his life. They ran the scene two additional times, isolating lines, digging for meaning. The lesson ended on encouraging words, but left Stephen feeling drained.

Milo gave him the "To Be or Not to Be" soliloquy from *Hamlet* to prepare for the next meeting. As conflicted as he felt, at least he wasn't suicidal like the famous Prince of Denmark.

On the way to the car, he ruminated about his acting. If he hadn't known of Kevin's good luck, the lesson would have gone better. Plus, Stephen wasn't happy with yet another Shakespearean scene, but Milo insisted his students be educated in theatre and film, that they have breadth and depth. They had to study the human condition. They had to have empathy. They had to be able to make an audience feel happiness or sadness, anger or fear, disgust or surprise. For now, Stephen's own feelings roiled with disgust and anger.

Before turning the key in the ignition, he rolled down the window. Hollywood's sounds settled around him. Maybe the character's final line held more truth than he wanted to believe. Had he become a "coulda been"? Maybe he didn't have what it took, that elusive thing called "talent."

Ever since he was young, Stephen wanted to be an actor. He'd seen movies like *Gone with the Wind, Of Mice and Men, The Lost Weekend, Key Largo,* and *Sorry, Wrong Number*—the classics. He'd practiced in his bedroom, reciting different characters' lines, adding facial expressions or distinctive moves. He'd starred in high school stage productions like *Arsenic and Old Lace* and *Oklahoma.* After high school he'd studied at the Pasadena Playhouse for a year, enabling him to land theatre work around Los Angeles. But all the acting classes, private coaching, and parts in plays still hadn't led to a break or an agent. His own damn doubt made him angry. All he wanted was to act in film, to stop the hammer of insecurity chipping away his confidence, to catch his star before it fell.

He decided against returning to his room or stopping at a bar to wallow in a self-pity drink. To muddle through his funk, he needed air. He started the car. From Hollywood Boulevard, he drove to Sunset and followed the winding road down to the Pacific Coast Highway. Once on the PCH, he stopped for gas at a Shell station near Will Rogers State Beach. On a full tank, he'd be free to go wherever and do whatever, maybe drive up the coast. The good news was his bellyache seemed better.

He waited for service, the only car at the pumps. The attendant in the station office looked through the plate glass window, pointing at the telephone receiver held next to his ear. Stephen drummed his fingers on the steering wheel, waiting for what became too many minutes.

He exited the car, walking past the pump's sign: "The Retail Gasoline Dispensing Safety Act Prohibits Customers from Pumping Their Own Gas." How easy it would be to just ignore the sign and pump the gas himself, but he wanted the kid off the phone, earning his money.

On the way to the station office, he welcomed fresh air wafting in on an ocean breeze. It pushed away the sour smell of city smog. He thought about one day having enough money to live in a pad in Malibu, either up on a nearby cliff or right on the beach. Being able to hear the surf.

Dream on.

At the office door, he said in his best gangster voice, "You gonna talk all night or you gonna pump my gas?"

The attendant, in his late teens, slightly built, with a bit of acne, said into the receiver, "Gotta go."

He followed Stephen back to his car. "What's your problem?" the kid asked. "I let you know I saw you."

Stephen turned, saw the name patch on the attendant's shirt. "My problem, Gary? I don't want to spend the night here."

Gary stopped, feisty like a bantam rooster. "Well, I only took a minute. I got a life, too, you know."

The attitude. The face. They annoyed Stephen. Just like Kevin Willis did.

"You punk," Stephen said through clenched teeth.

He grabbed Gary by the shoulders, shook him hard and shoved him. The kid fell back, a sprawl of arms and legs on the oil-stained pavement.

"Are you crazy, man?" Gary crab-walked backwards, trying to get away.

Stephen moved toward him, fists tight, wishing he had a piece of pipe or a tire iron.

"Get away from me!" Gary's voice turned from a cry to a shriek.

The fear in the kid's voice brought Stephen to a stop. What the hell was he doing? He opened his fists, put his palms up. Shaking his head, he extended his hand to help the kid up.

"Hey, Gary, I'm sorry. Bad day."

"Leave me alone!"

Gary hauled himself to his feet, ran back to the office, and slammed the door.

A Volkswagen van pulled into the station, music blaring through open windows. Stephen hurried to his car. He fumbled the keys into the ignition, glancing over his shoulder. The kid was on the telephone. Stephen's foot hit the gas pedal. He gunned out of the station, away from the beach, back toward Sunset, checking his rear-view mirror. The adrenaline rush, the action he craved to change his life, faded into feelings of stupidity for what he'd done. Why had he dumped his bag of frustration on a stranger? On a kid yet? He wove the Ford Fairlane back into Friday night Los Angeles traffic and bought gas on Olympic Boulevard, near the boarding house.

In his room, he fell on the bed, the word "stupid" repeating in his mind. Christ, he might have hurt the kid. He wanted his life to change—for the better, not for the worse. Did the kid call the police? Could the kid see his license number? He turned on the TV, an old western that did little to distract him.

Sleep finally came, but he woke in a sweat. The word "stupid" resounded again. He got out of bed, stumbled to the sink, filled a lone glass with cold water and, after a long drink, fell back onto the damp sheets. Several minutes of deep breathing calmed him enough to doze, only to wake up with the urge to pee. He lumbered down the hall to the bathroom.

In bed again, eyes closed and wanting to sleep, his mind wouldn't let him. It launched a parade of disappointments and shortcomings. There were no messages. There were no parts. He had no control.

The long night dragged by. Sleep visited in spurts until sunlight appeared through his window to announce Saturday morning—late Saturday morning. He groaned. He had to be at the Pantages Theater on Hollywood Boulevard by noon to help with the daily screening of *Cat on a Hot Tin Roof*, a part-time job that helped pay for his acting lessons.

He willed himself to get up. Running a hand through his disheveled hair, the gas station incident still in mind, he started to move. Towel and clean clothes in hand, he hustled down the hall to find a locked bathroom door. He pounded on it. Mr. Chang who lived in the room across from his called out, "Patience, my man, patience."

Stephen paced the hall. Finally, the bathroom door opened, and Mr. Chang emerged. Stephen rushed in. The clock's black cat leered at him and ticked 11:05. He showered fast and threw on his clothes even faster. As much as he hated the movie house job, it kept his head in the game.

Once at the Pantages, he parked in the rear lot and sprinted around the building into the lobby. Mr. Victor, his boss, wasn't in sight to know he was late. He hurried to his locker in the Employees Only room. Not having eaten anything except crackers since Friday's beef jerky, he rummaged for an Almond Joy candy bar he'd stashed on the locker's top shelf. He unwrapped the bar, took one of the halves and popped it in his mouth. Coconut encased in milk chocolate blended on his tongue, wafted to his nose. The signature almond crunched. The other half of the chocolate bar he'd save until he changed clothes.

Scrambling out of his jeans, he slipped into ivory-colored trousers with gold stripes down the outside of each leg. Next came white leather shoes, followed by a white shirt and a gold bow-tie. He topped the shirt with an ivory double-breasted jacket sporting brass buttons, gold piping on the sleeve cuffs, and gold epaulets on each shoulder. He completed the outfit with a matching ivory policeman style hat with gold braid above a gold visor.

Magic happened each time he put on the uniform. He stood straighter and angled the hat, adding a dash of panache. He felt handsome. Damn, he *was* handsome. His mood lifted for the first time since leaving his acting lesson.

In anticipation, he removed the rest of the Almond Joy from the locker, slipped it from the wrapper, held it in his fingers to savor the sight of it, and took a small bite, enjoying the slow crunch of coconut and almond and chocolate. He bit off another piece, chewing little by little, making the chocolate sensation last as long as possible. The third and final morsel lingered in his mouth as he straightened the front of his jacket.

In the lobby, he reached for a stack of playbills on the candy counter. Wanda, the counter girl, said, "Hey, your jacket's got schmutz on it."

He looked down in dismay to see chocolate smudges by the brass buttons. The stains reminded him of his soiled factory clothes. With haste, he took several paper napkins from the candy counter and wet them at the drinking fountain only to find that rubbing the spots made them bigger and worse. His good mood faded into agitation until he had an idea. If he held the playbills in front of him with his left hand, close to his body, he could hide the mess. He walked out onto the sidewalk, into the spring sun.

For the next few hours, he strolled Hollywood Boulevard, passing out playbills to tourists or excited moviegoers who were anxious to see Elizabeth Taylor and Paul Newman in their latest film. It felt good to be somebody people noticed, at least for a Saturday afternoon. Kids liked his uniform. Young girls gave him a lingering look, giggled when he handed them a flier. Women flirted. Old ladies smiled. He hugged the playbills close.

A familiar voice rang out behind him. “Hey, Stevie. You auditioning for a part? The leader of a brass band? You know, like Robert Preston?” It was Kevin Willis.

Stephen turned with a questioning look.

“Know what I mean? The musical *The Music Man*? The tune ‘Seventy-Six Trombones’?” Kevin added another punch. “You can’t lead a band, though, with your arm stuck to your chest. Right now, you look like Napoleon.”

Stephen clenched his teeth, his body stiffening.

The man moved on, calling over his shoulder. “Then again, every theater needs a good usher. Maybe you can show me to my seat. Heading to the Pantages now.”

About to follow Kevin, he felt a tug on his jacket sleeve. A young boy peered up at him. “Can me and my sister have one, mister?” It was then he realized his hand had curled into a fist. He uncoiled it to give the boy a flyer.

Stephen stifled his urge to go after Kevin Willis. He didn’t want a repeat of last night’s debacle at the gas station. He could punch someone, injure someone, let his frustration lead him into more dumb moves until he got himself into real trouble and accomplished nothing.

Maybe he should quit. Get out of the whole mess. Go back home to Colorado. Maybe he should keep trying. Get himself under control. He returned to the theatre, exhausted by his thoughts.

At five o’clock he changed out of his uniform, knowing his pay would be docked to cover the cost of the jacket’s dry cleaning. He drove back to the boarding house wanting to do just one thing—go to his room and lie down. But when he entered the foyer, Mrs. Kaminsky’s door swung open.

"Mr. Bowles," she called. "The rent's due on Friday. That was yesterday."

Stephen stopped. Oh hell, the rent. He'd forgotten all about it.

"Time got away from me. I'll bring it right down." He started on his way.

"Thank you, Mr. Bowles. I'll be right here," she said. "Oh, by the way, a woman, last name Myers, called Friday around five."

He stopped and turned.

"I posted a note on the bulletin board. You must have missed it. As you know, after a message is up for a day, even though I'm busy, I try my best to hand-deliver it." She reached in her pocket and extended a folded message.

He'd missed the note all right. He had other things on his mind, like his acting session, his night at the beach, his stint at the Pantages Theater. Kevin Willis.

"Thank you." He took the message, his curiosity growing.

"And will you please instruct your callers to leave name and number only, that you will return their call?" Mrs. Kaminsky said, her voice firm. "You know the rules. I am not, nor are the other guests, personal secretaries."

Mrs. Kaminsky retired to her apartment with the door left ajar.

Joan Myers. He knew that name. She worked at one of the agencies. Tall brunette, always friendly, not like some of the agency people he met. He unfolded the note. "Report to the United Artists' casting office at 10 a.m. on Monday." His eyes widened at the next line. "Auditions for *The Alamo*, John Wayne's next film." He whooped—and whooped again. Louder.

Mrs. Kaminsky's door flew open. She stepped into the hall, hands on her hips. "Mister Bowles!"

His noise stopped. His jubilant energy didn't. He wrapped Mrs. Kaminsky in a bear hug. Her feet left the floor.

"Mr. Bowles, puh-lease." She squirmed in his arms. "I am a lady."

"My apologies," he said as he put her down, waving the note. "It's the good news!"

"I am aware of your good news. However, remember your voice, *puh-lease.* We have day sleepers." Mrs. Kaminsky patted the henna curls around her powdered face and brushed at her rouged cheeks. Stephen thought he saw the downturned red lips soften to a slight smile as she stepped back into her apartment.

Bounding up the stairs two at a time, he read the note in his best Texan accent more than once, each time a little louder. Soon an inner voice joined in, gloating. It warned Kevin Willis to watch out. Mr. Smug wouldn't be the only student of Milo's who would land a part in a major production. Competition was on its way.

Stephen's steps slowed. He became aware of another inner voice, one he wanted to ignore. It grew louder. *What if I don't get a part? What if I'm not good enough?*

Rituals

Leonard parked his big rig at Wheaton's Truck Stop on Interstate 5 near Medford, Oregon, grabbed a burger with double fries for lunch, and asked his old friend Hank Wheaton for the loan of his pickup truck. He had to hunt down a damn cemetery. It was supposed to be in a nearby town according to his sister's directions—the sister he heard from only when she wanted something. A couple of bottles of good bourbon from a load of "spirits" he happened to be hauling to Seattle, and Hank's pickup was his to borrow.

By early afternoon he was on his way. Sun poured through the windshield as the pickup idled at a four-way stop. With a tight grip on the steering wheel, tighter than needed, he squinted at a road sign, its arrow pointing the way to the town of Jacksonville. He turned onto the old road with his jaw clenched. Sweet sister's grating voice still annoyed the hell out of him. After answering her call last week, he wished he'd let it go straight to voicemail.

"Len," she whined, "I want you to go to Ascension Cemetery up there in Oregon near Jacksonville. Remember it? I need pictures of our grandparents' gravestones for a family scrapbook."

"That'll be some scrapbook, Marge," he said, his sarcastic tone clear.

"Now don't be like that." She coughed. "You know how much I

love to travel. I'd do it myself but money's a little tight right now."

"Isn't it always?"

"I'm not asking you to make a special trip. You travel the West Coast in that big semi of yours all the time." Before he could respond, she added, "I'll email the directions. Just take pictures with your cell and send them to me."

Next thing he knew, the call was over.

Marge didn't ask for money for a trek from Stillwater, Oklahoma, to Jacksonville, Oregon, or anyplace else. She knew better. Sister-dear, along with her lazy mate, owed him three thousand dollars from when "they got behind." It'd be one lucky break if he ever saw that money again. After this final so-called favor, he planned to cut ties with his sister for good.

Family ties. They were nothing but trouble or disappointment. Marge had become a daddy's girl, an irritating little sister who accomplished nothing on her own. Jack, his older brother, lived life like their dad, full of dreams but no action. His mother had worked hard, trying to hold the family together, but she was always tired and never had time for him when he was a kid. Leonard felt he got his drive from her, but unlike her, he didn't have the hangers-on pulling him down. And he liked it that way.

His grandmother was the one exception to his thoughts about family ties. She'd made him feel special and always kept homemade chocolate chip cookies, his favorite, in the cookie jar. His grandfather had maintained a gruff attitude toward him and the other grandkids. Kids were women's work.

He passed another sign. "Jacksonville. Five miles." He sighed, his thoughts meandering like the road, recalling an unforgettable family reunion many years ago. After that, things were never the same. Family reunions. Another crock.

Deep down, something else troubled him. He'd been to Ascension Cemetery when he was nineteen for his grandparents' funerals. An out-of-control logging truck had hit their car, killing them instantly. He'd never been able to tell his grandmother how much he loved her or tell his grandfather about the life lessons learned at his hands. Thirty-five years later, a graveside visit would complete this unfinished business.

As much as he wanted closure with his grandparents, he didn't want the cemetery trip to take too long. Always on the prowl for another name to add to his little black book, he'd spotted a new waitress at Wheaton's. He liked her auburn hair and saucy smile. Other truckers would notice her, too. He had to hustle back before they started rolling in for dinner.

Not that he was looking for a wife. He lived by the motto "Play the field." His ladies were treated fine, but seeing the same lady too often led to problems. She'd start to get ideas. Marriage wasn't for him. Variety, that spice-of-life thing, was exactly that. In all truth, his family wasn't a front-page ad for matrimony. Or anything else, for that matter.

His thoughts were interrupted as he guided the pickup over a rise. Along the road's edge stretched a rustic rail fence with rows of gravestones beyond. A lane branched off to the right, framed by a wooden arch that held a faded sign dangling from two rusty chains. He peered up at the words, "Ascension Cemetery." With a grunt, he drove under the arch, past its open gates, and down the lane. Crushed stone crunched beneath the truck's wheels.

He parked in front of a clapboard cottage, English ivy clinging to its sides. He got out, dropping the truck keys in the pocket of his leather jacket. It hung open, revealing a white tee shirt underneath. Nearby, a man raked fallen leaves from a shedding maple tree into a pile.

"Afternoon. Help you?" The groundsman leaned on his rake.

"I'm here to check on a grave."

The man nodded toward the cottage. "See Vera."

Vera? Intrigued, Leonard adjusted his wide leather belt, careful to suck in a slight trucker's gut protruding over the silver buckle. He pushed his aviator style sunglasses up on his nose, ran a comb through his thick dark hair, and smoothed his sideburns. Ladies had appeared in some odd places in the past. It paid to be ready.

A small hand-painted sign pointed the way to the cemetery office. He strode up the walkway, trampling grass that poked from between used bricks, and climbed the wooden porch steps, their worn treads a cradle for the soles of his snakeskin boots. At the door, he took a deep breath, stood straighter, and turned the doorknob to enter. A woman looked up from her newspaper; a nameplate on the counter announced Mrs. Vera Conroy.

Leonard made a quick adjustment. The word *Mrs.* never bothered him, and Vera had a pretty face, but he liked his ladies younger, slimmer. "Morning, ma'am. Name's Leonard Kosloff." He strode to the counter. "I'm looking for the graves of Ed and Tessa Schneider. I'm in from California and in kind of a hurry."

"Well, how do you like our beautiful fall weather here in Oregon?" Mrs. Conroy smoothed her dress, fussed at a few curls around her face.

Pleasantries. Leonard didn't have time. "Like I said, I'm in kind of a hurry."

Sighing, the woman moved to a row of metal filing cabinets. "What was the last name again? The first names you gave me. Are those their Christian names?"

"Let's see." Leonard thought a moment. "Ed is for Edgar. Tessa is for Mary Theresa. Last name is Schneider. S-c-h."

She flipped through burial records. "Hmm. I have a Schaffer, a Schatz, a Schiller." The woman continued through the file cards. "Ah, here's a Schneider. But their names are Leon and Eleanor. We don't seem to have an Edgar and Mary Theresa."

Leonard's gut tightened, the same feeling he felt when his truck ran behind schedule. "I was told Ascension Cemetery off of old Highway 18."

Mrs. Conroy cocked her head, a smug look settling across her face. "Well, we have an odd situation here in Jackson County. There's another Ascension Cemetery farther down the road. Your relatives may be there."

"How come two Ascension cemeteries?" Leonard felt more hours dig into the afternoon.

Mrs. Conroy closed the records drawer. "The Protestants liked the name. So did the Catholics. We're the Protestants."

Leonard left, thinking about all the religious hocus-pocus, how it gave him a royal pain. Leave it to his sister to get holy and sentimental. He'd need a lawyer when he arrived at St. Peter's gates. Guilty as charged of living large.

He took pride in another reputation beyond his prowess with the ladies. L. Kosloff Trucking hauled anything for a price. If a certain cargo were needed by a certain time or a certain date, Leonard could be depended upon to do the job. His business operated just this side of the law, along with a dash of luck, laced with creative bookkeeping.

And now he was wasting valuable time, trying to find a cemetery. He shook his head in disgust and stepped on the gas.

Down the road several miles, he noted a wrought iron fence on his left. Beyond it stretched rows of gravestones. The other cemetery. Two stone colonnades flanked the entrance, one with a plaque announcing Ascension Cemetery of the Jackson County Diocese. He drove through the open gates toward a red brick building. The door, window trim, and shutters appeared to have a fresh coat of white paint.

Leonard entered the office, startling an elderly man watering a creeping Charlie plant in a wrought iron stand. The man stared over silver-rimmed glasses. "Yes?" He shuffled across the floor to place the water container on the counter.

Leonard rolled his eyes at the ceiling, delivering the information in a loud voice, time ticking.

The old man pushed his glasses up on his nose. "I ain't young, but I ain't deaf neither, fella. My name's Baxter." He opened a worn ledger. "Can't see worth a damn anymore."

Leonard saw lists of names with plot numbers.

"Let's see." The man rubbed his chin. "Year of death?"

Leonard leaned his elbows on the counter and thought a moment. "1982." At least his sister's information had been thorough.

"That helps." The man licked his fingers to turn the well-used pages. "Got this set up by years."

Leonard straightened, settling his weight evenly on both feet. His right hand slapped the denim of his pant leg as he watched Baxter tap a gnarled finger beside each name, willing him to move faster. He wished these old cemeteries had computerized tracking systems.

Several moments passed.

With a smile, Baxter exclaimed, "Yep, there it is. Edgar. Number 108A. Mary Theresa's right next to him." The man pulled out a tattered map, pointed to the plot. "Your grandparents are in the vicinity of the King of Peace and the Dome of Barbie."

Leonard tipped his head to one side. "What?"

"Oh, you can't miss the King of Peace statue. It's big. The Ellison family has money." The old clerk removed his glasses, leaving red indentations on the sides of his nose. "Barbie's nearby. She's there until it snows. The parents bring her back in the spring."

Statues. Domes. Leonard hopped in the truck, drove along the lane until a large marble statue in need of a cleaning appeared. Landmark number one. The King of Peace. Belching from too many fries, he brought the truck to a stop by two parked cars and glanced at his watch. Three p.m., time to get back to Wheaton's. The guys would be rolling in soon, making that waitress fair game.

He emerged from the truck, pulling his jacket around him, and walked through autumn leaves scattered on the ground. A green vinyl canopy stood in readiness nearby, a newly dug grave under it, waiting. Two men and a woman walked toward the tent-like structure where another woman sat by herself amidst several rows of folding chairs. The woman dabbed at her eyes. She glanced at Leonard and put her head down.

He lowered his gaze, wondering why all the ceremony. Dead was dead. End of story.

Near the King of Peace, he heard a clank. Then another. A thin, gray-haired man banged the sides of a metal urn with a hammer, causing pieces of caked-on dirt to fly onto the grass.

What was the old coot thinking, making all that noise?

From a nearby spigot, the man filled the urn with water, set it into a casing in the ground and slipped in a bouquet of flame-red gladioli. The graceful stalks fanned the rim of the bronze receptacle.

Leonard rubbed his brow. In his world, women were the caretakers, the weepers, the keepers of scrapbooks, the flower arrangers. Not the men.

The man bent down and, with short rhythmic strokes of a whisk-broom, swept the stone marker clean. With a hand on his lower back, he straightened, smiling at Leonard. "Married fifty-three years." He reached in his pocket for a handkerchief.

Leonard read the pink granite marker: "Yvonne, Beloved Wife and Mother." Etched rosary beads flowed around the name. He cleared his throat, feeling the need to say something, but no words came. The man nodded. Leonard returned the nod, walked on. He felt the urge to leave, smothered by the ritual. He looked for the other landmark.

Then it appeared: the Dome of Barbie, sitting atop a flat granite marker, sunlight dancing on the curved glass surface. Yellow, pink and green pinwheels, six in all, surrounded the small grave, their whirl-a-gig blades lazy in the slow-moving afternoon air.

The likeness of a little girl etched in the marker made Leonard uneasy as did the year of birth and death. Six pinwheels. Six years old. Her name, Deborah Jean.

The dome drew him closer. Under it stood a blond Barbie doll dressed in a gold evening gown, a little girl's treasure. Barbie. The pinwheels. The portrait. They pushed at his comfort level. He swallowed the distaste rising in his mouth. Useless. All of this was useless. The kid was dead. No domes or pinwheels could bring her back.

He walked on, following the numbered stone discs at the base of each plot toward 108A. Thoughts of the little girl lessened as childhood images of his own life closed in around him. He remembered when his grandparents moved to Oregon. All the family gathered at their house in Stillwater before they left. He pictured his porcelain-complected grandmother, barely five-foot-two, felt the gentleness of her touch. He remembered the heaviness of his grandfather's step, the man's tall frame, his craggy face.

His gut tightened. His mind lit up like an HDTV screen. He saw himself playing with the other grandchildren at his grandmother's house. He was ten.

"I gotta go," I call to my cousins. "I'll be right back."

I run to the house and gallop up the stairs to the bathroom. Everyone is down in the yard. The house feels kinda spooky with no one in it. All of a sudden, I hear noises. My grandpa's voice, gruff and scary, booms from a bedroom.

"Don't tell me what to do!" Grandpa yells.

I don't move, my ears wide open.

"But, Ed, you've had enough." My grandma's voice. She sounds tired.

"If I want a drink, I have a drink. I earn the money. You lie around at home."

"That's not fair," she says.

I nod my head. I know that's not fair. My grandma's house is always real clean and full of flowers she grows herself.

Footsteps pound across the hardwood floor.

"I'll show you what's fair!" my grandpa thunders.

I hear a whack. A moan.

I freeze.

I hear a thump.

Before I can stop myself, I'm running into the bedroom. My grandpa bends over Grandma, shaking her by the shoulders. Her head bobs. I see blood by the corner of her mouth. Her cheek is red. He raises his arm to hit her again.

"Stop, Grandpa, no!" I grab at him.

"Get out of here, you little weasel!" He backhands me. I tumble against the wall. I'm scared. My face hurts. He looms in front of me, reeking of beer.

"You say one word to anyone," he threatens, "and you'll be mighty sorry!"

I inhale a sob. I windmill my arms at him, slapping and punching. "You're hurting her!"

Grandpa tries to backhand me again.

I jump aside. "I hate you!"

"Get the hell out of here," Grandpa snarls.

"Bastard!" I scream.

I run to Grandma to help her up.

"Go, Lennie," Grandma says.

"But, Grandma . . . " I'm crying, pleading.

"Lennie, go! Now!"

I run from the room, down the stairs, into the yard. My chest aches, my heart feels like it will burst apart. I'm crying. I'm running like the wind.

My uncle, sprawled in a lawn chair, calls to me, laughing. "Sure are runnin' fast, Lennie. Your hair on fire?"

I don't stop until I reach the lake, panting. Panting.

Leonard could feel his accelerated breathing. He stood still to settle himself, looking out over the grounds. He'd kept the terrible secret and stayed away from his grandfather.

When he grew older, he talked to his mother about his grandparents' marriage. Her words filled him with anger.

"Len," she said, "the family knew about Ed and how he treated your grandmother."

"Why didn't someone stop him? Get her the hell out of there?"

His mother shook her head. "Times were different then. We asked her to come live with us. Lennie, your grandmother wouldn't leave him."

The images pounded in his head, yesterday's ghosts still a nightmare.

Leonard moved on, his steps deliberate, until he stood at his grandfather's grave. He clenched and unclenched his fists. His long-buried words erupted into the stillness.

"You fucking, old bastard. I hate you. For what you did to my grandmother. For what you did to me. I admit I'm no angel. I cut corners in my trucking business and I sure know my fair share of women. But, unlike you, there's two things I've never done, you rotten son of a bitch. I've never struck a woman, and I've never been a drunk."

Leonard squatted in front of Ed's gravestone; his head overflowed with loathing. "May you rot in hell for what you did." He spat.

Saliva trickled from the word "Edgar" down the stone. He spat once more into the earth, releasing years of disgust and anger.

He pushed himself up and backed away, unfinished business finished. In a few steps, he stood at his grandmother's gravestone. Removing his glasses, he dropped them in his jacket pocket. "Grandma," he said, his voice unsteady. "I'm sorry no one ever stopped him. That I never stopped him."

Kissing his fingertips, he placed them on the word "Theresa," whispering, "Dear Grandma Tessa. I hope you always knew how much I loved you."

His eyes moistened, recalling the days spent in her care while his mother worked every day, while his father shifted from job to job, unemployed for weeks at a time. He remembered old Ed sitting at the kitchen table every night with a half-empty glass, staring into space.

"Enough, enough," Leonard whispered.

With two quick clicks of his cellphone, the pictures were taken. It was over. He dropped the cell back in his pocket, took a last look, and walked away, tucking his grandmother's memory deeper into his heart.

Consider the cord cut, Marge. Mission completed.

With each step, he distanced himself from the graves, but also with each step, an unusual weariness crept into his body. He considered himself a fine specimen for a fifty-four-year-old, boasting of "a lot of fire in the fireplace." But he couldn't deny a sense of fatigue.

He lowered himself onto a nearby bench, pushing his hands against his thighs. Despite the cemetery calm around him, he felt uneasy. Something more than weariness battled within him.

He stared out into the grounds, massaging his temples for what felt like the start of a headache. But the ache grew. It spread through his body, burrowing into his feelings until it touched a private place buried deep inside him. A soft cry escaped his lips. The eerie sound startled him. He glanced about to see if anyone might have heard, then folded his arms against his body, holding himself in his own embrace.

The dam broken, questions flooded into his mind, questions about what would happen when his time came. Who would tend his grave? Who would weep for him? Who would miss him? Would a wife have loved him? A child? Questions without answers. They knocked on his survival wall, held at bay, like an enemy.

Perhaps it wasn't too late to allow his guard to drop, to remove the wall. He could marry, buy some land, build a house, own a dog. Tranquil images floated in his mind until, with a jolt, he remembered his role models, and the unhappiness. He paused his Pollyanna thoughts and shook his head. He could own a house and have a dog without any entanglement. Closing his eyes—along with the door to his feelings—he stretched and sat, letting the quiet settle around him.

Suddenly, he slapped his thighs and stood. He walked toward his friend's pickup, checking his watch. The walk turned to a trot. He had to hurry. It was time to meet that new waitress.

Bingo and the Gown

Bingo Jensen crept along the alley toward Alice Wilson's house. With quick glances left and right, he slipped past a crooked fence post and a broken gate into her backyard. Overgrown oleander bushes, ocotillos, lantanas, and bougainvillea spread before him. He edged toward the house, dodging thorns, crooked sprinkler heads, and scattered rocks sticking up in the sandy soil. Untrimmed fronds on a Queen Palm hung low, brushing his shoulders.

He stuck out his lower lip, took a deep breath and blew a whoosh of air up on his face. After this quick stop at Alice's, he'd wave goodbye to Beaumont Corners and hop on his Ninja for a thirty-mile bike ride up to the little town of Idyllwild where the temperature changed from Mojave Desert heat to San Jacinto Mountain cool. He called it his "weekend escape."

Life always felt better up in the Village, and this trip promised to be the best yet. First, he'd drink a few Friday night beers with his buddies at Big Red's Biker Bar. When the bar closed, Red would let him crash at his pad for the night. Saturday morning, he'd be with Lindy, a girl he met at the Idyllwild Ice Cream Shop last weekend.

He picked his way through the yard, his thoughts on Lindy. She had a smile that turned his insides queasy, eyes blue as a desert sky and a smoking-hot body, one he wanted to touch all over. He pulled his tee shirt up to wipe the sweat from his face.

They'd agreed to meet at the Mile-High Café and spend the day together. It was a great plan, one that should have kept him happy all week, except he had problems. His landlord had cornered him about the rent. His biker's insurance came due. Plus, the guy who'd done the custom paint job on his Kawasaki Ninja motorcycle three months ago wanted the rest of his money. He hoped his little visit to Alice's would solve his financial issues.

An ocotillo grew dead ahead. He slipped around its spiny arms, wishing he could hang his problems there and leave them. Having no cash proved the least of his troubles. Early in the week, he discovered Lindy's cell phone number had disappeared. Poof. Kaput. The napkin she wrote on must have fallen from his jacket pocket. He should have put the number in his cell phone contacts, but he liked having something she'd touched and given to him, something he could hold and look at. He'd been unable to call her. Would she show up? Would he see her again?

Without warning, a small beacon of moonlight poked through the clouds, its hazy glow unleashed into the night. He hunkered down closer to a bougainvillea, avoiding its prickly spines, retied a lace dragging from one of his Nikes and took off his beret, the one old Alice made for him back when his father Elroy was married to her daughter Diane, back when they all lived together. He smoothed his shaggy black hair, shoved some wispy strands behind his ears, and put it back on, Green Beret style. The beret—coiled cotton yarn of red, orange, yellow, green, blue—made him feel good, despite its history.

With a glimpse around him, Bingo stood to hoist up his low-slung khaki cutoffs, making sure they were firm on his hips. He darted from behind the oleanders over to a hedge of thick lantana bushes near the side door of Alice's house. He edged to the door, key in hand, praying the old lady hadn't changed the locks. The key slid into the slot. Click. *Bingo!*

He gave the door a gentle nudge. It moved. He gave it a push. It stopped, double-chained from the inside. He pulled the door shut. *Damn.* He crept along the hedge toward the front of the house. If she'd left a light on at the front door, he'd have to go in through a back window.

He knew from occasional surveillances that the house would be empty. Alice's Friday night routine hadn't changed. Her friend Thelma Watson picked her up and they played bingo until midnight at the Beaumont Corners Community Church. As a little kid, he used to go, too, yelling "Bingo!" for Grandma Alice. Soon, everyone called him Bingo. It was better than being called Elroy, like his dad, or worse yet, Junior. Diane's daughter Sandra, his used-to-be stepsister, only came home on Saturdays since she stayed in Palm Desert to go to Cal State. Diane had moved to Los Angeles a while ago.

He moved along the lantana bushes closer to the covered front porch. Its wooden railing would be easy to climb over. He nodded when at last he had some luck; no porch light shone in the darkness.

Alice's Social Security check would be in by now. He knew from times past she kept money stashed around the house. She owed him. Hell, the whole family owed him. What had happened hadn't happened because of anything he did. He wasn't the one who'd played around.

They all used to live with the old woman. When their parents married, Sandra and he, both four years old, became like brother and sister. Everything blew up when Elroy got a girlfriend. And it wasn't the first mistake. Diane threw his father out.

Thinking back made Bingo's body flush, his face turn red. He felt the hurt, he felt the shame, like it happened yesterday. He'd been cheated out of a family. Out of a home. Out of a love he craved. It all disappeared with the slam of a door.

Bingo bit his lip, remembering how he'd cried, how he'd wanted to stay with Grandma Alice, but he'd had to go with his father. He was twelve years old. Elroy rented a place on the other side of town where they lived until Bingo turned eighteen. He moved out the day after his birthday, leaving Elroy to his apartment and his girlfriends. Alice had told him her door would always be open, but stopping by never felt right after what his father had done. Bingo took a deep breath, proud that he'd worked steady and taken care of himself for the past four years just fine.

Don't get sentimental now. Screw the memories.

He had an immediate problem with a solution at hand. Alice used to give him money. When he asked her as a kid, she'd give him loose change, maybe a couple of dollars. Candy money. Well, tonight the Bank of Alice could help him out again.

Go.

He legged it from the bushes to the porch, grabbed the wooden railing and swung himself over. A splinter pierced the heel of his hand. He landed cat-like on the wooden floor, his breathing shallow and fast. He tried to remove the sliver, but it broke, leaving a stinging sensation. In the commotion, his beret slipped from his head onto the porch floor. He grabbed it, put it back on. All five feet ten inches of him stood straighter. He became strong like Samson, wise like

Solomon. Alice had taught him the Bible stories well. The burn of the wedged splinter became non-existent, the past forgotten.

Something rustled in the bushes. He froze, waiting, looking for a dog or neighbor out poking around. Nothing. No one. He stepped to the door. The key used to fit this lock, too. He inserted it, held his breath. *Bingo!* The deadbolt turned.

He slipped into a cramped 1950s-era room with a kitchen on one side, a living room on the other. He relocked the door, conscious of the sweet smell of apple pie lingering in the air. Apple pie. Man, oh, man. He'd love to taste a big slice right now. Alice's pies were famous all over Beaumont Corners. She used to sell them at a small stand in her front yard with his and Sandra's help.

Alice always kept a red cookie jar on the counter beside the sink. He made his way in the semi-darkness, thanks to hazy moonlight drifting into the room. He saw the red crock but decided to leave it for now. It might hold enough for a beer or a slice of pizza. He had a bigger score in mind.

He made his way down the hall, passing what used to be his parents' room. He continued past Sandra's room. At the end of the hall, he stopped in the doorway of his old room, a converted porch at the back of the house. He still could smell the fresh-ironed sheets Grandma Alice put on his bed every Friday, their surface smooth against his skin. They always made him feel safe, clean, and loved.

The old lady's room was across the hall from Sandra's. He headed for a chest of drawers opposite the bed and opened the top drawer. From his pocket, he took a penlight and, shielding the glow with his hand, rifled through handkerchiefs, a collection of cotton stockings in a quilted satin box, four scarves, a hymnal, church bulletins, two

Beanie Babies. But no cash. The rest of the drawers yielded nothing. Underwear, nighties, sweaters, cotton tops. All neatly folded.

He moved to the closet. With the penlight in his mouth, he dug inside shoeboxes, purses, loose shoes. He rifled in a bag of clothes labeled "For Church." He unzipped a garment bag. The inside reeked of mothballs protecting a man's clothes. They must have belonged to her husband before he died.

Bingo closed the closet door. Penlight still in hand, he looked under the mattress. Nothing. Beneath the bed sat an old suitcase. Inside, nothing.

The nightstand beside the bed remained. He opened the drawer. A Bible stared back at him. He leafed through the worn gilt-edged pages, passing an occasional page with the corner folded down. Beneath the Bible, he discovered the mother lode. *Bingo!* A crooked smile curled the edge of his mouth as he counted a small stack of money in a white envelope. Nine hundred fifty dollars. *Thank you very much, Bank of Alice!*

He started to stuff his find in his right pocket where he kept the keys to the Ninja, but he stopped. *Aw, shit,* he thought.

Bingo couldn't do it. Couldn't take it all. Three hundred fifty would be plenty. He could gas up his cycle, go to Idyllwild, and treat Lindy to a good time. Putting the rest of the money back, he noticed a loose photo of Sandra, Diane, Grandma Alice, and him, eating pie at a picnic table in the front yard.

He slammed the drawer shut and made his way back to the kitchen. At the counter, he shook the cookie jar. Coins rattled. He placed the crock on the table. Before opening it, he looked through the front kitchen window, but saw nothing unusual. He removed the lid, slipped his hand into the crock—*Bingo!* Not only change, but bills. He shoved the money in his left pocket, where he kept the penlight and a Swiss Army knife. He replaced the lid.

All at once, the room grew brighter. What the hell? Through the window he saw the sharp beam of headlights bob into the driveway. Was old lady Alice back from her night out so soon? He couldn't have taken that long. Sure enough, Thelma's white Taurus stopped by the walkway to the porch.

Alice pulled herself out of the car, thanked Thelma, and with the aid of her cane, started up the walk. She stepped right along for an old gal. Thelma waited to let the car's headlights guide Alice's way. Bingo's mind raced. Should he run for the side door? Dive out a window? No. He'd hide. She'd be asleep in no time, an old woman like her.

On cat feet, he rushed past the kitchen table, bumped into one of its chairs, and stumbled into the living room. He heard Alice on the steps. He looked around. Alice was on the porch. He rushed toward the sofa. Alice was at the door. He dropped onto his knees. Alice's key jostled the lock. He wiggled between the wall and the couch, jamming his hand with the sliver on the hardwood floor. It hurt. But something more felt wrong. He touched his head. *No beret.*

The door opened, followed by the click of a switch. Light from an overhead fixture filled the room. He heard her cane tap along the floor, the shuffling of her feet, then a scuffing sound, like a chair pushed on linoleum, then rummaging sounds. A cupboard door banged. The old woman cleared her throat.

He heard, "Elroy Junior, if you're here, you'd better come out. Your beret's on the rug by the coffee table, big as life. If you're not

Elroy Junior, you still better come out."

Shit. He crawled from behind the couch, grinning. Alice stood on the other side of the table, holding a baseball bat.

"Now, Alice, don't do anything silly. It's just me—Bingo. You're home a little early, aren't you?"

"Yes, since you're asking. Thelma's lumbago acted up. This a social call?"

"Just dropped in, like you said I should."

"When I'm not home? Hiding behind the couch? What do you want? As if I don't know." Alice lowered the bat and glared at him. "I keep that red cookie jar on the kitchen counter by the sink. Done it for years. I never leave it on the table." Her cane lay beside it. "How did you get in?"

"The front door."

"I guess my porchlight burned out while I was gone. I suspect it saved you from crawling in a window. I'll have to change the locks after all these years. Until I do, you can put that key of yours on the table."

Bingo moved closer to the beret, keeping an eye on Alice and the bat.

"I'd recognize that beret of yours anywhere," she said. "Made it for you for your twelfth birthday, back when you were just a boy being a boy."

He picked up the beret, taking his time to shape it before placing it on his head. He tossed the key on the table.

Alice studied him. "Haven't seen you much."

"Yeah, it's been a while." He shrugged.

She shook her head, pointed at the crock. "You'd really steal from me?"

"Aw, hell. Here. Don't know what I was thinking."

Bingo pulled the money he'd taken from the crock out of his pocket and put it on the table. She counted eighteen singles, plus three dollars and seventy-six cents in change. She put it back in the cookie jar, replaced the lid.

"Like I told you many times, I got just enough to get by. Besides, you're young, you're healthy. Work regular, so I been told."

"Yeah, at the Morongo Casino. In maintenance."

"Why do you need money?"

"Met a girl," he said. "A nice girl."

Alice scowled at him. "You don't steal for a nice girl or any girl. You don't steal, period. You work for your money like my husband and me did."

Bingo looked at the floor, avoiding her eyes. An awkward silence followed. In a soft voice, he said, "I know, Grandma. I know."

Another awkward silence accompanied by a rush of memories, a flood of feelings. He stopped the flow. He didn't like being shamed. Again.

"You wouldn't really hit me, Alice, would you?" He eyed the bat. "You know, I could pull that away from you real easy."

He saw the skin on Alice's knuckles grow taut as she tightened her grip on the bat. "Maybe you'd better stay away from me, from Sandra, and this house until you get yourself straightened out."

"Whatever you say." He moved toward the door. "You know I'd never hurt Sandra. Or you. I'd never hurt anybody. I'm not like my old man."

"I hear you've gotten into a fast crowd at the casino." Alice held his gaze. "Right now, you best be on your way, young man."

"No problem."

Bingo opened the front door, gave a semi-salute, and left. He heard the lock click behind him. Heart pounding, he clumped down the front steps past a bicycle chained to the porch railing next to a big pot of geraniums. Close call. It pained him that she'd said to stay away. They used to have fun together. *Damned old woman.*

He walked toward the bushes. Best to stay out of sight. Once hidden, he looked back at the house where he'd been so happy. What had happened wasn't his fault.

He kicked at the dirt. Now he had another problem. Alice knew he'd broken in.

Just then, lights lit the yard again. He squeezed closer to the foliage. Had Alice called the police? Could they respond that fast?

His stepsister's old blue Ford Fiesta Coupe pulled into the driveway, a day early. He relaxed. It came to a stop by the porch walk. Out hopped Sandra. She removed a plastic bag with what looked like groceries and a big flat box. She juggled her packages while she locked the car, then bounded up the steps, unlocked the front door and shoved it open. He heard, "Grandma, your light's burned out. Look what I have! Big day is tomorrow."

The door closed. Followed by the click of the lock. Again.

Curious, Bingo edged his way back to the house, crept by a side window to watch from the shadows. Sandra hugged her grandmother. Grandma Alice put her hand to her ample breast, smiling. From the box Sandra pulled out a black cap followed by a gown. She shook the gown. It unfurled to its full length. She placed the mortarboard on her head and held the gown against her shoulders. Standing model straight, she walked, like strutting across a stage.

Sandra must be graduating from college. Bingo turned away.

That could have been him, *should* have been him, too. His face grew hot. His lips pursed into a firm line. He sneaked another look. The cap and gown lay on the couch. The two women sat at the kitchen table, talking, Alice's hand on the cookie jar.

Time to leave. The old lady would be talking about him, about what he'd tried to do. Well, she didn't know what he'd really done. With each step he felt meaner. He pulled an open pack of Wrigley's Doublemint gum from his back pocket, unwrapped a stick, folded it into his mouth and chewed. The wrapper slid from his fingers as he dug in his right pocket, then his left. *Where the hell was it?* Found it. He gripped his knife as he neared the Fiesta.

He chose the blade he wanted. Using his right thumb, he pried it open. After a quick glance back at the house and out to the road, he squatted by the driver's side front tire, trying to shove the blade through the tire wall. No luck. Working fast, he unscrewed the valve cover and used the knife blade to damage the valve stem. He did the same to the other three tires. Air seeped slowly.

For a final touch, he shoved a wad of gum into the lock of the driver's side door. Quickly opening another stick, the wrapper flying, he chewed the piece fast and wadded it into the lock on the passenger side. A last look at his handiwork felt good, and he hurried to the front sidewalk. His rapid walk through the night shadows became a jog that turned into a run.

You folks enjoy your Saturday ride to graduation—if you ever get there.

He grabbed the beret from his head and ran, air rushing by, his Nikes pelting the sidewalk. When he reached the Convenience Mart parking lot, he bent at the waist, hands on his hips, breathing hard. His lungs were about to burst, his heart pounding.

"Hey, Bingo! What's happenin', dude?"

He looked up as Len Hawkins walked out of the mart, a hot dog in his hand.

"Goin' to Idyllwild," Bingo replied. He caught his breath. "Just picking up my bike." He pushed his hair behind his ears, re-angled the beret on his head. His motorcycle waited in a parking place where he'd left it earlier.

"My Yamaha's parked over by your wheels." Len pointed, chewing. "Every time I see your Ninja, I want a blazin' paint job like you got. Must have cost you a few. Want some company?"

"Yeah, sure. Okay, but I'm in a hurry." Then he asked Len, "You got any money?"

Len shrugged. "Yeah, enough." He shoved the rest of the hot dog in his mouth.

"I'll hit the head. Then we'll gas up and take off." Bingo hurried into the mart, anticipating wind in his face, Ninja roar in his ears. Nothing like a night ride into the mountains.

When he came out of the store, drinking an orange soda, he saw Len talking to a girl on a bicycle. *What the hell?* It was Sandra. He walked toward them.

"I saw your Ninja parked in the lot when I stopped to buy bread and milk for Grandma Alice," Sandra said.

"How'd you know it was my bike?" Bingo asked.

"It's hard to miss," she responded. "I've seen you on it a few times around town. I wondered where you were. Now I know. We have to talk."

"About what?" he wanted to know, feigning innocence.

"I said we have to talk." Her voice was firm.

“What’s going on?” Len asked.

“Give me a few,” Bingo said. He walked over by his bike. Sandra followed, lowered the kickstand on her bicycle, propped it up and stepped in close to him.

“We know what you did,” she said in a low voice.

“Yeah? Like what? I gave the money back.”

“I’m not talking about the cookie jar. You took three hundred fifty dollars from the nightstand. Grandma Alice needs that. If you give it back, she won’t call the police.” Sandra waited. “Did you think we wouldn’t look around after finding you in the house?”

Bingo assessed Little Miss Do-Right. He considered the deal. Give the money back and no police. He’d miss the trip to Idyllwild, miss seeing Lindy.

Lindy or the police? A lousy choice.

But wait. He could borrow a few bucks from Len. He’d loaned the guy plenty of money in the past. Maybe he couldn’t take Lindy to the expensive Aroma Café or Stone Creek Inn for a dinner, but he’d at least see her. He dug in his pocket for the money and put it in Sandra’s hand.

“Here. Now leave me alone. I planned to give it back next week.”

“Sure you did.” She paused. “There’s more, Bingo. I won’t call the police if you fix my car. We need it to get to graduation.”

“What do you mean, fix your car? What’s the matter with it?”

“Oh, come on, Bingo,” Sandra answered. “The flat tires? The gum in the locks?”

“What makes you think that was me?” Bingo asked.

“Your unscheduled visit, wrappers from your favorite gum.” Sandra leaned in closer and said, “A flare of temper I remember from when we were kids."

He glared at her.

Fix her car? Get the gum out of the locks? Repair the valve stems? He didn't have time to get all that done. Hell, he'll have to find a car and borrow money from Len until payday for sure. Car or the police? Another lousy choice.

"We used to be family, Bingo. Despite everything, I've never forgotten that." Sandra reached for his hand.

Bingo pulled away.

"I want you to come to my graduation on Saturday. Tomorrow," she said.

"Yeah, I bet you do." Bingo's insides grew tight. His voice had a slight quiver.

"It starts at two," she continued. "Meet us at Alice's at noon. And," she paused, "let's start over."

Suddenly, she wanted him at graduation. Suddenly, they were all family again.

"You know what you have to do, Bingo." Sandra kicked up the stand on her bike and rode back toward Alice's house.

Bingo felt the weekend slip away. Lindy. The mountains. The good time. Up in Idyllwild, people thought he was a great guy. Everyone called him BJ. They didn't know about his father, renowned Don Juan of Beaumont Corners. They didn't know he had a once-upon-a-time stepsister and grandmother—who had finally noticed him.

He kicked at a stone in the parking lot. The wheel of luck had a funny way of turning. There would be no Lindy. He had no money. He had to fix a car. That'd take Saturday morning and maybe all of Sunday. He had to find a car for Saturday afternoon. There were no choices left.

Bingo watched the people entering and leaving the mart, his thoughts churning at how fast life could change. He kicked at another stone, but stopped. An idea began to brew.

"Hey, Len," he said, as he walked toward his buddy. "Change of plan."

"Yeah? What's up?"

"I need to do something for Sandra."

"Yeah?"

"Yeah," Bingo replied, then said, "I need some wheels."

"So?"

Bingo paused. "I need to use your pickup truck tomorrow."

"What?" Len asked, clearly surprised at the request.

"You heard me. And I need to borrow some money."

Len scratched his chin and narrowed his eyes at him. "I don't know, man. That's one hell of a big ask."

"Aw, come on. I'm in a real bind. I'll owe you a favor."

Len cocked his head, took his time to respond. "Okay, Buddy," he said, a gleam appearing in his eyes. "I have one condition. I get to tool around on your Ninja this weekend and next."

The Ninja? The Ninja! Bingo stared at Len. His insides tightened. The Ninja.

Slowly, he nodded.

The Simian Society

A rhesus monkey sits on Lori Anderson's left forearm like a short-distance runner about to push away from a starting block. It quivers. It glimpses up at her but doesn't move. Despite the humid summer air in her neighbor's garage, Lori's mouth is dry, and her hands feel cold. She's never been this close to a monkey.

She nods toward a large wire cage sitting on the floor next to a workbench. Above its door hangs a scrap of wood with *Jimmy* scrawled in black paint. "That's his house?" she asks.

"Yep," her neighbor Daff answers, clutching the end of a short leash attached to the monkey's harness.

"How old is he?" Lori observes the animal's compact little body.

"Dunno. Someone else owned 'im before me." Daff holds out a dish with his free hand. "Give 'im some of this."

She takes a slice of peeled banana from the plastic bowl. "Here, Jimmy."

Jimmy grabs the fruit, shoves it in his mouth, glances from her empty fingers to her face, then back to her fingers. She offers another piece.

"Jest move slow," Daff advises.

"This isn't natural," Lori says, shaking her head.

"Jest feed 'im. He'll be okay."

Jimmy snatches away another piece. Then another. While he eats, Lori looks at him more closely.

He has perfect nails, shaped like a human's, except they're black instead of pink. Spikey brown fur, like a man's brush-cut, tops his head, only to give way to longer fur down his neck and back. His chest has a pinkish hue. Deep-set brown eyes, a long nose, and incisors that protrude over his lower teeth form his face. Unlike the soft warm look in her dog's eyes, Jimmy's eyes appear glacier cold.

She picks up the last banana bit from the dish. Even though Jimmy's cheeks bulge like a squirrel's, he shoves it into his mouth. He looks up at her face, down at her fingers, now void of banana, back to her face. He glances at the empty dish in Daff's hand.

Lori feels the monkey's feet grip her forearm. She tenses. In a blur of movement, Jimmy leans across her chest and clamps his teeth onto her right biceps like he's eating an ear of corn. She screams.

"What the hell!" Daff pulls the monkey away with a rough jerk of the leash. He shoves the screeching animal into its cage. The dish clatters onto the garage floor.

Lori covers the bite with her hand, startled, clenching her eyes. Daff's loud, angry voice meets Jimmy's high-pitched screams. She opens her eyes, the cacophony subsiding, except for her heavy breathing. She's cold. Her pulse pounds.

"Don't know what the hell made 'im do that," Daff mutters. He looks at her. "I gotta get ya to the hospital. Ya look pale."

"What do you expect?" Lori says, fighting back tears. "Your caged monkey just bit me! Animals like him belong in the wild."

"Come on, Lori. We been here before. Let's jest agree to disagree."

Daff offers to help her to his pickup; she brushes his hand away.

He opens the door, offers his help again, which she refuses. She climbs in. The pain in her arm throbs. She wipes her eyes with the back of her hand.

She waits while Daff folds his six-foot frame into the driver's seat. He takes a camouflage baseball cap that sits on top of the dash and puts it on. Strands of graying red hair sprout from beneath it. His weathered, seventy-year-old face now hides in shadow. She watches him turn on the air conditioner and throw the truck in reverse, backing down the drive onto the road. The blast of cool air feels good on her clammy body. The truck lurches forward.

"Ya mad at me?" he asks.

"What do you think? The damn thing hurts!" She peers down at the perfect set of teeth marks in her upper arm, at the bruised skin, the surface blood. "He could be rabid or diseased."

Daff shakes his head. "Nope, no way. Jimmy has had his shots. I got papers."

"I hope so." Lori digests this news but can't stop herself. "Why in hell did you get a monkey?"

"Aw, people buy 'em all the time for pets. They're smart. Hell, they even sent one into space."

"Doesn't make it right," she says and looks again at her wound.

"I'm sorry, Lori." Daff sounds sincere.

"Me, too, but I'm really mad at myself for going along with your . . . craziness; for holding and feeding him in the first place. Jimmy should be in an animal sanctuary."

"Aw, ya got it all wrong," Daff grunts. "And I ain't crazy."

He grows silent. A truck with *Fallbrook Produce* scrolled above images of avocados rumbles past, leaving behind a plume of exhaust.

Lori digs in. “You know, you don’t have the greatest track record with animals.”

Daff gives her a sharp look. “What’re ya talkin’ about?”

“What am I talking about?” she asks in disbelief. “Did you forget? Your two black Labradors killed some of my prize-winning Yokohama chickens.”

“I paid ya for ’em. Got rid of the Labs.”

“Then Monty, your Brazilian macaw, came along,” Lori reminds him. “On his outside perch, he squawked or talked so loud the neighbors reported you.” She momentarily remembered the string of curse words in Monty’s repertoire.

“I gave ’im to a zoo.”

“What about that black horse named Rebel? Huge animal. Seventeen hands. He gnawed through your wooden corral fence and ran off. The Sheriff’s Department had to capture him.”

“He was a mean bastard.” Daff rolls down the window, spits. “Hope someone made glue outta ’im.”

“You’re impossible, Daff.” She stares straight ahead. “And put that window up. The hot air is coming in.”

Lori isn’t surprised that, over time, her neighbor’s given name of Dan Taff has morphed into Daff. She’s often wondered what causes his fixation with exotic or bizarre animals. Maybe it’s the great white hunter syndrome or the alpha male instinct or . . . loneliness. His wife died five years ago.

A pain shoots up her arm. She grimaces.

“We’re here.” Daff’s voice interrupts her thoughts. He makes a right turn into the Hospital Emergency Entrance.

Once inside, Daff says, “Glad it ain’t busy, Lori. I’ll be here in the waiting room."

With a nod to the contrite tone of his voice, she checks in. Moments later, she's shown to a small exam room. While she waits, she picks up a *People* magazine from a counter. A child film star on the cover holds a Shih Tzu puppy. She thumbs through the pages, thinking of her own animals. Her adopted Rhodesian Ridgeback, Barney. Her Appaloosa named Ember. Her chickens. They have a good home on the small avocado ranch she operates with the help of her foreman, Diego.

Jimmy's bite reinforces her belief about wild animals. They're not meant to be caged in a garage next to a cluttered workbench, a case of motor oil, and a pickup.

A doctor enters, gives her a benign smile. "So, you have a monkey bite? An interesting man in the waiting room assures me the animal has had its shots."

"He's my neighbor," she explains. "He's a character, but he's sincere."

"Good to know," the doctor says.

A thorough cleansing of the wound is ordered, plus an antibiotic shot, followed by a tetanus shot. After the doctor leaves, a nurse arrives who does the procedures with a minimum of discomfort.

The next day, Lori's bandaged arm aches, but she manages to squeeze her still trim fifty-year-old body into jeans. She clumsily buttons a denim shirt. After tying back her long brown hair, noting its strands of gray with a sigh, she walks across the road to Daff's with one thing on her mind—to convince him to put Jimmy in an animal refuge.

She finds the two of them in the garage. But before she can

launch into the subject, Daff apologizes again for Jimmy's misdeeds, then adds, "Ya know, when I have 'im trained, I'm gonna take 'im to a meeting of The Simian Society up in Hollywood."

"The Simian Society?" Lori raises her eyebrows.

"Animal owners gather with their monkeys to network," he explains. "Agents might be there. It's a good place to make connections, get Jimmy into the movies. Or on a TV show, like *Friends.* For that show they used a capuchin monkey."

"I can't think of anything worse," Lori says. "Aren't there laws? Licenses? Permits?"

"Dunno."

"You'd better find out."

"Aw, I ain't hurtin' anyone," Daff answers.

She's sad to see Jimmy harnessed and leashed. More disturbing, he's dressed in tiny, water-proof pants. Daff's large, rough hands have slipped the animal's six-inch tail through a small opening in the back of the garment. They fit the twelve-pound, twenty-four-inch animal perfectly. She asks, "Where'd you get the pants?"

"From Wild Bill's place up in Oceanside. He deals in all kinds of animals, takes good care of 'em. Come on," he says. "Let me show you what Jimmy can do."

"Count me out."

"Aw, come on. You'll change your mind." Daff takes her hand. "Wait 'til you see his tricks. He's really a cute little bugger. Maybe you won't be mad at me or him anymore. He was just nervous the other day."

"So was I. And I'm not mad . . . at him."

Her curiosity wins. Daff holds Jimmy close on their walk from the garage into the house where he picks up a slender black wand, about five feet long, leaning in the corner of the living room. The monkey squirms, but Daff holds him tighter.

Surprised, Lori asks, "What are you doing with a harness racing whip? You don't own a horse. Or a sulky."

"I'll show ya," Daff replies. "I've been trainin' this ole boy."

The supple fiberglass wand has a free-swinging piece of black leather about a foot long hanging from its tip. At the other end of the whip, a wrapped handle like one on a golf club gives the user a good grip. Lori's seen drivers wield this whip on their horses during sulky races at the annual Avocado Festival.

Daff places Jimmy on the tile floor, plops his foot on the leash. "I ain't able to move fast like he does or stay close enough to him, so when he misbehaves, I can reach out and snap 'im." He flicks the whip in the air. The free-swinging piece of black leather pops. The animal flinches and tries to edge away.

Lori plants her hands on her hips. "You what?"

"Aw, come on. It don't really hurt 'im. Just gets his attention. Watch what he can do." To begin the show, Daff clicks his heels together, bowing like a circus ringmaster. His foot slips from the leash.

Jimmy's coat of brown fur bristles. He leaps into the air, grabbing onto the folds of a flowered drape, his short leash loose and dangling. With a nimble glide, he attaches himself to sheer white curtains covering the window between draperies, grabs onto the far drape, swings for momentum and catapults onto the scalloped wooden valance above the window.

Pop, snap goes the tip of the whip. Jimmy proves the faster.

"He's showin' off," Daff says, attempting an excuse.

"Stop that. You'll hurt him!" Lori steps toward Daff, but he puts his hand up like a stop sign.

Daff grumbles, tries to grab the leash, but Jimmy bounds onto the back of a well-worn green couch. He jumps down, scampers across the floor, then leaps onto the back of a dining room chair. With a short hop, he lands on the dining room table. He scuttles across it, whisking a decorative runner from its surface, along with a large wooden bowl filled with plastic oranges, pears, apples, bananas. The runner, the bowl and the fake fruit clatter onto the floor.

Pop, snap goes the whip.

"Daff, don't."

"Stay outta this, Lori."

"Stop it! Stop hitting him!"

"Aw, I can't let him get away with this." Daff makes another lunge for the leash.

Lori retreats to the safety of the doorway. She wants to grab Jimmy in her arms. She wants Daff to feel the flick of that whip.

With the bowl's contents scattered, Jimmy scampers about the room, dodges the whip, and bounds down a hall. Daff stumbles around the obstacles, goes after him, shouting. He tries to snap Jimmy with the whip; he tries to grab the leash, but the confines of the hallway restrict him. He falls against a wall, cursing.

Jimmy bounces back past Daff, leaping once again onto the living room valance. Jimmy's eyes gleam, full of play. Daff's eyes narrow into slivers of deception. He hauls himself to his feet.

He leans the whip against the living room wall, puts his hands in his pockets and gives a long look to Jimmy who returns the look. After a beat, Daff takes the bowl and runner, puts them on the dining room table. Using slow, casual movements, he picks up a fake apple, a fake orange. With each piece of fruit he drops in the bowl, he edges nearer to Jimmy.

Jimmy watches, scratches his shoulder, then steals a look at Lori.

At that moment, Daff lunges for the end of the leash, grabbing it, yanking Jimmy down from his perch. The man drops into an easy chair, his face red. Lori cheers silently: *Jimmy: one. Daff: zero.*

"Daff," Lori begs, "get rid of that whip."

"Hey, ya gotta punish bad behavior to get 'im to do what ya want," Daff insists.

"Have you ever tried rewarding his good behavior?"

Daff waves a dismissive hand at her. "Gotta make an animal respect ya."

Jimmy sits on the rug by Daff's chair, quivering. Lori wonders if Jimmy feels fear. Or anger. She starts to say more to Daff, but she can only manage a disgusted look before she turns toward the door, exits, and slams the door behind her.

The next morning, she drives to San Clemente to visit her parents for two days. While away, she can't put the image from her mind of a five-foot whip being used on a twelve-pound animal. She calls the San Diego County Humane Society from her parents' home. She reports Dan Taff, aka Daff, and gives his address. She also mentions a place in Oceanside called Wild Bill's.

The morning after her return, Lori's at her mailbox down by the road's edge. After she slips a letter to her sister inside, she raises its red metal flag to alert the postman. Just then, a van with SDCHS painted on its side pulls into Daff's drive. Two men get out of the cab. She lingers, weeding around the mailbox post, straightening the decorative stones, glad she's made the call. The men come out moments later, empty-handed.

She wonders what Daff has said to make the men leave without Jimmy. After lunch, she walks across the road, up her neighbor's drive to find him in his garage, drinking a beer. A large gauze bandage swathes his right hand like a boxing glove. Jimmy's cage is empty.

"You call the Humane Society on me?" Daff's tone hovers between anger and hurt.

"I sure did. You know how I feel. Jimmy belongs where he has trees, fresh air, freedom." She looks at his hand. "What happened to you?"

Daff's face flushes with anger. "After you left, Jimmy chewed the hell outta my hand, but I yanked him away before he did any real damage."

"Well, I wonder what made him do that?" she asks, a bite of sarcasm in her voice.

Daff scowls. "Well, whatever you think, I sure fed 'im enough. Kept 'im safe, too."

"Safe from what? Your whip?" She looks at the empty cage. "Where is he? The Humane Society left empty-handed. Are you hiding him?"

"I took that critter back to Wild Bill's real quick. Got my money back." He paused, then added, "Ya probably got Bill in trouble, too. I had to tell those Humane Society guys about 'im."

A bad feeling rises in her stomach. "What's Wild Bill going to do with Jimmy?"

He points to his hand. "That monkey's one mean son-of-a-bitch. He's gonna have t'get rid of 'im."

"How?" Lori asks.

"That ol' boy'll be put down."

"Oh, Daff." Lori puts her hand on her forehead, shakes her head. She leaves the garage, feeling heartsick, vowing to never let him abuse another animal, vowing to call the Humane Society if it happens again. She adds a prayer that the Humane Society gets to Wild Bill's place fast.

Lori walks back across the road, feeling the slight pound of a headache. She calls for Barney, whom she finds sitting in front of the barn where he's been waiting for their daily routine to begin. In the tack room she grabs a blanket, a bridle from its hook, and a black saddle from a wooden stand. Ember neighs from a nearby stall. Barney's tail wags against her leg.

"We're coming," she calls.

She places the equipment beside the stall door, then slides it open to enter. She strokes Ember's nose, feeling its soft warmth. When she slips on his harness, he nudges her, neighing softly as she leads him from the stall, shuffling his hooves while she drapes the saddle pad over him. After she heaves the saddle onto his back, securing the cinch around his belly, he tosses his head. Her foot in the stirrup, she swings up onto the saddle. Barney barks.

Soon, they're on their afternoon trail ride in the nearby San Diego Hills. She inhales the ocean breeze coming off the Pacific to the west. With a gentle hand, she pats Ember's neck. Barney runs along the path ahead of them.

As a rule, out on the trail, her mind sheds its worries. Ember's rhythmic sway, the loyal Barney nearby, an occasional squirrel scampering among the black oaks . . . these all bring her peace.

But not today. Her eyes moisten. She pictures the small primate quivering on her arm. She can feel his warmth. She recalls the one moment she witnessed his sense of play. The gleam in his eyes. The fun. The freedom.

Oh, Jimmy, I wish I'd made my call the day I met you.

III

The Tap of Metal on Glass

"Uneasiness followed him out the door, with a good chance it would follow him from now on."

—Nick Ferrelli
"Ferrelli's Fall"

Funny Man

Denny Jackson stopped practicing his comedy routine in the middle of a joke, an oldie about a lazy pimp. It didn't fit with his shtick. His gut told him it could fizzle like a cheap firecracker, and he trusted his gut. Tonight wasn't the night to bomb.

On the truck seat beside him sat a grimy notebook with "Denny's Babies: Jokes for the World's Greatest Comic" scribbled across its cover. He flipped through the pages until he saw a joke about a golfer and a gopher, *Caddyshack* style. Perfect. It would add the right mojo for a desert town offering golf courses around every corner.

Satisfied with the change, he relaxed, his thoughts switching to the evening ahead. He'd waited a month for another Open Mic Night for Comics at the best casino in town. His dream of being a stand-up comic like Jerry Seinfeld or Chris Rock hung close. He had never felt more ready.

A tap of metal on glass startled him back to the moment. He rolled down the window of his delivery rig. Behind him, other trucks waited in line, their engines idling.

"Hey, Funny Man!" A voice like crushed gravel whooshed in with the day's heat. "Park your load of two-by-fours down by those cement slabs so we can get them unloaded." Joe Fallon, the construction super, held a soiled clipboard. With a ballpoint pen, he checked off the lumber delivery.

"Okay, Mr. Boss Man." Denny grinned at Fallon's red face, a roadmap of capillaries, sweat pooling in the man's pockmarked cheeks.

"Yeah, yeah." Fallon scratched his bulbous nose. Then he asked, "Hey, ya know your load's shifting? We gotta get that thing unloaded before I got a pile of timber on my feet."

Nodding, Denny rolled the window up fast. Late afternoon heat seared the sand. At least the truck for the world's lousiest job came with air conditioning. He realigned his sunglasses on his nose and looked out at Morgan Ranch, an exclusive housing development underway in the middle of sand and tumbleweed, forty miles east of Palm Springs. Even if he had money, he'd never live out in the boonies, miles from people and casino nightlife. He needed more than coyotes and roadrunners for company.

He drove through the open construction gates, knowing there'd be another five- or ten-minute wait before the offload. Uneven, hard-packed sand of the temporary roadway jostled the truck. He checked the rearview mirror to make sure the load held steady and parked by a "Drug Free Work Zone" sign, its red letters faded and dusty. Time would be tight. It was a bad day to get stuck with a late delivery.

After unloading, he'd have to rush back to Palm Springs, drop off the rig, pick up his car, and race home. He'd have just enough time to run his routine in front of a full-length mirror hanging on the bathroom door and hype himself up for the biggest night of his life—five minutes in front of an audience at the Black Hawk Casino, the best casino in Palm Springs. He wanted his deadpan look to be just right, his timing to be spot-on.

His clothes for the night were spread out on the bed—a New York

Yankees' cap, jeans with a baggy ass, and a lucky Hawaiian shirt with palm trees and surfboards. Black high-top Keds with bright colored laces sat by the nightstand.

The casino emcee's voice played in his head: *"Give it up for the Big D. J., Denny Jackson, the King of Dyn-O-Mite Jokes!"* Denny mouthed the words. The name sounded good. Better than Dennis. Better than Denver, like his buddy suggested.

He'd be onstage where it counted, not in a meat market joint full of sloppy drunks. Important people would be in the audience. Maybe tonight he'd land a stand-up gig in the casino lounge or a chance to open a headliner's act in the big room. He'd been well received at the last two open mics he'd done at the Augustino Casino. But the Black Hawk was the casino with connections. He stood on the edge of a breakthrough. The feeling raced in his bones.

The desert by night excited him with its hot chicks, big crowds, and bright lights. He could see "Denny Jackson" in red neon on a casino marquee.

By day, the desert siphoned him dry. If he didn't take care, the yellow polyester shirt spanning his chest with Desert Builders Supply stitched on its back would squeeze him into a dead-end life of dust and dirt, complete with a wife and kids, before he'd had a chance.

"Mama," he said out loud, "this is the night your boy is gonna get noticed."

He revved the truck engine. Matt Larsen, from Sunshine Plumbing, pulled in behind him with a haul of PVC pipe. The man got out of his truck and stretched his wiry frame. Denny hated to leave his air-conditioned cab but decided to get out. He hadn't seen Larsen since the guy had his accident.

Within moments the polyester shirt clung to Denny's back and chest. He ran his hand over his shaved head where the sun's rays beat like hammers on his scalp. Heat rippled up from the raw desert floor. The Coral Mountains nearby appeared too hot to touch.

"Summer in the desert's a real bitch," Larsen said and spat in the sand. He limped with a slight tilt to the right, causing a short time delay with each step.

Denny leaned back in the cab to get his cap. "Glad to see you back on the job. How are you?" He eased the cap onto his head.

"How do you think, Funny Man? I'm not runnin' any races, am I? My boss don't know it, but I'm gonna sue his sorry ass. His friggin' fault a load of old galvanized steel pipe rolled on me at the scrap metal yard and broke my legs. That truck's rigging was shot. Then he makes nice, givin' me a charity job drivin' deliveries." Larsen rubbed the back of his neck, eying Denny's new truck. "I still got pain."

"Yeah, that was a bad deal." Denny squared his shoulders.

"You still tryin' to be a comedian?" Larsen looked him over, a sneer on his face. After casting a quick look around, he pulled a small white envelope from his side pocket, shaking three white pills into his palm. He popped them in his mouth, swallowing several times.

Denny watched. "Those pain pills? Hope you're not taking too many."

Closing the envelope, Larson slipped it back in his pocket and gave him a sly look.

"Yeah, pain pills with benefits. Not to worry, my friend. Not to worry." Larsen smiled, his eyes slits. "Must be kind of a downer, slummin' with the construction apes."

"Come on, Larsen."

The man shook his head. "I had dreams, too. Runnin' the Los Angeles marathon. The Boston Marathon. Then to New York for the big one. Hell, now I got trouble chasin' the dog." He spat again and wiped his lips with his tongue. "Dreams got a way of gettin' crushed flat."

"I'm sorry, man." Denny glanced away for a moment. He wasn't going to let the guy pull him down. He looked back at Larsen and said, "Hey, I'm doing an open mic at the Black Hawk tonight. Come on by. I'll give you a few laughs."

"Won't happen. I got things to do." Larsen scratched his groin. "Y'know your load's leanin'?"

"It's okay," Denny said. "It's still solid. Fallon knows."

Larsen scowled, the line between his eyes a deep crag. "So, drivin' a truck ain't good enough for you?"

Denny caught his breath. The guy was always wired tight, hard to handle. "It's okay for now."

"Well, don't quit your day job," Larsen said, taking another shot. "Last joke you told me stunk like a pile of manure."

"Hey, I've gotten a lot better, man," Denny replied.

"Says you, says you."

Denny didn't get it. He'd never done anything to Larsen. He put his hands on his hips to air his armpits. "Hope we unload quick. I gotta get out of here. Tonight's big for me."

"In a hurry, huh, big guy?" Larsen reached in his pants pocket and took out a knife. With a quick flip of his wrist, the blade flew open. "Well, I'm just gonna slow you down, let you know what it feels like to be out of the race. To miss the big one."

"Put that away. Are you crazy?"

"Crazy like a fox, Denny Boy."

Bright lights and fame, that's what Denny wanted, not a knife in the belly. He wasn't going to mess with the drugged-up, jealous bastard. He ran for the super's shack.

Larsen stood where he was, yelling, "Runnin' away, Funny Man? Was a time I coulda caught you easy." The words blended into the din of workmen's shouts and noisy truck engines.

Sweat rolled down Denny's forehead. He swung the shack door open. A blast of cold air from a noisy air conditioner hit him in the face. "Hey, Fallon, I need your help. Larsen's acting weird. He pulled a switchblade on me."

"What the hell?" Fallon grabbed his safety helmet and hustled from the shack. He motioned to a trucker crouched under a scraggly palm. The man stubbed his cigarette in the sand and ran over.

"What's up?" The man squinted in the glare.

Fallon shook his head as he pulled out his cell phone. "Got a crazy with a knife. I'm callin' 911."

The man grabbed a piece of two-by-four from a nearby scrap pile.

Denny ran back toward his truck in time to see Larsen fumbling with a strap, one of three holding the unstable load in place. Alarmed, Denny cried out, "What the hell are you doing? Get outta there!" If the lumber fell, he'd never make it to the casino on time.

Larsen slashed the strap from its iron ring. His feet kicked up dust as he scuffed along the truck's side toward the middle strap. With speed and precision, he slashed it.

The man could move faster than Denny realized. Heart pounding, Denny wished he had his pry bar.

Fallon and the trucker drew near. Fallon yelled. "Get away from that truck."

"Stuff it, Fallon," Larson shouted. "Stay back, losers, or I'll cut you, too."

Biceps bulging, Larsen sawed on the last strap, but swung around as the men came in closer, crisscrossing his knife in front of him, chanting "Funny Man! Funny Man!" at Denny.

"Grab the crazy bastard!" Fallon and the trucker rushed at Larsen from one side, Denny from the other. Larsen slashed out at the two men, but suddenly turned and cannoned into Denny, slamming him into the side of the truck, his head cracking against an iron ring. Denny's knees folded under him as he sank onto the sand. A blurry Larsen dodged away. The strap snapped.

The lumber's soft groan became a loud rumble, an avalanche of wood tumbling from the truck bed, pressing Denny into the sand like pick-up sticks in a game gone wrong. He heard Fallon shouting, Larsen laughing, the other man cursing. Flashes of light zigzagged, burst, and faded. Pain radiated through his chest. He couldn't breathe.

A faint voice whirled around him in the cloudy grayness.

"Okay, folks, put those hands together and give a Black Hawk welcome to Denny Jackson, the desert's number one Funny Man!"

Darkness engulfed him, followed by silence.

The Waiting Room

The walls are dull, institutional green. In the background, an air conditioner drones nonstop against the hottest August in Medford that anyone can remember. Even though the room is cool, sweat beads on my skin. I lean back in the wooden chair to rest my head against the wall.

The waiting room door opens and Leanne Westlake walks in carrying two bottles of water from a vending machine in the hall. She drops onto a wooden chair beside me. I take the bottle she offers and hold its cold surface against my forehead before opening it. My mouth is dry. I unscrew the cap, taking small sips.

"I spoke to the nurse," she says. "When Brad comes out of surgery, he'll be taken to ICU. I can't see him yet." She opens the other bottle of water, puts it to her lips. After a slow swallow, she adds, "They're moving Drew now, Cathy." Her voice trails off.

A short time ago, after watching the Medford Rogues play the Chico Heat, our husbands were on their way home from Miles Baseball Field over near Jacksonville. Now Brad is in surgery. Drew is dead.

Nothing matters. Things I thought important no longer are. Not Drew's new job at the Medford Water Commission. Not the cosmetology license that came in yesterday's mail. Not the blue couch I want to buy at Nelson's Furniture.

I'm a widow at twenty.

Earlier we called our families. Leanne helped me when my voice broke. Now we sit in silence. I close my eyes. I've seen enough of the brown vinyl floor, the basement windows hung with Venetian blinds, the dusty fluorescent fixtures suspended from the ceiling. The walls close in around me.

Pictures of happy times I'd posted on Instagram float through my mind. High school graduation. An August wedding, even though our parents had wanted us to wait. Our small apartment. A new puppy we named Jazz. Our first-anniversary party.

There's nothing happy to post now. Nothing.

I open my eyes. My hand tightens into a fist, the other closes around the water bottle. I'm angry. At the world. At Brad. At Leanne. I want to kick the wall, throw the bottle across the room. I want to scream until I have no voice. Does Leanne sense how much I resent her?

Brad's car swerved off the road at high speed, careening through a fence into a tree. One fatality . . . Drew. I'll never again feel his touch on my skin or watch him shave or wash his work clothes or tell him to hang up his towel. We'll never . . .

The memories make me ache.

Sad, bitter thoughts collide into each other, out of control. I drink my water until it's gone, the bottle empty like me. I hold it tight in my hands as the early morning telephone call from the Sheriff's Department continues to ring in my ears.

It comes at thirteen minutes after midnight, waking me as I doze in front of the TV. I had expected Drew home from the game around eleven. I grab my cell. I think I'll hear his voice; hear they've had car trouble or gave a friend a lift home and they're on their way.

"Mrs. Connery?"

A woman's voice. Why do I hear a woman's voice?

I reply with a scratchy, "Yes?"

"This is the Jackson County Sheriff's Office. We regret to inform you your husband has been in an accident. He's at Providence Hospital."

Panic grabs me. My heart races.

"The paramedics told the officers it's serious. Do you need transportation?"

I tell her no; I'll get to the hospital as quickly as possible. I hang up, light-headed, scared. I pull my baby-doll nightgown over my head. Each piece of clothing I touch tangles in my fingers. Jeans, tee shirt, flip-flops. I pull my hair back into a ponytail and cinch it with a scrunchie. The phone rings again. Nerves pound in the back of my head. It's Leanne. She's gotten the same call about Brad. I hold my cell tight in my hand, talking to her, and run to Drew's pickup parked in front of the apartment.

Leanne and I meet at the hospital. A nurse takes us down a long hall to a secluded alcove, a distance from the hospital lobby. Several minutes pass. A trauma room doctor enters the alcove through double swinging doors; as the doors swing closed behind him, I see a "No Admittance" sign on one, "Authorized Personnel Only" on the other.

Leanne learns Brad is in serious condition, still in surgery, but expected to survive.

The doctor turns to me. His voice is soft but to my ears, it sounds like thunder. Drew died in the ambulance.

I collapse against the nurse who helps me to a nearby chair. My sides constrict with a wave of nausea. Someone gives me a paper cup filled with water. Someone else talks to me, but I don't hear. I cry.

The admitting nurse apologizes about procedures and then extends hospital forms attached to clipboards for each of us to sign. The two of us attempt the paperwork. I want to run away. I want to curl up into myself. I want to bury my head in my arms to stop it from pounding. The forms completed, another nurse guides us to an elevator and down to a basement room, the room where we wait.

It seems as if we have waited for days. My thoughts, my regrets, my constant remembering tire me. I drop the empty water bottle into my purse, an old habit. Drew always recycles. I correct myself . . . Drew used to recycle.

We wait, two people abandoned, longing for rescue.

My sweaty hands tuck pieces of hair behind my ears, shorter strands that have slipped from the ponytail. I think about the plans we had. Driving to San Francisco in the fall to see the Golden Gate Bridge. Saving for a house. Starting a family in a year or two. I wipe at tears with my fingertips. Leanne is talking to me.

"Remember when you sprained your ankle two days before prom?" Pale pink lipstick frames Leanne's smile. "You still made it, crutches and all. Even did our hair. You were always good with hair. You're strong, Cathy."

I see kindness in her eyes as she puts her hand on my arm. It grates on me.

"So easy for you to say." I pull away. "My husband's dead, not yours."

The look on her face seems to fade from surprise to pain. She responds, "Brad could have died, too." She glances down at her hands, at the chipped nail polish. “I don’t know why it was your husband and not mine. I don’t know why it had to be either one of them.”

She stands abruptly, walking to the other side of the room, her back to me.

I can’t stop myself. “Brad was the one driving, the one with the hopped-up Mustang, the one who likes his beer. Thanks to him, Drew is dead.”

A heavy silence settles between us.

Leanne turns and says, “I know you’re angry.”

“You don’t know anything.” My voice grows louder. “You didn’t lose your husband. I’m the one left alone. I’ll be the one crying at night. I’ll be the one listening for the door to open when her husband should be coming in from work. Except he won’t ever open it again!” I’m shouting. “Brad will get well. Your life will be like before.”

Suddenly, I’m choking on tears.

Leanne folds her arms around herself, looks down at the floor, and then at me. She starts to say more but stops as the waiting room door opens and a man in green scrubs enters.

“Mrs. Connery?” He looks at Leanne, at me, his eyebrows raised.

I wipe my face, struggling to find my voice. “I’m Mrs. Connery.”

“I’m Dr. Stanton. This way, please.”

Leanne takes a step forward. “Do you want me to come with you?”

I clasp my hands in front of me. I don’t want to go alone. I manage to say, “If you want to,” and walk to the door.

Dr. Stanton takes my arm. Our footsteps echo in the silent corridor. Leanne walks on my other side, trying to take my hand, but I push it away. As we walk, I see flashes of Drew standing beside me. I think about the secret we kept between us as we promised each other we would. We didn't want to hear, "I told you so," or "You were too young." But I couldn't bring myself to say the words Drew wanted to hear about our secret.

I realize if I don't say them now, I won't have another chance.

The doctor pauses by a metal door. Two words stenciled on it stare back at me. "Hospital Morgue."

I feel hollow.

Inside, we stand beside a gurney, Drew's body outlined beneath a white sheet. The doctor waits while I compose myself. I vow that after I make the identification, I'll ask to be alone. I'll ask to be alone so no one will think I'm crazy talking to a dead man.

Dr. Stanton clears his throat. "There's no easy way to do this, Mrs. Connery. Are you ready?"

Leanne who has patiently waited beside me takes my hand. This time I don't push her away. I nod. I close my eyes and hear a gentle rustle of cloth.

A scream startles me into opening my eyes before I'm ready.

"Oh, God," I whisper.

My hand goes to my mouth. Leanne leans into me. She begins to cry.

I feel a rush of adrenaline. "That's not my husband."

"I beg your pardon?" Dr. Stanton opens the file he holds.

"That's not Andrew Connery," I murmur. "It's Brad Westlake. Bradley. They were in the car together."

I fold Leanne into my arms. She's sobbing. Each in our own way, we're trying to process what has just happened. I'm afraid I might be dreaming. Neither of us has words. Leanne steps to the gurney to kiss her husband's forehead but collapses onto his body. The doctor and I help her stand. He replaces the cloth and steps back.

Leanne and I stand by the gurney, each in our own worlds. The grief hanging around my shoulders slides onto hers. I regret my words to her.

Drew and I have a second chance.

The doctor walks to his desk and makes a call on his cell phone. "Those accident victims brought in this morning? The deceased is Bradley Walker. Who the hell is handling the paperwork up there?" He ends the call and looks at us. "I regret what just happened. Please accept my apology. And my deepest sympathy."

My arm around her waist, Leanne and I walk from the morgue toward the elevator. I keep my good news close, shedding my grief, my anger. I promise to be a better wife, a better lover, a better friend. My bargains with God spill like diamonds onto a jeweler's tray.

The elevator doors open. Leanne looks pale, like she might collapse. I steady her. I have no idea of Drew's condition. I have yet to find out.

"I'm sorry for my ugly words," I murmur. "I wish I could take them back. All of them."

Leanne looks at me. "I wish I could take things back, too."

I nod, acknowledging the tests to our friendship, recent and past. I help her into the elevator. I hope our families arrive from out of town soon. We need them.

I want to see Drew.

Leanne watches the elevator doors rumble to a close. She takes deep breaths, trying to collect herself. "Cathy, you have to call the bowling alley. I can't lose my job."

I assure her I will.

We arrive at the first floor. She walks out of the elevator into the hall. I take her hand. I'll help her with paperwork like she helped me. It's my turn to make the calls, to provide comfort.

I realize I'm all right doing this. The past no longer matters.

She stops. "Someone has to cover my shift. Ruthie Hanson owes me."

Ruthie Hanson.

"I'll take care of it," I say.

We continue toward the hospital lounge to wait for whatever comes next.

Ruthie Hanson. I remember her well.

Ruthie is the one who told me about Leanne and Drew. About their one-nighter last winter after too many bowling alley beers.

Did Leanne know Drew told me?

We'd kept it our secret. We wanted our marriage.

But I never said the words Drew wanted to hear.

I never said, "I forgive you."

Now I can. And I'll mean it.

Hannon's Folly

Hannon stood on the edge of a deserted viewpoint high above Palm Springs. A slight breeze ruffled his hair as he looked out across the valley into a clear, starlit night, indifferent to the rugged beauty of the San Bernardino Mountains silhouetted against the sky or the maze of headlights, neon signs and lighted buildings sparkling below. He felt ill.

To steady himself, he sat on a stone bench near the vista's safety rail. His body ached. Sweat slipped down the small of his back, despite a slight coolness to the night. The pounding in his temples felt almost unbearable. He kept asking himself the same question: *Why did this happen?*

An image rushed into Hannon's troubled mind. He stood with a freckle-faced seven-year-old boy and the boy's mother in the entryway of a house that once had been his home, too.

"Will the tooth fairy come, Daddy?" the boy had asked.

"Check under your pillow in the morning, Danny," Hannon replied. "Come on, it's time to go to the stadium to see your first baseball game."

His son put on a pint-sized cap that Hannon had brought. It had the team's logo of a bighorn sheep above the visor.

"Bye, Mom," the boy said.

She wasn't "Mommy" anymore. The little man was growing up. Hannon and his ex-wife Karen exchanged a brief glance. He had detected a moment of softness in her look, before her cold glare returned, reserved only for him.

Hannon shook himself back to the present. He reached inside his lightweight jacket for a crumpled cigarette pack and a book of matches. Across the matchbook cover blazed the name of his favorite bar, The Red Pony, a place he frequented after the divorce. He pulled out a cigarette, placed it between his dry lips and lit it. He coughed, wiping his mouth with the back of his hand.

Hannon's thoughts returned to the day he'd picked up his son. He and Danny had jostled through the crowd at McCallum Stadium to watch a game between the Palm Springs Bighorns and the Tucson Trailblazers. They had seats along the first-base line.

With the opening pitch, Danny's questions began. "What's the pitcher chewing, Daddy? Why does he nod to the catcher?" Hannon answered and the boy listened. He learned fast.

After several innings with the Bighorns down by two, Hannon felt a tug on his sleeve. He turned to see Danny wiggling in his seat, holding up one finger. The signal. Hannon sighed. The Bighorns had men on first and third bases. The next batter was walking to the plate. He looked at his son and knew there was no extra time. They made their way to the men's room. On the way back to their seats, Hannon checked the scoreboard. The Bighorns led by one, thanks to the batter's homerun.

Hannon punched his arm in the air and shouted, "Go, Bighorns!" Danny did the same.

"Fist bump," Hannon said, his fist meeting his son's.

When the seventh inning stretch arrived, Hannon felt another tug on his arm.

"Restroom again?"

"No, I'm hungry, Daddy." Danny took off his hat to scratch his forehead.

Hannon put his hand on the boy's head and rumpled his hair. "Hot dogs and fries sound good? Hang on to my hand."

Danny put on his cap, grabbed his father's outstretched palm.

At the food stands, a hungry, thirsty crowd milled about, the smell of hot dogs mingling with buyers' voices and loud laughter. Taking their place in one of the lines, Hannon heard his name.

"Neil, Neil Hannon?"

He turned to see a pretty, tanned face framed by long blond hair.

"Well, hi," the blond continued. "I haven't seen you in a while."

The face belonged to the owner of a business card given to him at The Red Pony two weeks before, a card he'd lost. The woman had attracted him that night and he hadn't forgotten, feeling he'd stumbled onto something good. He didn't plan to lose contact again until he found out.

"Hey, hi, Anne. Didn't know you were a Bighorn fan. You're looking good. This is my son, Danny." Hannon watched his son stand tall and extend his hand like he'd been taught.

"Hello, Danny." Anne shook his hand. "I'm happy to meet you."

"Hi," said the little man of the house, the house Hannon made payments on every month. Danny grinned, gap-toothed, adding, "She's pretty, Daddy."

"Thank you, Danny." Anne laughed. "Is he going to be tall like you, Neil?"

Hannon felt Danny lean against him. He looked down. His son seemed overcome with shyness.

"Probably." He shifted his weight and patted Danny on the shoulder. He paused. "Haven't seen you at The Red Pony lately." He slipped his hands into his pockets.

Anne shook her head. "No, I've been busy. Real estate is hot right now." She ran her hand under her long hair, combing it with slender fingers.

"Can I buy you a drink?"

"Oh, I'm getting drinks for my friends," she said, "but thank you."

Hannon drew Anne into line beside them. She ordered four large Cokes. As the drinks became ready, she put them in the cardboard carrier the server had given her. She pulled loose bills from her large shoulder purse and paid, adjusting the purse's strap back up into place.

"Let me try that again," Hannon said. "Can I buy you a drink at The Red Pony? Tomorrow night?"

Picking up the drinks' carrier, Anne turned to Hannon. Before she could speak, the strap of her large handbag slipped from her shoulder. The heaviness of the purse pulled her arm down with a thud, tipping the box of drinks until ice and liquid flew. The cups bounced onto the floor.

People jumped back, brushing Coke and ice from their clothes.

"Oh, I'm so sorry," Anne said, pulling napkins from a metal holder on the counter to hand to those who needed one. She repositioned her purse on her shoulder and reordered. Drinks emerged quickly.

"Now that all the excitement is over, I repeat," Hannon said. "Can I buy you a drink at The Red Pony?"

"Yes, I'll see you there tomorrow night about 8:30." Anne picked up her order, waved goodbye, and made her way through the crowd.

A man with "Maintenance" tagged on his uniform materialized to clean and mop up. People stepped around him.

"Well, I didn't expect all that," Hannon murmured, mindful Karen would pump Danny for details about what had happened at the game. Sighing, he stepped to the counter and said to the server, "We're ready to order."

To Danny, he said, "Ready for that hot dog, Big Guy?"

He looked down beside him.

"Danny?"

Hannon looked to each side, and behind him.

"Danny?"

Hannon swung around, calling his son's name.

"Danny!"

Someone, he didn't know who, asked what was wrong.

"My son! He's been standing right here with me. He's gone!"

When had his son wandered off? *I talked to Anne for only a moment. Danny always stays by me. Always.*

"Always," Hannon said into the night air, the memory vivid, gut-wrenching. He moaned as he hugged himself, rocking forward and back. Sobs shook his frame. Fits of coughing punctuated his shallow breathing.

A quiet desert night couldn't silence the cacophony of self-blame pounding in his head. He watched the glistening valley swim before his eyes. His stomach tightened.

Stadium security had responded at once. A young security guard placed a hand on his arm. "Don't worry, Mr. Hannon. If he's here, we'll find him."

An older man, a supervisor, asked questions: "What's your son wearing? What color is his hair? Do you have a recent picture in your wallet?" With his phone, the man snapped a photo of the image Hannon produced. He sent it to the security staff and assured Hannon all his people would be in constant communication.

Hannon checked the nearest restroom, hurried through the crowd calling Danny's name. He returned to their seats on the chance his son had been a big boy and found his way back on his own.

The Palm Springs police arrived. They pressed for more details.

"Did you see anyone talking to your son? Who was standing nearby? When did you miss him?" Hannon told the officers everything he remembered.

An Amber Alert lit the signboards above the freeways. The boy had vanished.

His call to Karen, the call before the police had arrived at her house, began another nightmare. "Danny? Danny's what? What did you say? Danny's not with you? He's missing? How did you let this happen?"

He tried to tell her.

She broke into tears. "Oh, Danny! Danny!"

And the call had ended.

Hannon looked out into the desert night, shaking his head, the memories overwhelming, his guilt unbearable. He clasped and unclasped his hands. Reaching into his jacket pocket, he fumbled past his cigarettes and matches, and retrieved a crumpled newspaper clipping, ragged from constant folding and unfolding. He knew the headline. He knew the contents. Like Lot's wife in the Bible, he looked back, again and again.

"Boy's Body Found in Desert."

Hannon's fingers coiled around the news article, crushing it, his fingernails digging into his palm. He grimaced and uncurled his fist. The wadded paper dropped to the ground.

If only I'd found the sick bastard who took Danny. Found him before the police.

He reached inside another pocket and removed a handgun. He placed it on the bench beside him.

A bright movement in the sky distracted him. He looked up to see a shooting star. Danny would have liked that. He could hear his son: "Oh, look, Daddy. God's moving His furniture."

Hannon looked down, picked up the gun and placed its muzzle against the soft skin beneath his chin.

Thelma's Cry

Thelma Walz lay in bed listening to strong winds rattle the windows of her room at the Whitfield Parish Nursing home. She hadn't slept well. Yesterday afternoon, her roommate Irene had said a hasty goodbye and left with her daughter. Being alone in the room at night, especially now, wasn't to Thelma's liking.

During breakfast yesterday morning, Thelma had watched a TV newsman report on a powerful hurricane hitting the Louisiana coast. The grave situation had caused the governor to issue a mandatory evacuation order. She and the other residents in the dining room had cried out with concern.

Thelma knew about tropical storms. She'd survived Hurricane Andrew. The thought of going through another barrage of wind, rain, floods and destruction overwhelmed her.

Evacuate, she thought. She couldn't move herself from the bed to her wheelchair unassisted. She waited every morning for caregivers Deborah or Winston to transfer her, every bone in her body crying, *Be careful! I'm fragile.*

Thelma was glad her ninety-year-old mind had stayed strong. She longed to have her say with that Deborah who had a smart mouth. But the woman took revenge every time Thelma responded to her sass or nastiness: roughness during a bed bath, clumsiness during a transfer from bed to wheelchair. Worse, Deborah might leave her alone too long in her chair, until she soiled herself. Thelma knew that woman's games.

Deborah entered the room, Winston behind her.

"Gotta move you, Thelma Jean. It's everyone to the rescue." Deborah grabbed Thelma's wheelchair from the corner and brought it over to the side of the hospital-style bed, banging it into the bed's metal frame.

"Here we go, Thelma." Winston slid his arm behind her back, sitting her up and easing her onto the side of the bed. He didn't hurt her.

"Anyone coming to evacuate you?" Deborah rambled on, her hands on her hips. "Your son, James, maybe? The guy who dropped you off a year ago? The guy who hasn't been seen much since and seldom calls?"

Winston shook his head and cast Deborah a long look. "Give me her bathrobe," he said.

Deborah scowled. She grabbed Thelma's chenille bathrobe from a bedside chair and tossed it to Winston. "Good thing you're here, Thelma Jean. Keeps me in a job."

Not allowing Deborah to bait her, Thelma kept quiet. Winston waited while she pulled the collar of her flannel nightgown up around her neck. Carefully, he eased her arms into the robe's long sleeves and snugged the pale pink garment around her body.

"Where are we going?" she asked. "It's too early for breakfast." Thelma winced as they transferred her into the wheelchair. Deborah pulled a blanket from the bed and gave it to Winston. He tucked it around Thelma's knees. They wheeled her down the hall, faster than usual.

"We're going to the dining room. Vehicles are coming to take you to higher ground," Deborah said. "This hurricane is on a real rant. Stuff's down all around us. Water's rising. Got your boots on, Thelma Jean?"

Thelma fidgeted, watching rain pelt the hall windows. Outside, trees bent and bowed under the wind's force. The building itself seemed to moan. Winston placed a hand on her shoulder.

Thelma joined the haphazard arrangement of disheveled residents being assembled in the dining room. She counted seven in wheelchairs, eight in beds, and nineteen sitting at the dining room tables, some able to walk unassisted, some with their walkers beside them. *They must be frightened like me.*

Peggy Dalton, the administrator of the home, walked into the large room. "Ambulances and vans will arrive shortly to move you inland," she said in a flat voice and hurried back to the lobby.

A low murmur arose. Thelma noticed Deborah standing in the doorway, this time with a purse on her arm. The woman glanced around and left the room. She saw Winston cast a glance at the cold coffee pots, at the empty bowl usually full of bananas for daily potassium, and at the lights in the ceiling, which should have been on. He moved around the room, reassuring the residents. He had often told them of his wife and children, shown them pictures.

Winston was a caring man, but even on a good day, Thelma didn't like living at the nursing home. She'd been so comfortable in her little house. She'd owned it, free and clear. But she began to fail. First came the cane, then the walker with the tennis balls on the ends of the legs, and finally the wheelchair. By then she knew it was time to move. She came from good genes, but, as her daddy had said just before he passed, "My parts are just wearin' out, honey." Her parts were pretty worn out, too. James lived in her house now.

"Ma," James had said, "I can't take care of you and you can't take care of yourself. Let me find you a place where you'll be safe, with good meals every day."

Thelma sighed. Deborah was right; James didn't come around or call very often. Thelma had to give him power-of-attorney over her small savings and social security. To her embarrassment, the administrator had come to her room several days ago to tell her the rent had arrived late two months running and the check for the current month had never arrived.

Thelma grimaced. The administrator went on to say she'd called James. He'd said he was hard at work and it had slipped his mind. Thelma wondered how that could be. She'd talked to her son a month ago. He was collecting unemployment. It was time she and James had a "behind the woodshed" talk. With the storm, she didn't know when that would be.

Just then a loud voice filled the room. Thelma turned to see Old John Walton starting one of his tirades. But this time it wasn't about dry meatloaf or watered down coffee or cardboard pancakes. "Hey, the floor's wet!" Old John yelled. "There's water on the floor!" Others took up the cry.

Thelma rolled her wheelchair nearer a window and looked out. Where were the ambulances and vans? Where were the workers' cars? She saw Winston standing by his old blue pickup, one of the few vehicles left in the lot. Was he leaving? Going to help his family? Where was everyone?

The unthinkable paled Thelma's already wan skin. *Is no one coming? Is no one here?* They were never left alone. The attendants might all be on the patio with a smoke and a coffee, but *someone* was always around. What about residents who needed life-saving medicines? Who would dispense them this morning? Thelma didn't take many pills—just baby aspirin, Tylenol and vitamins. Occasionally, she was given Lorazepam for anxiety. But what about the others?

John Walton started up again. "Might as well sing while we wait for them t' come git us." He cleared his throat. "What a friend we have in Jesus . . ."

"Praise the Lord," Thelma's friend Ethel cried, waving at her.

"Oh, there ain't no one comin' for us!" Old Dan Hodgkins shouted, always the naysayer. "Just a bunch o' bunk. Who needs us?"

Despite Old Dan's words, Thelma joined the other residents for several hymns until, little by little, the room quieted.

Someone's supposed to come, she thought. Just who would that be? Maybe James? He lived two hours away. Bayshore Hospital ambulances? Vans? Hearses? But she hadn't seen anyone. Her heart beat a little faster. She grew warm and felt her cheeks flush.

Thelma prayed, trying to calm herself. *Our Father, who art in heaven . . .*

Time passed and the telltale odor of urine and soiled diapers rose in the room. A woman cried out for water. People moaned or murmured to each other or fell asleep. Thelma grew more upset, clasping and unclasping her hands. Her heart began to thump. She tried to take a deep breath but couldn't. The room blurred; her thoughts tumbled into each other. Her eyes drifted closed. She blinked them open, but they closed again. She slumped against the wheelchair's arm, her head down, in a daze.

Was that James who seemed to be walking toward her, smiling? No, wait, it wasn't James. The man was too tall. Could it be Winston? Maybe he'd come back. No. Who was it? A man in a white uniform? No, no, it was a woman, smiling at her. No. That wasn't right. Who was it? Who was here?

A scream rose in her throat. But it wouldn't come out.

She had trouble breathing. People and voices jumbled together.

She felt herself being lifted from the wheelchair. Someone helped her to lie down. A blanket settled over her.

"Fasten the gurney's safety straps," a voice ordered. "Get the oxygen going. Check her vitals. We've got a lot of people to move."

Something cold covered her nose and chin.

A voice urged, "Breathe, ma'am, breathe."

Thelma felt tapping on her chest, fingers on her wrist, a band tightening around her arm.

"Breathe deep, ma'am," the same voice said. "Breathe deep."

She tried but couldn't.

Someone grunted behind her and the gurney began to move from the dining room and into the lobby. The automatic doors to the home whooshed open. Wind and rain pelted her.

A motor rumbled nearby. The gurney jostled from side to side until she was no longer out in the weather. A vehicle door slammed. Jarred by the noise, she opened her eyes, returning from the haze and confusion she'd been drifting in. Breathing became easier. She turned her head.

A man sat beside her amid monitors and equipment, writing hurriedly on a clipboard.

"You're safe, ma'am." Smiling, he covered her with a dry blanket. "You're in an ambulance. Trip won't take too long."

He adjusted her oxygen mask.

Thelma nodded and closed her eyes.

HELIOS

New York Times, October 10, 2030
"Phoenix I Launch a Success"

Los Angeles Times, October 10, 2030
"Phoenix I Runs for the Sun"

Three and a half months had passed. Dr. Andrew Hollenbeck placed a mug of coffee on the commissary table of the Copernicus Institute, stretched his lanky frame, and eased onto one of four wooden chairs. The cafeteria hummed with the activity of scientists and techs filling coffee cups in anticipation, a palpable sense of excitement in the air. His eyes burned, strained and bloodshot from monitoring the morning's solar activity. He rubbed the bridge of his nose between thumb and forefinger. An unhurried swallow of coffee did little to quell his uneasiness.

Excitement filled the air with good reason. Phoenix I now neared its goal to begin an orbit of the sun. But he was apprehensive. He didn't know whether to be concerned about the morning's observations of the sun's surface or not. He had scrutinized each solar sector, but he felt troubled.

Ten minutes ago, agitation in Solar Sector 248 had exceeded all previous energy outbursts. Like a fever, the flare in the sun's corona had spiked beyond the norm but then subsided. He wanted no surprises for Phoenix I, the first craft capable of circling the sun and withstanding its temperatures—so long as it traveled out of the reach of coronal flares. Years of charting the sun's activity had determined the craft's orbital route.

The recent eruption in Sector 248 had pushed past the normal A and B levels on the Solar Flare Scale. It climbed into the upper range of Classification C before quieting down. The flare had failed to reach Classification D or the high-danger levels of M or X. With the spaceship's landmark mission to circle and study the sun about to begin, after years of study and preparation, the flare's strength worried him.

He found being a part of this watershed event invigorating but nerve racking. His eyes screamed for rest. He closed them, placing his fingertips gently on their pale, veined lids. After several deep breaths, he settled his nerves enough to enjoy the coffee's aroma. Sighing, he managed another swallow of the dark brew and closed his eyes again.

He'd joined the Copernicus Institute five years ago, his previous position being at NASA where he'd worked in the space program. After the lift-off explosion of Mariner III, rumors circulated that his department may have been culpable. Some of his colleagues felt he'd rushed the data analyses. After many reports and an investigative commission, nothing had been proven. The cause of the explosion had been attributed to irregular weather patterns. He'd felt vindicated, but a pall hung over his work.

Lethargic for several months after the Mariner III mishap,

he'd consulted a physician who treated him with anti-depressants. He weaned himself from them over time, tapering to the use of a strong sleeping pill, when necessary. The doctor urged him to make a change—a new place to live or a new job. He'd chosen to find a new job.

After a difficult interview, The Copernicus Institute, world research leader in the study of global warming, had offered him a position. His initial work focused on the interdependence of the atmospheres of the sun and earth. He often wondered if an associate had pulled strings to get him into The Institute—or worse, if someone had maneuvered to get him out of the space program.

Whatever the circumstance, he valued his new position and worked hard to prove himself. The Institute, cooperating closely with NASA, shared his findings with scientists in the Phoenix Program. After years of collaborative research, Phoenix I (the first manned spacecraft to explore the sun) now neared its destination. He felt blessed and lucky to be involved. Even so, the importance of his responsibilities weighed on him.

Checking his watch, he realized it was time to get back to his station. Dr. Samuelson, the administrative astrophysicist, would be looking for him. He downed the last of his coffee and exited the lounge.

The lab at the end of the hall housed Big Zeus, a solar vacuum telescope The Copernicus Institute operated in the Quinlan Mountains near Tucson. There, twenty-four-hour monitoring of the sun took place, the findings of highest priority for the current solar craft mission.

Always invigorated by the sight of Big Zeus with its cutting-edge technology, he entered the lab to resume work. Dr. Samuelson removed his ear buds and pushed away from the computer console. Picking up a file, he nodded and left. The doctor was not one to banter. Hollenbeck suspected he hadn't been Samuelson's first choice during the hiring process, a committee decision.

Sinking into the leather chair, he slipped on his headset and rolled into position at the controls. All but one of the fourteen screens in front of him showed different areas of the sun, each focusing on dynamic but normal activity. Dark sunspots appeared and disappeared. Bright flares of discharged energy exploded outward. The fourteenth screen showed the progress of Phoenix I toward the sun and kept him in touch with SPACE Control, the agency responsible for the spacecraft.

"Okay, Big Zeus, let's take a look," Hollenbeck murmured. One after another, he enlarged the image on each screen and charted his findings. On the next to last monitor, Screen H-13, he viewed Sector 248, the area he'd been studying before his break. Its extraordinary energy and color continued as before, fascinating him.

Hollenbeck pushed a button to talk to the head of the Phoenix Program, asking him, "Dr. Da Silva, anything new over there?"

"She's on schedule," Da Silva replied.

Hollenbeck signed off and adjusted the controls on Screen H-14. Phoenix I appeared, traveling at more than 36,000 miles per hour, nearing its destination after almost 106 days. He nodded to the image, an acknowledgement of achievement.

Over the years, scientists persevered in experiments with communication systems, heat resistant shields, and robotic probes. Now, before him, their dream spacecraft approached the sun. He leaned toward the screen, hand to his chin, and followed its movement. A chill went through him. He rubbed his neck and returned to viewing the other screens.

He was aware of staff filing into the room behind him, filling the lab, their eyes on the large screens before him. They spoke in hushed tones, anticipation in the air.

Hollenbeck's routine observation and charting continued. Again, his gaze fell on Screen H-13, on the energy and color of Sector 248. The flaring movement lay within high normal parameters but with increasing agitation.

Without warning, Screen H-13 flashed brilliant white. A tumultuous discharge of magnetic energy erupted from the sun's corona, an intense, far-reaching spike. Hollenbeck gasped. The flare gathered momentum, penetrating farther into space, emitting surge upon surge. Heat intensified. Temperatures soared amidst exploding solar energy and winds. The computer gauges jumped like a volcano spewing lava. He had never seen a flare of this intensity and magnitude. A rush of voices behind him filled the lab.

He jolted upright in his seat and brought up Screen H-14. His words exploded like the sight before him. "If that flare doesn't subside, Phoenix I will orbit into it!" He checked the Solar Flare Scale. "Good God!"

His eyes stared at the rising numbers, measurements never seen before. The intensity registered at X45, the most powerful eruption he'd ever observed. He calculated the speed of Phoenix I. The spacecraft could not withstand the amount of radiation produced by a solar wind of this magnitude, no matter what previous testing claimed. It *must* be diverted.

He punched the SPACE Control button. Next, he flipped an

emergency switch to rouse Dr. Samuelson.

"Mayday SPACE Control, Mayday SPACE Control!" he shouted. "Divert Phoenix I! I repeat: Divert Phoenix I! An abnormal, high-energy flare is jetting from the corona, right in its path. Divert at once!"

"What?" Da Silva's voice. "Hollenbeck, are you sure?"

"I'm looking at an X45 intensity!"

"Sweet Jesus!" Da Silva exclaimed. "How long have we got?"

The two men calculated the speed of Phoenix I against the time needed to send radio signals to the spacecraft.

"It's close, but we can do it!" Da Silva concluded.

"Do it!" Hollenbeck shouted.

"Roger!" Da Silva signed off.

Hollenbeck held his breath. Their computations attested to enough time for the radio signals to reach the sun-bound craft. Samuelson loomed beside him.

With all the technology available at his fingertips, Hollenbeck felt helpless. On Screen H-14, he traced the path of Phoenix I. He followed the activity of the powerful flare on Screen H-13. As his associates stared at the screens, they gazed in horror at the approaching catastrophe.

Samuelson slammed his hands on the counter and cried out, "Why the hell doesn't Phoenix I divert?"

Hollenbeck again contacted SPACE Control. "Da Silva, get Captain Hernandez and his crew away from that flare. Veer right. Head into space. Abort! I repeat—abort!"

After a brief silence, Da Silva's reply stunned them. "We've lost contact. The magnetic field? The heat? The solar wind? We're unable to reach them. Nothing. We're out of time." His voice cracked.

The horrified group watched the pending calamity, images on

the two monitors clear and detailed. The flare persisted in duration and intensity. Phoenix I held its course toward the unprecedented solar storm. Then the unstoppable, tragic encounter occurred. Screens H-13 and H-14 filled with fiery brightness.

A communal gasp went through the lab. Heads dropped, hands went to mouths, eyes moistened. No one spoke. Slowly, Hollenbeck stood and walked toward the door. Associates stepped aside, stunned. Others stood frozen. Some turned away.

Samuelson's assistant Dave Beck appeared in front of him. He placed his hands on Hollenbeck's shoulders. "The flare was an anomaly. Never in all the studies did . . ."

Hollenbeck interrupted. "I'll begin the report. Give me a couple of hours."

He was aware of Samuelson speaking to the group as he exited into the hallway, thrashed by his thoughts. Pre-launch monitoring never produced a shred of evidence of such activity, never hinted a flare would exceed the safety range he had established. Why hadn't he told Samuelson about the rogue flare? What had held him back? Hedging his bets? Wanting to be part of this epic achievement? Incompetence? A feeling the eruption would simply subside and never repeat?

Something else gnawed at him. The radio waves should have had enough time to relay the communication. He ran the figures in his head again. What had happened? What had gone wrong?

He leaned against the wall, eyes closed, arms folded in front of his body. His shoulders slumped as he buried his face in his hands and wept.

Bewildered, he made his way down the hall toward his office, oblivious to the rush of movement around him. He closed the office door and opened the briefcase sitting on his desk. Among the papers lay several medications. A bottle of aspirin. An over-the-counter sinus medication. Sleeping pills prescribed after the Mariner III disaster. And the one he wanted—a small vial of Prozac with a few capsules left.

His office door flew open. Hollenbeck slammed his briefcase shut. Samuelson stood in the doorway, his face a study of grief and anger.

"I'm calling a meeting. Conference Room 10. At 1400 hours. What the hell happened?"

Hollenback shook his head. "I've never seen a solar explosion like this before."

"Bullshit!" Samuelson snapped back. "I think you saw flares like these before but failed to report them, rushing the data again. I knew hiring you was a mistake!" Samuelson turned abruptly and left.

Hollenbeck walked to the door, closed and locked it. He returned to his desk, looking around his office a final time. From a side desk drawer, he took a sheet of letterhead paper and an envelope. He wrote his resignation, put Samuelson's name on the envelope, and placed it on the desk.

Briefcase in hand, he left his office, walking in the opposite direction from the conference room, down the hall to the exit. His career over, laden with guilt and sadness, he didn't intend to listen to Samuelson's condemnations. He'd hear his own for the rest of his life.

New York Times, January 26, 2031

"The Nation Mourns Phoenix I"

Los Angeles Times, January 26, 2031
"Phoenix I, We Grieve for You"

On a Saturday morning eight months later, Hollenbeck sat at his kitchen table in a worn bathrobe, unkempt, and fifteen pounds heavier than the day he'd left the work he loved. His job at a local solar firm paid the bills but held little challenge. In front of him was a large manila envelope with a return address he'd never expected to see again: The Copernicus Institute. Ratcheting it open with his thumb, he removed a folder with a note stapled to the cover.

"Thought you'd like to see this before it hits the papers. Best, Dave Beck."

Hollenbeck opened the folder, reading the first page.

PHOENIX I INVESTIGATION
Congressional Report
September 15, 2031

He turned the page, where he saw a single paragraph:

After a thorough investigation into the Phoenix I disaster, a special Congressional Committee has found that the Solar to Earth Transmission System (SETS) developed by Claymore Technologies, Inc., used for communications between Earth and Phoenix I, malfunctioned. Congressional inquiries reveal that the competitive race for the lucrative government contract led to cost-cutting measures and rushed analyses. The SETS system did not receive the full battery of field testing necessary to warrant a Failsafe Certification for so important a mission. Details on ensuing pages.

Nodding, Hollenbeck closed the cover. "I knew there was enough time to send radio signals to the spacecraft, enough time to divert," he murmured. "I knew it."

Ferrelli's Fall

Nick Ferrelli walked beside the Niagara River, unable to shake a pensive mood or ignore an October wind chilling his bones. In the distance, lights from downtown Buffalo brightened a clear night sky, but he felt neither bright nor clearheaded. He pulled the collar of his leather jacket up around his neck. His hands soon felt the cold. He shoved them back into his pockets.

The river appeared calm, but beneath its surface swept an erratic current, one that grew more dangerous as it flowed toward Niagara Falls. The water's turbulent nature reminded him of Maggie, his former girlfriend. Three months ago, she'd stormed out of their Palm Springs condo, accepted a new job, and moved to the other side of the country. He hadn't heard from her until, one evening, she called with an unusual request. She asked him to apartment-sit. His inner voice immediately warned him to be careful. He wasn't interested in more turmoil. But the pull had proved to be too strong. He wanted to talk—about the break-up, about their relationship. He wanted her back. He'd flown to Buffalo, only they still hadn't talked.

Immersed in his troubles, Nick continued along the riverfront, his way lit by vintage streetlamps. Fallen leaves from nearby maple trees blew across the sidewalk. They crunched beneath his shoes, the sound drifting into the autumn night. Idly, he picked up a leaf and settled it on his palm. Its once rich hues of reds and golds were gone, replaced by lifeless, mottled brown. He turned the leaf over with his fingers. It broke apart. He brushed the fragments from his hand, watching them flutter to the ground, struck with an odd feeling: Was this an omen predicting how his relationship with Maggie would end? In pieces? Or was it a reminder to treat the relationship gently to keep it whole? He weighed the questions, wanting answers.

Suddenly, a male voice called out, "Behind you, on your left."

Nick heard the steady cadence of a jogger's shoes striking the walkway and moved to the right to make room. All at once, he felt a hard shove. Thrown off balance, he fell to his knees on the sidewalk. Before he could move, a sharp blow to the base of his neck landed him face down on the concrete. He rolled to his side and looked up. A male figure jogged in place in front of him, the man's well-built shoulders moving in rhythm with his runner's legs. A black jogging suit clung to his body.

"You dumb bastard!" Nick rubbed his neck. "What do you want?"

The man threw down an envelope, said nothing, and jogged off into the night.

Nick raised himself to his feet, grunting, knowing his body would soon ache all over. He picked up the envelope, surprised to see his name scrawled across it, and moved to a nearby streetlamp. No one in Buffalo knew him except Maggie. He ripped it open and read, "Meet me at the Anchor Bar tomorrow night at eight. I'll find you."

Nick jammed the note into his pocket. Anger reddened his neck, the same anger he'd felt when his older brother used to bully him. At sixteen, Nick discovered his own fists. After that, big brother left him alone. After that, nobody knocked him down. Until tonight. He vowed there wouldn't be a next time, not without a fight.

"Mr. Jogger, I owe you one," he muttered.

Edgy, nerves honed like a knife, Nick kneaded his lower back and eased himself onto a park bench. He massaged his knees. He was in good shape at forty, but not prepared for a mugging in a park. Or, for that matter, meeting a man he didn't know in a bar.

A man and woman, her auburn hair blowing in the light breeze, walked past him. The man had his arm around her waist. Nick turned away from them, his thoughts drawn back to Maggie—tall, athletic, blond Maggie who came into his life ten years ago at the Los Angeles Book Fair. Their stormy relationship struggled through break-ups and reconciliations, a perpetual merry-go-round. Despite their history, he couldn't shake the emptiness gnawing at his insides. He wanted to touch her hair, smell her perfume, feel her body against his. He put his head in his hands.

The trip to Buffalo had spiraled out of control fast. He'd hoped they'd have an opportunity to talk *before* her business trip; but when he arrived, she'd already gone. The manager gave him an envelope and a key. According to her note, the date for her New York City trip had changed—or so she said. He wondered if that was true. He wondered, with their history, if they could ever move past their ambitions, their competitive natures, or their strong-headed independence.

He rubbed his temples, amazed at the way a solitary stroll to sort out his thoughts could turn into one lousy, miserable night. He'd met a wacko. He felt depressed. He longed for Maggie, for the sound of her voice.

Her call had surprised him. Alone on the deck of his condo, watching the sun drop behind the Santa Rosa Mountains, he'd been tempted to let the cell phone ring and not interrupt a quiet evening, but he'd answered at the last moment.

Maggie's low-pitched voice had greeted him. "How are you?"

Nick took his time responding. "Are you on your way back to the desert?"

"No, I like my new job." she said. "I realize neither of us seems ready for commitment. But I do have a proposition."

"I'm always ready to be propositioned," he said.

She didn't laugh at his humor. "Would a change of scene interest you?"

"It would. Want to run away to Belize?"

"No, Nick. I need to go out of town for work. I'm ghostwriting a book. I have on-site research and interviewing to do, which means my place will be empty for a few weeks. You could do your freelance writing here where it's cooler. You know how hot October is in the desert. You could have a change of scene. Use my car."

"No, thanks."

"My building has a state-of-the-art gym," she added.

Nick wasn't buying. "So does mine," he answered.

"There's a golf course nearby."

"Maggie, Palm Springs is a golfer's paradise."

"Oh, Nick, please? My home office is all set up. It has everything you need from paperclips to a computer."

"In case you've forgotten, I have a fully equipped office. A condo. A car."

"I know that." Her voice softened. "I have a spectacular view of the Niagara River." She paused. "Do I have to beg? A little change might be good . . . and maybe we can talk."

Nick's next flip answer vanished.

At the end of the week, he'd flown to Buffalo, only to find her gone. His anticipation collapsed like a punctured balloon. Maggie called his cell once to make sure he'd gotten there, picked up the key and read her note. It was a quick, rushed call.

Nick pulled himself up from the bench. Across the river, lights from the Canadian town of Fort Erie glimmered in the darkness, their lonely look matching his own. He needed to unwind, to relax about Maggie and the mystery jogger.

He left the park and headed for a neighborhood bar he'd spotted called The Falls Inn. It sat less than a block from Maggie's upscale apartment complex. He needed a little liquid therapy.

When he reached the tavern and opened its door, a blast of heat hit his face. He stood a moment, warming up, looking into a long, narrow room with a bar stretching down the right side. Behind the bar, shelves mounted on paneled walls displayed bottles of liquor and sports memorabilia. Framed photos of sports teams like the Buffalo Sabres and the Buffalo Bills hung on each side of the shelving. On the opposite wall stretched a large, sepia-toned photographic mural of Niagara Falls.

Nick walked over to a well-used stool and sat. Three men down at the far end of the bar glanced his way, nodded, and went back to their conversation. The place reminded him of the old TV show *Cheers*, emanating local color, but he missed the rhythm of his own watering hole back in Palm Springs and his usual beer. Since he was just across the river from Canada, he decided to try a Canadian brew. He said to the bartender, "Give me a Molson's Dry."

A booming voice interrupted his first swallow. "Avast, ye landlubbers!"

A stocky, craggy-faced man wearing an unkempt Navy pea coat and rumpled white sailing cap thumped in. He eased his ample weight onto a stool next to Nick. The men waved at him, one calling out, "Yo, Captain."

"My usual, mate!" the seadog bellowed at the barman.

The fellow nodded and filled a mug from a Labatt's keg.

The man's gaze turned to Nick. "Enjoyin' the place? Captain Jack MacGregor here, Retired. Folks claim I spin more yarns than a Scottish knit shop."

"Nick Ferrelli, writer. From California."

"Call me Captain Jack. A writer, huh? Guess you'd call me a talker." He raised his glass in toast, taking a long swallow. Nick did the same.

The captain gestured to the wall behind them with his near empty glass. "That mural over there? That's the Canadian Falls. Shaped like a horseshoe, they are. I used to pilot a boat called the Maid-of-the-Mist up close to the inferno at the base of the Falls. The old girl's still navigatin' those waters today. New men are at the helm. Take a good look. You can just see her, a safe distance from the rocks, shrouded by mist."

Nick focused on the mural, spotting the image of a sturdy double-decked craft the size of a large commercial tug. Sightseers on board, clad in rain gear, leaned on the rails, waving.

"What's it like, Captain," Nick asked, "to be in those waters?"

"It's a churning cauldron, son. Never dull. Gotta know where the rocks are. They're tumblin' down from the top of the Falls all the time." Captain Jack finished his drink, smacked his lips, waved to the bartender for another. "And the people? Always somethin'. Like when I was all set to perform a weddin' on board, the groom suddenly went missin'. My mate found 'im in the galley. Hidin', he was. Said he'd changed his mind. The bride-to-be tossed her bouquet overboard and told the guy to go get it. A sturdy little lass, she was. She meant it."

Nick gave a short laugh. "I've been a little commitment-shy myself—or so I've been told."

"Take your time, mate. Take your time." The captain wiped his mouth with the back of his hand. "Also had a pretty little lass—in her twenties, she was—try to jump over the rail. Kept yellin', 'Get away! Let me go!' My mate and I barely pulled her back."

"Poor kid." Nick thought about Maggie, the night she'd stomped out of the condo. He knew all about life's unexpected turns, how it could zigzag out of control with a finger snap.

"Yep, these waters, these Falls draw 'em all, more than just honeymooners or jilted lovers. The suicides and loonies flock here like gulls to dead fish." Captain Jack leaned in, peered at Nick with watery eyes. "Ever want to kill yourself, son?"

Nick gave the captain a long look before he answered. "Interesting question, but the answer is no. I'll hang around, no matter what life tosses my way."

"Glad to hear it," the captain continued. "Just watch the newspapers. Poor souls walk into the rapids above the Falls or leap from the Rainbow Bridge. Some blow their brains out." He shook his head. "I guess things just pile up on folks."

Nick swirled his beer. "To me, life with all its warts beats the alternative."

"Hard to know, son." The captain scratched his nose. "Ever kill anyone?"

"Whoa, Captain. Are you kidding?" Nick shuddered. "I couldn't go that far."

"That's the way I felt until I served in Korea in the 1950s. I could and did. With my bare hands, with anything I could find."

"That's war, not so-called normal life. I could never commit murder. My moral compass won't go there."

"Well, my friend, you just don't know what you'll do until you get your shorts in a twist. That compass needle could start spinnin'." Captain Jack cradled a handful of pretzels from a dish on the bar, popped one in his mouth. "Around here the loonies often get trigger happy. Domestic squabbles, robberies, murder. Just watch the newspapers. These tumblin' waters must mesmerize the poor buggers." He chewed on another pretzel. "Anyway, how long you been here? Met any of our loonies yet?"

"I've been here a week." The jogger in the park jumped to mind. He added, "Not sure about the loonies." This wasn't a great way to soothe a troubled mind, he thought, talking about suicide, crazy people, and murder. He drained his second bottle of Molson's. "Gotta run. Thanks for the conversation."

"Anytime, son," the captain said.

Nick returned to the high-rise and took the elevator to Maggie's ninth-floor apartment. He opened the door, reached inside, and flipped a switch. A table lamp came on in the living room. He tossed his jacket on the couch. The strange encounter with the jogger and the odd conversation with Captain Jack bothered him. He massaged his neck, moving his fingers out along his shoulders. His muscles felt like taut rubber bands.

What had he stumbled into? Maybe he had met one of Captain

Jack's loonies. Nick switched off the lamp and stood by the expanse of windows. A night view of the river and city lights stretched before him. Glow from a waxing moon sprinkled the room with shadows of gray and black.

The next day, Nick paced and hung out in the apartment. When night arrived, he took the elevator to the subterranean parking garage, the smart key to Maggie's dark-blue BMW X3 in his pocket. He gripped the driver's-side door handle. The door unlocked. After buckling himself in, he pressed the start button on the dash, programmed the Anchor Bar's address into the car's GPS and slowly drove from the parking stall.

Maggie kept the transponder for the security gate clipped to the visor above the steering wheel. He pressed its button. The iron gates opened with a dull whirr. Following the system's directions, he drove north along River Drive, turned left onto Lafayette Avenue, right onto Main, into the heart of downtown Buffalo. He gripped the wheel, not enjoying the drive. This meet-up with the jogger worried him.

A red neon sign announced the historic Anchor Bar. He glanced at his watch. It was 7:50 p.m. He parked in the restaurant's lot, locking the car door with a touch to the sensor on the handle. He entered the restaurant, jostled through a line of people waiting for tables, and found his way into the bar. He eased onto an empty stool. In the mirror behind the bar, he watched servers rush by with pitchers of beer, baskets of steaming Buffalo Wings, plates heaped with French fries and onion rings. The smells. The food. They didn't interest him.

"Any preference, mister?" The bartender waited.

"Carling Black Label," Nick said.

In a nearby booth, a young couple held hands across a table, glasses of red wine between them. He looked away, reminded too much of a scene with Maggie. Next to him a bald man in a plaid flannel shirt and faded jeans sat with a beer.

Nick unzipped his jacket, a gift from Maggie—she'd said it made him look like a James Bond type. He waited, not knowing what to expect. Maybe he'd have to dust off some old boxing moves. His brown eyes scanned the mirror. He didn't touch his beer.

The bald man, scratching his chest, threw money on the counter and turned to leave. In the mirror Nick watched him weave past a wiry, sandy-haired man about Nick's height who slid onto the empty stool. Nick checked his watch. It was 8:10.

"Nick Ferrelli," the man said, not a question.

Nick nodded.

"I'm Jason Tucker. We met last night in the park."

"I have just two questions," Nick said, not wasting any time. "What do you want, and how do you know my name?"

Tucker looked at Nick with wary eyes. "What do I want? I want to make sure I have your attention. We have a mutual friend."

"I repeat, what the hell do you want? What mutual friend?"

Tucker sneered, "Looks like we're off to a bad start."

"No kidding. Talk to me, Tucker."

Nick waited while the man ordered a Sam Adams. The bartender popped the cap from a bottle and set it in front of him. Tucker took a swallow, leaned his elbows on the bar. When he turned toward Nick, his eyes shone like polished steel. "All right, big man. I want you outta here. Maggie told me all about you. You're messing up her life."

"This is about Maggie? Maggie's our mutual friend?" Nick shook his head, surprised. "What business is it of yours? In case she forgot to tell you, I happen to be apartment sitting."

Tucker swiveled around on the stool, jabbing a finger in Nick's chest. "I want you to go back where you came from."

Nick grabbed the man's wrist. "Who the hell are you? I'm in Maggie's place at her invitation."

Tucker yanked his arm away, rubbing his wrist. "Look, Ferrelli, you've been hanging around her life for years. She's tired of it. Butt out. She and I have a good thing going."

Maggie had never mentioned someone else. Nick began to wonder why the hell she'd called him. "Well, Tarzan, what's your next act? Beat your chest? Swing through the trees?"

"Listen, Ferrelli, just pack up your gear. She's mine."

"Personally," Nick said, "I think she still has a thing for me." The man flinched. Nick let the dig sink in. He stood, threw money on the bar.

Tucker grabbed his arm. "You've been warned."

Nick pulled away. "Keep your hands to yourself."

Tucker slid from the stool, stepped in close, blocking the way. Beer breath hit Nick's face. "You stay away from her."

"Out of my way, Tucker," Nick said, attempting to elbow past the man.

Tucker seized Nick's arm, pulled him around, and delivered a sucker-punch to his chin. Nick fell back into a booth occupied by two women. They screamed while he disentangled himself and lurched toward Tucker who danced in front of him. Three men in bright blue bowling shirts cheered, hopped off their bar stools, and pulled tables out of the way. The bar crowd started clapping. Someone yelled,

"Fight! Fight!"

Nick landed a solid jab to Tucker's jaw. The man staggered back, Nick in pursuit. They fell to the floor and rolled, pummeling each other.

A crash, followed by a blast of cold water, brought an avalanche of ice cubes onto Nick's head. Icy water stung his ears, splashed in his eyes. Tucker sputtered and slapped away pieces of ice. A burly waiter with thigh-sized biceps pulled Nick up, pushing him aside. He hoisted Tucker to his feet. Two husky men stood nearby holding a now empty Gatorade cooler between them, "Brawl Breaker" painted on its side.

"Knock it off, gentlemen, or we call Buffalo's finest." The waiter looked from Nick to Tucker. The crowd laughed. A young man appeared with a mop while the two husky men put down their cooler and moved the furniture back into place. Customers returned to their drinks.

Nick wiped at his jacket. He spotted the waiter's name on his red apron. "Okay, Angelo. I'm leaving." He grabbed a cocktail napkin from the bar to blot water and blood from his face.

Angelo spoke to Tucker who returned to his place at the bar. The man dabbed at his cheek with a handkerchief from his back pocket. He checked his hair in the mirror.

Nick hustled toward the exit, happy to step into the fresh night air. On the walk to the car, he cooled down, deciding to stay at Maggie's place until she returned and let her explain what was going on. He wondered how she'd found Jason; more importantly, how the dumb bastard fit into the picture.

Nick pulled the BMW out of the Anchor Bar parking lot into

light evening traffic. Steering with one hand, he rubbed his jawbone with the other hand, moving his jaw from side to side; it was sore but not broken. He glanced in the rearview mirror at the beginnings of some facial bruising. He didn't come to Buffalo to be beaten up. He also didn't travel from the west coast to be dumped. Again. She'd blindsided him with a boyfriend. He should leave, save the melodramatic encounter for the soap operas.

"Son of a bitch. No way," he mumbled. He'd have his say.

Tucker's wild cannon actions should be reported to the police, put on record. But the thought of a police sergeant's possible response made Nick laugh. *Sorry, fella, we solve break-ins, not break-ups.*

Stopped at a traffic signal on Main Street, he noticed a road sign: Scenic Delaware Park, Five Miles. He turned, following the arrows onto Delaware Avenue, knowing the car's GPS could get him back to Maggie's later. He just wanted to drive.

The busy street of blighted buildings became a gentrified avenue lined with restored Victorian era homes. Tall, old elm trees, their foliage gone, formed a skeletal canopy, allowing moonlight to cast checkered shadows on the road. From Lake Erie, a freshwater breeze blew through the open car window. He took a deep breath, enjoying Nat King Cole's "Red Sails in the Sunset" on WKSN, an oldies radio station he'd discovered earlier in the week. The roadway began meandering through the gentle hills of Delaware Park.

In the rearview mirror, headlights appeared from around a curve, approaching faster than the thirty-miles-per-hour speed limit. He moved right to allow it to pass, but the vehicle slowed and closed in behind him. Nick went on red alert. What now? Some kid playing car games? He'd had enough game-playing for one night. He accelerated.

The driver behind did the same. Nick slowed. The vehicle remained behind, matching his speed.

Nick rammed the accelerator to the floor and sped ahead, white knuckles on the wheel. He checked his rearview mirror, catching sight of a black SUV closing in on him. The two high-powered machines rounded the curves, tires squealing.

Like a shot, the SUV slammed into his rear bumper. Nick's body jerked forward, then snapped back. The SUV fell away but struck again seconds later. Then it pulled out and swerved in beside him. Dark tint covered the windows.

Nick's car hit the curb, jumped back onto the roadway.

"You crazy son of a bitch!" Nick shouted. He clutched the wheel, trying to watch the road, ignore his racing heart, the flop-sweat under his arms, the taste of fear in his mouth.

The passenger window on the black SUV lowered. The driver hung onto the steering wheel with his left hand, leaned toward Nick. For a moment, a streetlight illuminated Jason Tucker. In his right hand, metal gleamed. A switchblade flipped open. He waved it, yelling, "Watch your six, Ferrelli!"

Tucker's SUV surged ahead. Nick followed what he now knew was a black Land Rover. Squinting through the windshield, through the glare of his headlights, he made out a New York ego-plate along with a dealer's name advertised on the license frame.

Nick stayed close behind Tucker, gunning the BMW. But he took the next curve too fast. The car spun and hopped the opposite curb. He pumped the brakes. The vehicle skidded across grass, sliding to a stop. He popped the seatbelt and hauled himself from the car only to be greeted by the loud quacking of ducks, disturbed from their nighttime slumber. He realized he stood on the edge of a lake. He bent over, hands on his knees, breathing deeply. His neck and back hurt.

An inspection of the car revealed deep dents in the rear bumper, expensive dents that would be on Nick's tab, but first he intended to take them out of Tucker's hide. He wouldn't forget the Land Rover, the license plate or the dealer name.

After a late breakfast and another healthy dose of Tylenol, Nick drove onto the lot of Manchester Motors, Buffalo's only Land Rover dealership. He pulled into customer parking near the service bay where three vehicles waited, the last in line a black Land Rover with ego plates he recognized: "LR4JT." This would be easier than he thought. He strode into the showroom where a slick salesman with a breezy, outdoor manner approached him.

"Maybe you can help me." Nick looked through the window and pointed to the SUV. "I'm looking for the owner of that black Land Rover in the Service line."

"That beauty belongs to our top sales producer. Your lucky day—he's in." The salesman gestured toward a glass-walled office with its door closed. Nick could see Tucker on the business-side of a desk, deep in conversation with a couple seated in front of him.

Nick smiled. "Looks like he's busy. I'll just have a seat."

"I'll tell him you're here, Mr. . . .?" The salesman waited.

"Smith. Just say his friend Mr. Smith is here."

The salesman pulled out his cell phone and called Jason Tucker, who looked out through the glass wall. His glare washed over Nick like sulfuric acid. Nick waved a glossy Land Rover brochure at him, a wide grin on his face.

Thirty minutes later, Tucker escorted the couple out. He motioned Nick over to his office, lowered the privacy blinds, closed the door.

"You're a slow learner. I've given you several warnings." Tucker walked behind his sleek chrome and glass desk. "How did you find me?"

Nick watched Tucker, keeping an eye on the man's hands. "Hardly rocket science; your ego plate, the dealer's name on the license plate frame, your SUV in plain sight." Nick stood across from Tucker, holding the man's cold stare with his own. "I'm a step away from calling the police. Mess with me one more time, I'll land your ass in jail for assault and stalking."

Tucker studied him, like a hawk eying its prey. "This is my final warning. Get the hell out of Maggie's apartment. Get the hell out of her life."

Nick leaned his palms on the desk. They smudged the thick glass top. "And if I don't?"

Tucker's eyes narrowed. "I mean what I say, Ferrelli."

Nick slipped his hands under the desk's edge, tipping it. Tucker scrambled to stop papers, files, and a laptop from sliding to the floor. Nick let the desk down with a thump. Tucker grabbed a letter opener.

Nick lunged for the man's wrist, slamming it onto the desktop. "I'm sure someone will call the police if we break the place up."

Tucker glared at him. "Get out."

"Careful." Nick smirked. "Don't hurt yourself with that opener."

He sauntered to Maggie's car, feeling good, aware of Tucker glaring at him through the showroom's large plate-glass windows.

He made eye contact with the man one last time, followed by a "see ya later" wave. Before Nick drove from the lot, he turned on the radio. Another oldie was playing: Creedence Clearwater Revival's "Bad Moon Rising."

That night Nick's cell phone rang. Stretched out on the couch, half asleep, he wrestled the phone from his pocket and grunted, "Hello."

"Hi, Nick. It's Maggie."

He took a deep breath and sat up.

"Are you enjoying the apartment?" she asked.

Nick stood, walked to the window, and looked out on the river. Anger flushed his face. "The place is fine. Me? Not so much. Maggie, what's going on? Who the hell is Jason Tucker?"

She laughed. "How in the world do you know Jason?"

Nick straightened his shoulders. "Let's just say your boyfriend introduced himself the other night. What's he to you?"

Maggie laughed again. "I'm car shopping. He's just a salesman I met. I'm considering a Land Rover."

"That's not the way he tells it."

"Are you drinking, Nick?" Maggie's tone sounded accusatory.

"No, I'm not. He told me to get out of your life. If that's what you want, you could have called me, sent an email. Hell, you could have sent a 'Dear John' text."

"Oh, come on, Nick."

"Look, he knocked me down on the river walk. The next night he picked a fight with me at the Anchor Bar. After that, he tried to force me off the road in Delaware Park. I damn near drove into a lake."

"If this is your idea of a joke, Nick, it isn't funny."

Nick replied, "You're right about that. I paid the guy a visit where he works and told him to back off. I'm not sure he got the message. What the hell are you doing with this Neanderthal?"

"He showed me an SUV. We've had a few casual dates." Maggie stopped. "I don't have to justify my actions to you."

"He says you're his girlfriend."

"Nick, this conversation isn't going too well." Maggie paused. "If you feel you should leave, then leave."

"At this point, Maggie, I'm wondering why you called me in the first place?"

"A weak moment."

Her hard, sarcastic tone stung.

Neither spoke. Nick felt like he'd received a blow to the gut.

In a soft voice she said, "Forgive me for that remark. It might be that I miss you, Nick. It might be I'm a little mixed up about us."

Again, neither spoke.

Nick broke the silence. "You know I miss you."

After a pause, Maggie murmured, "Will you stay?"

"Yes," he said. The connection ended.

Nick sank back onto the couch, realizing the turmoil was back. They seemed to thrive on it. Restless, he walked into Maggie's office, turned on the desk light. He had an article to write about gun violence, part of a series he'd pitched to a national magazine. The flash drive was in his pocket. He'd use her iMac to distract himself and get something done.

At the desk, trying to work, his eyes roamed over Maggie's awards hanging on the far wall—letters and pictures from people she'd interviewed for various publications. Her journalism awards.

His thoughts wandered back to their conversation. At least one good thing had happened. She wanted him to stay.

His cell rang again. He didn't recognize the number scrolling across the top of the screen. Wrong number? Telemarketer? He hesitated a moment and answered.

"Hello."

"Get out, Ferrelli."

Nick's grip tightened around the phone. "How the hell did you get my cell number?"

"Easy, Ferrelli."

"Answer me, Tucker."

"Since you're so curious," came the smug reply, "I got it from Maggie's contacts list. Her cell phone just happened to be sitting on the restaurant table one day while we had coffee. I appropriated it when she went to the restroom."

"You're a real prince."

Tucker laughed. After a pause, his tone changed. "I'm saying this for the last time. Get out, Ferrelli."

"Go to bed, Tucker. Sleep it off." Nick ended the call.

He ran his hands through his hair, needing a break—from the computer, the phone, the apartment, Tucker. Maybe even Maggie. He spent a restless night.

After finishing his morning coffee, Nick decided to take a day trip to Niagara Falls, Canada, for a change of scene. The Horseshoe Falls that Captain Jack talked about might bring him some luck.

He crossed from Buffalo via the Peace Bridge into the small town of Fort Erie, Canada, and followed the signs onto a two-lane road called Scenic Parkway Drive, soon driving along the Niagara River with Buffalo's skyline receding from view across the water. Traffic remained light until near the city of Niagara Falls where it became bumper-to-bumper; cars, buses, minivans, and delivery trucks crowded the way. Exhaust fumes seeped into the BMW.

The river, placid near Buffalo, home to pleasure boaters and fishermen, had turned to turbulent, forbidding rapids. Near the edge of the falls, he saw a rusted steel barge caught on the rocks, a macabre warning.

Nick lowered the car window. A thunderous roar from tons of water cascading over the Horseshoe Falls erupted in his ears. He powered the window back up and drove into a busy parking lot, jockeying the BMW into a place just vacated by a jeep. As he exited the car, he found himself walking in a rainy mist created by the tumbling water. Tourists held jackets or umbrellas over their heads or simply walked bareheaded through the shower. A fragile rainbow hung in the fine spray.

Nick zipped his jacket closed, pulled up the collar, and hurried across the street toward an iron safety rail crowded with sightseers. He edged himself between a tattooed biker and a blond man with a backpack slung over his shoulder. In front of them, the Niagara River hurled onto the fallen rocks below.

The biker turned to Nick, his voice a shout. "Folks go over them falls in a barrel! That's some kinda crazy!"

Nick leaned on the rail, watching the *Maid of the Mist* navigate a safe distance from the base of the Falls. Transfixed by the sheer power before him, his thoughts wandered inward to the strange turn of events with Maggie. Their relationship, like the river, had gone into the rapids, fallen over the precipice and crashed onto the rocks. Also like the river, they'd always managed to move on, together. At least, that was true in the past.

Jason Tucker added a new complication. During Nick and Maggie's time together, a liaison with someone else had never been an issue. Wisdom hinted that, maybe, if he didn't force the situation, his free-spirited Maggie would return to him. Wisdom further suggested that it would be smart to report Tucker to the authorities. However far his wisdom stretched, he knew one thing: he wanted a showdown.

Hands buried deep in his pockets, he left the crowded rail to return to the parking lot across the street. He stepped off the curb, his mind elsewhere. A blaring horn jolted him.

A minivan driver shook his fist, yelling, "Wake up, buddy."

"Hey, sorry." Nick stepped back onto the curb to wait for a lull in traffic. The near-accident reminded him to get his head together. He returned to the car, exited the lot and pulled out onto the busy road.

The drive north along the highway took him past rose gardens, souvenir shops, and a casino with garish neon signs promising fortunes. The Rainbow Bridge leading from the city of Niagara Falls, Canada, to its counterpart stateside came into view, but he wanted to continue along the scenic Canadian route.

The farther north he drove, the lighter the traffic, the darker the sky. Gray clouds eased in. The river disappeared, flowing now at the bottom of a deep chasm. Only the opposite side of the gorge with its layered limestone rim could be seen.

After a few miles, the road curved inland. He drove past woods of oak, maple, and slender white ash. A rabbit dashed across the road in front of him only to disappear under low bushes next to a sign pointing to the Great Gorge Hiking Trail. A walk would feel good, he thought, even if it did rain. Markers directed him toward a parking area hidden from the main road by trees where he parked, the only car in the lot, and walked across the road to the trailhead.

Nick ambled along the wooded pathway edged with dogwood, holly and clusters of ivy, enjoying both the scent of approaching rain and the quiet of being the only one on the trail. Before long, a Mile One marker appeared on his right. He thought about turning back but, taking pleasure in the walk, decided to continue. The trail turned toward the gorge, until only a rustic fence and, on its opposite side, a wide, protruding ledge of loose dirt and scrub brush stood between them.

A warning sign posted on the fence told hikers to "Stay on the Trail." He had no desire to go any closer to the gorge or to stand at its edge, risking vertigo. He checked his watch. It was only 3:00 p.m. He'd have time for a glass of Cabernet at a local Ontario winery if he left now.

In the woods behind him, a rustle like the sound of a small animal on the prowl interrupted an inner calmness Nick was feeling for the first time in days. The movement stopped for a beat, but then resumed. After yet another beat, more rustling followed. He turned. A form suddenly loomed in front of him. The form lunged. Nick's hands flew up to protect himself. Pushing back with all his strength, he landed on top of Jason Tucker.

The two men scrambled to their feet. Nick moved in, kneeing Tucker in the crotch. The man grimaced, bending forward to cup his groin.

"Are you fucking nuts?" Nick yelled as he backed away, gasping for air. "You're good, man. I wasn't sure about the rustling sounds until the third time. Three strikes and you're out. I want to knock you senseless, but instead, I'm going to the police." He turned to walk back to the parking lot.

The cock of a handgun stopped him. He looked back.

"Climb the fence," Tucker demanded. He held the weapon with both hands, arms extended, his voice tranquil and eerie.

Nick scanned the area. No one approached in either direction. With no choice, he climbed over. Tucker followed. The drop into the gorge lay straight ahead. Nick's fear-churned gut made him queasy, siphoned his mouth dry. His heart raced. He had only moments to stop the inevitable.

Tucker poked him in the back with the gun muzzle. "Keep walking."

Nick whirled. His two hands swung like a cleaver, slicing down on Tucker's wrists. The gun fired into the ground. Tucker struggled to bring the weapon up, but Nick wrenched it away, hurling it into the brush.

Tucker sprang, his hands clutching Nick's neck, his thumbs pressing into Nick's Adam's apple. The grip grew tighter. Nick struggled to breathe. In a burst of strength, he inserted his forearms inside Tucker's arms and pushed outward, breaking the chokehold. He grabbed Tucker's head, his thumbs pressing at the man's eyes. Tucker twisted himself out of Nick's grasp.

They reeled away from each other. Tucker fell backward, teetering on the edge of the gorge. Nick grabbed his arm, pulling the man to safety, only to have Tucker pivot and try to whirl Nick toward the edge. The two men grappled.

A scream pierced the air. Nick fell to his hands and knees, the sound of his heavy breathing crashing in his ears, the sight of Tucker falling into the gorge seared into his brain. Nick hauled himself to his feet, backing away from the edge as rain began to fall from the darkened sky, stippling the scuffed ground of their battlefield. Several hundred feet below, the river swept Tucker's body downstream.

Nick stood, pondering what had just happened, wondering what he should do. He began to look around. The trail was deserted. He dug in the brush and dirt until he found the gun and shell casing. What should he do with them? Keep them? Turn them over to the police? Had anyone heard the gunshot? The revolver seemed too hot to touch, like a burning coal. He hurled it and the casing into the gorge, to vanish beneath the fast-moving water.

The rain now pelted in earnest, settling the dust, obliterating signs of their encounter. He climbed back over the fence onto the trail, running to the parking lot where he stood for a moment with his head turned upward, letting rain stream down his face, as if trying to wash himself clean.

The lot now held two vehicles—a white Land Rover with dealer plates from Manchester Motors, its wheels turned at a sharp angle, and Maggie's car. He unlocked the BMW and jumped in, wondering what to do next. Rain battered a heavy staccato on the car roof. He pushed the start button and pulled out from the lot, wanting to get back to Maggie's apartment. His vision blurred in the torrent of rain, the windshield wipers slapping a predictable rhythm in counterpoint to the turmoil in his head.

What should he do? He could go to the Provincial Police, tell them about the stalking and an unavoidable incident. But was it?

Did he want Tucker to topple over the edge? Could he have somehow moved the fight away from the rim? Was it justifiable homicide? Was it survival? Was it murder? Would he spend the rest of his life in jail? Would he stand trial in Canada? Could he be extradited to the States? Were there any witnesses? His mind whirled.

Maybe he should call a lawyer. Maybe he should do nothing.

His moral compass spun. His judgment clouded.

He had no memory of the return trip. Back at Maggie's he sat on the couch with the replay of the encounter fresh in his mind, along with Captain Jack's question.

Could I kill a man? Sadly, Captain, I can.

Several days later, the *Buffalo Evening News* reported the recovery of a body from the Lower Niagara Gorge. The victim, found by hikers amid rocks along the riverbank, was identified as Jason Tucker, a male in his late thirties. His car had been found in the parking lot for the Great Gorge Hiking Trail, several miles upstream from the body discovery site.

Canadian authorities suspected a hiking mishap, that the unfortunate American tourist had ignored signs posted along the Great Gorge Hiking Trail and gone too close to the unstable edge. Suicide, however, had not been ruled out.

That night, not wanting to be alone, Nick walked to The Falls Inn. Captain Jack bought him a beer, telling him, along with anyone else who would listen, that another "loonie" had jumped, this time into the gorge. Some guy named Jason Tucker, a hotshot car salesman. His bloated, battered body had surprised a group of hikers. Nick didn't have the stomach to listen to more. He finished the beer to be polite and left.

Maggie called his cell the next day. He broke the news to her, the official version of Tucker's death—a hiking accident or suicide. He told her nothing about what had really happened at the gorge. After a long pause, she replied, "I never intended that to happen."

"What?" Nick's eyes narrowed. He shook his head as if to clear his hearing. "What did you say?"

"I only wanted him to scare you," Maggie said.

Nick waited a moment, stunned. "What the hell are you talking about?"

"I hired Jason to help me," she answered. "I'm ghostwriting a book for a well-known psychologist who's interviewing and studying crime victims—their reactions. What they do. What they think. What they feel. He's doing a deep dive into the fright, fight or flight response."

"What's this got to do with me?"

"I'm trying to tell you, Nick. I developed a research idea that I wanted to pursue on my own. What if a skilled interviewer knew, really knew, the victim, an articulate victim like yourself? Would more in-depth information come forth? Could I discover new data or shed light on any of the doctor's findings?"

"You were to be the skilled interviewer?" Nick queried. "My life was in the hands of a journalist playing at being a psychologist and an unbalanced car salesman?"

Maggie went on, sounding more excited. "I felt you would be a good study, that you would be able to articulate your experience with accuracy. Jason was to put you through several situations, each one more intense than the last, like what happened in Riverfront Park, the Anchor Bar, Delaware Park, and whatever else he might think of. Then I would interview you when everything was over."

"You knew, of course, that victims like me, your old buddy Nick, would fight back."

In a more somber tone, she continued, "I counted on it. But Jason must have cared about me more than I realized. He must have lost his objectivity, his sense of mission."

"Evidently, and become a little delusional perhaps? How did you team up with him?"

"He was former military; confident, tough, smart. Successful. Gutsy. Maybe a bit of a showboat. I didn't realize he was so jealous or possibly suicidal."

"He was angry all right." Nick gripped his phone. "And listening to you, I'm growing angrier by the minute."

"But just think, Nick. Your observations and thoughts could make a valuable contribution to the research," Maggie pressed on, unfazed. "I'm anxious to know your 'in the moment' actions, reactions and details. I'm looking forward to our interview. I'll reframe the actual events."

"That's not going to happen. A man is dead. You'll never hear my story."

"We can't control an accident or suicide. Sadly for us, Nick, we've both harmed Jason. It's now our secret."

"I had no intention of harming anyone." He looked out at the river. "Let me make sure I have this right. I'm just research? You got me here to be your guinea pig?"

"Like I said, things went wrong."

Nick felt as if he were in a bad dream. "I didn't come here to be a laboratory mouse, running through mazes for your enjoyment. I came to apartment-sit and discuss our relationship. I thought that's what you wanted, too. I didn't come to be thrust into a bunch of mumbo-jumbo 'research' conducted by two rank amateurs, which was evidently the scheme from the very beginning. You used our emotional connection to get me here. God, Maggie, what were you thinking? When did your drive to compete and succeed reach such a crossroad? Just when were you going to tell me all this?"

"When I got home. Which, by the way, will be the day after tomorrow. We have much to do. And I want to talk about us, too."

"I think we already have." He ended the call.

Standing at the living room window, Nick watched the wide flatness of the Niagara River wend its way toward turmoil but a few miles away. Like the river, he appeared calm. But beneath the surface his anger seethed. He dug his hands into his pockets.

He held genuine remorse for Jason, a man who'd been manipulated to his own death.

Nick could never undo his part in that. He also discovered himself to be nothing but a pawn. Maggie had used them both. One conclusion became apparent: The door to their relationship would be closed. By him. In his values book, bad faith and broken trust remained just that, bad and broken—impossible to be made good, impossible to be repaired.

His anger and, yes, hurt, rose to the surface. He wanted to hurl something through the window. Vent. Punch his fist through the wall, but, after some deep breathing, reasonable thought intervened. In the basest of terms, it had simply become a case of survival of the fittest. He'd won. He'd emerged the last man standing. No lawyer or police were involved. No one had seen him. No one had reported a gunshot. The gun and casing remained lost in the fast-flowing water. Loose ends seemed to wrap themselves.

And Maggie? Her misguided thinking started the chain of events, making her complicit in the loss of a man's life. To protect herself, she would never be able to tell her part in the story, nor would she ever know the whole story.

He thought again about Captain Jack's question: "Could you commit murder?" He shuddered. He regarded himself as a law-abiding, peaceful man. But he couldn't avoid a final showdown with Jason. The only outcome he had sought was to stay alive.

The debacle would have made quite an interview for Maggie, except there would be no interview. Ironically, Nick did garner first-hand information for his series on gun violence. He had primary research, the best kind. Or maybe the worst.

After a call to Uber for a ride to Buffalo International, he threw the apartment key and the smart key for the car on the kitchen counter and pulled the condo door closed behind him. If Maggie wanted him to pay for the car repair, she could call him. He'd be happy to talk about fault. Right now, he wanted to get away from the loonies before he became one.

Uneasiness followed him out the door, with a good chance it would follow him from now on, complicating his life even more. He knew everyone had flaws. People fell from grace all the time. But some people fell further than others.

He wondered what bothered him more—Jason's fall? Maggie's fall?

Or his own?

The De Luca Effect

Celia De Luca, Teacher

The imminent arrival of Celia De Luca's last class before lunch, the one in which all student eyes focus on the clock and stomachs rumble like railroad cars, makes her sigh. Freshmen. They're a squirrely bunch, agog at high school life. They wriggle and rustle about in their seats, drop notebooks and poke each other. A second sigh escapes her lips, this one deeper and more prolonged.

Celia De Luca, Miss De Luca to her students, prefers teaching her junior and senior classes that meet earlier in the morning for two reasons. First, they know how important it is to earn good grades. Second, their advanced Latin curriculum interests her more. Ninth grade Latin classes study Caesar and the Gallic Wars, boring her to her very fingertips. After thirty years of teaching, she can recite the passages from memory.

At least she looks stylish, thanks to her new navy-blue shirtwaist dress. It's the latest spring style for discerning women of the 1950s, according to Florence at the Sample Shop where she bought it. Not that this class will notice. She does hope Mr. Arens, the divorced biology teacher and her peer, appreciates her efforts. He's quite friendly in the teacher's room during coffee breaks.

With the index finger of her left hand, she repositions her glasses on the bridge of her nose and watches the class file in. Wily Jimmy Davis slinks in; sooner or later she'll catch him in a lie. Roberta Miller, a good student, follows. A tall girl is next. *What's her name?* She thinks a moment. Oh, yes, Janice White, who is awash among the upper classmen and low on the totem pole of a large suburban school like Lafayette High.

Janice is an awkward girl. She daydreams and looks out of the classroom windows instead of listening. Once in a great while she answers a question in a timid voice. Why doesn't the girl speak up?

Unsmiling, Miss De Luca watches the rest of the class arrive. She likes instilling a little fear in the adolescent pissants. The older students seem to know how to survive her histrionics, but these young ones lack savvy. Like a cat, she enjoys toying with them.

She calls the class to order, takes attendance, and picks up her worn Latin textbook, its margins filled with notes. Tabs of white paper protrude from between the pages, marking various passages. Latin, a logical language, disciplines the mind. Except for this class. In her thoughts, she groans at the mangled translations and mispronounced words she's about to hear. Her efforts here are wasted.

The college position she applied for last summer never materialized. The memory brings a scowl to her face; in all likelihood the job was awarded to someone younger, someone cheaper on the pay scale, and prettier. She should have moved to the university level years ago. Now she's stuck. In a public high school.

Shaking her head to remove the unpleasantness, she picks up a piece of soft chalk, a dust maker for her hands and new dress, and writes, *Noli cedere cognoscere.* Under it she writes the translation. Turning to the class, chalk in hand, she taps it on the blackboard under the words.

"Never cease to learn," she says with emphasis.

Her chosen opening statement is followed by the introduction of new vocabulary, the conjugation of some verbs, and more of the story of the Gallic Wars. With ten minutes of class remaining, it's time to call on a few scholars to translate passages from last night's homework, after which they'll hand in their papers. She shudders at another mind-numbing night spent correcting inept work. Tomorrow, she'll have to talk about the multitudinous mistakes.

"Who would like to start the translation?" she asks the class.

Roberta Miller puts her hand up at once, as do Dale Cameron and Beverly Lawson. Jimmy Davis sinks down in his seat, trying to disappear, as usual. She looks for slackers, someone to surprise. She begins her stroll, the eyes of the class following her every move. She locks a target in her sights, one sitting in the third row, the third seat. The student flinches and looks down at her open notebook.

"Janice, please translate the first sentence," she says.

Silence. Miss De Luca's hand balls into a fist. She feels her pointed nails dig into her palm.

"Janice, Miss White, did you hear me?" she asks her seemingly diffident student. "I asked you to translate the first sentence."

At last, words reach her ears. "All Gaul is divided into three parts . . ." And Janice's voice fades.

Miss De Luca stiffens. "Well, go on, go on," she insists.

". . . one of which the Belgae inhabit, the Aquitanians another . . ." The girl stops, clears her throat. The girl appears to have nothing else to say.

Just as suspected. Homework incomplete, if done at all. She stares the flustered freshman down. The girl lowers her head. *Good, you deserve it. Wasting my time.*

"Are you finished?"

"I, um . . . yes," Janice stammers.

Miss De Luca massages her forehead with the fingertips of her right hand, shaking her head. She says, "Oh, Janice. How can you be so stupid?"

She walks to the front of the class. *I'll let fear hang over the room for a moment. Ah, the tension is divine. I'm surrounded by dunces.*

She glances at the clock, enjoying the effect on the fear-filled, silent room.

"Roberta." She smiles at her star. "Please translate the first few sentences . . . or as far as you wish." She hears a collective sigh of relief, the shifting of feet, the turning of pages. She sees the glances between students as Roberta translates the first paragraph, the second, and the third, the scholars knowing they are safe for another day.

"Thank you, Roberta." She scans the class. "It pays to do your assignment."

Miss De Luca walks to her desk, sits, drumming her nails in a staccato cadence on the scratched surface. In a matter-of-fact voice she says, "Translate the first three paragraphs on page thirty-eight for homework. Be ready to read your work." She looks at Janice.

Just before the bell rings, she adds, "*Monitus es,*" in a somber voice.

Janice White, Student

Miss De Luca's brown eyes, their once clear outline blurred into the surrounding white, focus on me from behind large round lenses set in clear plastic frames. She gives me "the stare."

My ninth grade Latin teacher is short. She's known for her temper and wild gestures. She reveals her white teeth at me ever so slightly, clenched behind thin lips. I feel she might take a bite out of me.

A short-sleeved blue dress with padded shoulders and gathered skirt covers her slight body. Around her neck is a white Peter Pan collar. Her permed, graying hair frames her face. She looks nice, but she isn't. She presses her lips together, her eyes continuing to focus on me. The prolonged eye contact shrivels my insides. I look down. On toothpick legs, her small feet in navy blue pumps, she begins to move.

I'm sweating. My mouth is dry. I want to disappear.

Miss De Luca's steps draw her down the third row to the third seat where I sit. I see the veins on the tops of her hands, the skin slightly sagging from her forearms. She holds an open Latin textbook in one hand, flattens the gathers of her skirt with the other. I can tell she's ready to aim words at me. She's distracted for a moment by the sight of chalk dust on her skirt. She brushes at the fine powder with the back of her fingers.

"Janice, please translate the first sentence," she says.

I've done some of my homework. Sometimes I don't understand and I'm afraid to ask questions. Translating the story of Caesar and Gaul from Latin into English isn't on my list of exciting things to do. Not when I can play on the freshman girls' basketball team and do volleyball and soccer in after-school sports. Not when I can run the athletic field and feel ever so free. I wish I could run now.

"Janice, Miss White, did you hear me?" she asks with that edge in her voice. "I asked you to translate the first sentence."

Goodie two-shoes Roberta Miller gives me a cat-like smirk, letting everyone know she can do it. Jimmy Davis slides down in his seat. I feel twenty-eight pairs of classmates' eyes burn into me in silent celebration that it isn't one of them under the De Luca curse. I find my voice.

"All Gaul is divided into three parts . . ." I stop.

"Well, go on, go on," Miss De Luca says. She sounds impatient.

". . . one of which the Belgae inhabit, the Aquitanians another . . ." and I begin to fade, tongue-tied, afraid, unable to continue with what I've written. I'm afraid the words are wrong.

"Are you finished?"

"I . . . um . . . yes," I stammer.

Miss De Luca rubs her brow, shakes her head, the actions telegraphing to the world there's no hope for me. "Oh, Janice, how can you be so stupid?"

Her question bites into me like a tick. It sucks at the little confidence I have. Like a tick, the words hang on. They already haunt me.

Her glasses slip down her nose. Using the index finger of her right hand, the white nail tip filed to a point, she pushes the frame back into place. Her nostrils flare. She turns from me and moves up the aisle to the front of the room, the clicking of her heels and the swishing of her skirt around her legs the only sounds. She stands by her desk. Tension stretches across the room. She calls on Roberta Miller who translates three paragraphs on cue like a parrot.

"Well done, Roberta," Miss De Luca says.

After she gives a warm look to her star, she allows her gaze to wander from face to face. This slow, mind-numbing process is followed by the De Luca silence. I squirm, shuffle my feet, look down at my hands. Someone coughs. I sneak a peek at the clock. Miss De Luca walks around her desk, sits primly in her chair, taps her pointy nails on the desk.

"Translate the first three paragraphs on page thirty-eight for homework. Be ready to read your work out loud in class," she says. It sounds like a command.

Miss De Luca gives me a significant look, penciled eyebrows raised. Today we have her controlled undertones of rage. Tomorrow we'll be treated to handwringing, loud disapproval and anger. The class has been through this before. And it panics me.

"Monitus es," she says just before the bell rings.

Roberta Miller translates for all to hear, her voice a smug, loud singsong: *"You have been warned."*

I'm scared. I know I should do my homework. I want to do my homework. I'll try, even if . . . I'm shy . . . and stupid.

IV

EVERYONE KNEW THE STAKES

"Everything sounded hollow. Logic usually worked, but not tonight. He could find no logic in what he'd done."

—Penn Chalmers
"The Rule of L. Pennington Chalmers"

Not Even Gloria

Jingo slipped a Harley key into his jeans pocket and shouldered through the Friday night crowd at The Golden Cue, a local gathering place in mid-town Indio. He grabbed a draft beer at the bar, white foam sloshing over his fingers. After riding in from Desert Hot Springs, fighting wind, dust, and semis on Interstate 10, he found The Cue a good place to grab a cold one and cool off. But the main reason he dropped in wasn't for the beer. He wanted some action—pool hall action. He settled himself on a stool near the tables.

Boozer Diggins, a regular at the place and a fairly good player, spotted him. "Hey, Jingo Sparks," he called. "Good to see ya, man. How 'bout we shoot a few? Twenty bucks a game?"

"You're on, Boozer," Jingo hollered back. He slid off the stool, setting his drink on a ledge beneath a sign that read, "Players, Park Your Drinks Here." He ambled over to a wall rack where cue sticks stood on end, side by side.

With Boozer racking the balls, Jingo pulled a stick from the cue rack. He needed to hustle a few bucks. Gloria, his new, high-maintenance girlfriend, liked fancy things. Cost him plenty, but she made up for it in the "makin' love department" where it counted.

He hefted the polished stick in his hand, sighted down its length, held it out to feel the balance, rolled it on the table. It had a slight warp. He took another stick from the rack, repeated the process. Then another. Finally, he found a stick that passed all his tests. He grabbed the pool cue chalk and prepped the tip of the cue, thinking about Gloria.

Man, he loved to flash her around—make his friends jealous, especially Spike Grogan. The guy would dangle his little finger at Jingo and say, "Hey, Wee Willie. You'll never keep Gloria."

Oh, yeah? Gloria was Jingo's way of saying to the world, "Everything's workin' just fine."

Tonight, Gloria had to stop by her Aunt Mabel's. The old lady suffered bad from shingles, she said. That was good, Jingo thought. Her visit gave him time to raise some extra cash. Last night he took her to the Flying J for a sandwich. She threw a tantrum. Damn near chewed his ears off. He got it; she liked the good life, the local casinos, not a truck stop.

"Well? You gonna stand there thinkin'?" Boozer asked, leaning on the pool table, chalking his cue stick. "We gonna play or not?"

Jingo nodded. "Oh, yeah."

They played. Most of the night. Jingo kept sinking his shots, soon up a couple hundred bucks. Guys hung around the table, the smoke thicker than morning haze on the mountains. His eyes burned. Adrenaline raced up and down his arms. God, he loved this game. Too bad Gloria wasn't there to see him in action.

Around eleven, Boozer quit. "Ya got me, brother," he said. "Good playin' with ya. You're hot tonight."

Others echoed Boozer's words. Made Jingo feel good, knowing the guys liked and respected him.

Before someone else stepped up to play, Jingo decided to go to the head. At the mirror, he slicked back his unruly brown hair and smoothed his black Johnny Cash tee shirt into his black jeans. He also tucked his money in his boots. Had to be careful about flashing cash. Counting what he came in with, he had almost four hundred bucks.

On the way back to the pool tables, he glanced into the lounge to see who might be around. What the hell? Gloria was sitting there with some guy. Jingo recognized him—Lenny "One-Shot" Guardino. He'd won a big pool tourney last month and came through town occasionally, looking for a game. Had a real set of hands—in more ways than one.

Hold it, buddy. Gloria was his, Jingo's one and only. Hoisting his jeans, he walked to the booth where One-Shot and Gloria heated up the red vinyl seats.

Gloria looked up, trying to sound casual, but the shocked surprise on her face didn't look casual. "So what are you doing here?" she asked. "You said you were gonna work on your car."

"So how's your Aunt Mabel's shingles?" Jingo said, not moving.

Damn it. A panic punch hit him in the stomach. He'd never find another girl like Gloria. It'd been a great night, all the guys wanting to shoot a game with him. She should have been there, hanging around, sitting on a stool near the pool table, guys saying stuff like, "That's Jingo's girl. Man, he's one cool dude."

Jingo glared at One-Shot. One-Shot stared back.

"Oh, Jingo, just go," Gloria said as she flipped the back of her hand at him, waving him away.

Jingo's body stiffened. Nobody waved him away. When he was ready to go, he'd go. He put his sweaty palms in his pockets, cool-like, and shifted his weight. He hoped his face was poker-calm, that it masked the hurt stabbing at him. He had to decide. Was Gloria worth a dust-up? His mind raced. Yeah, she was.

One-Shot was a first-class pool player. Taking on a guy like him could build Jingo's reputation, get him into some tournaments, give him a chance at winning real money. Gloria'd want to be in *his* arms then, not in a paunchy older guy's. Words flowed from his mouth before he could dam them up.

"Hey, One-Shot. Got a proposition. Let's shoot a game, just one game. Hundred dollar buy-in. Winner gets the pot." And before he could stop, he added, "And the winner gets Gloria."

"Say what?" Gloria tossed her curly mop of blond hair, her face flamethrower red. "Who do you think you are?"

Jingo looked at her. "Just wait, sweet cheeks."

One-Shot unwrapped his arms from Gloria, raised an eyebrow, looked Jingo up and down. "You got guts, kid. Tell you what. One game—open table, real casual. Sink any ball, any order, down to the eight and the cue ball. Then sink the eight. I'm gonna up the ante. The lady, the pot, *plus* two hundred bucks."

"What's going on? I'm not a thing. I'm a person. With feelings!" Gloria grabbed her purse, pushed by Jingo, and stomped all the way from the booth to the ladies' room.

Jingo swallowed. He was playing for his girl. For all his night's winnings. He inhaled. His head nodded yes before he knew it. He followed One Shot back to the tables. Everyone stepped aside for the pool hall legend.

They lagged for the break. If One-Shot won the lag, Jingo'd never get a chance to shoot. The guy would run the table. Jingo hit his ball square on. One Shot did the same. Jingo held his breath. To his surprise, One-Shot's ball lagged short of his. *Great!* Or was it? Was the guy messing with him? Letting him shoot first, waiting for him to blow it? Waiting for him to choke?

In the wall mirror behind the table, he saw Gloria sifting through the crowd, closer to the action. She sat on a bar stool, lit up, crossing her right leg over her left, swinging her ankle back and forth. Her face seemed to say having two guys duke it out at the pool table wasn't the worst thing that could happen to a gal. He turned away and chalked his cue.

Jingo called his first shot and potted the ball. He sank the next and the next. His cue stick lit up, touched with magic. Onlookers collected nearby, watching him sink his shots.

"Go for it, Jingo," someone said. His gut grabbed; his hand tightened on the cue stick.

A low murmur settled over the room. Word had spread. Everyone seemed to know the stakes. He could become a hometown hero—the guy who put everything on the line for his girl, the guy who beat Lenny "One-Shot" Guardino. Or he could lose everything.

Gloria stood, put out her cigarette, and moved a little closer.

Then it happened. Jingo missed his shot.

"Guess you choked, kid," One-Shot quipped.

Poker faced, One-Shot stepped to the table. He played fast, the cue stick and his hands a smooth machine. The balls dropped, until only two remained—the cue and the eight. Jingo bit his lip. The man lined up the winning shot—*and missed!* The crowd gasped. One-Shot winked at him and stepped back.

Jingo shook his head. *He's gotta be jabbin' me. Thinks I can't handle the pressure.* He glanced over his shoulder. Gloria was right up front. Shadows played on her face, making the dimple in her left cheek deeper than ever.

One-Shot left him a lousy pop shot. The cue ball touched the wood railing with the eight ball right in front of it. Jingo wasn't a righteous man, but he offered up a pool hall prayer fast. *One-Shot's tryin' to psyche me out, Lord. Don't let me do somethin' stupid now.*

He arched his left hand on the rail, extended his thumb, angled the stick high, and popped it onto the cue ball. His stomach sagged. The stick hit the cue ball half-assed. The cue ball hit the eight ball half-assed. The black ball rolled, wobbled toward the pocket. Closer. Closer. And stopped. On the pocket's edge. It didn't move. It didn't drop. The crowd inhaled. The game was over.

Son of a bitch. Goddammit. With one lousy shot he'd just become a poolroom joke, a guy dumb enough to bet his girl and his stash on a game against a pool shark. Jingo bent down to pull the money from his boot. Suddenly, voices erupted around him. Someone shouted through the noise. "The damn ball just dropped." He jolted up, hitting his head on the table's edge.

His eyes weren't playing tricks. The ball no longer hung above the pocket. It was *in* the pocket. He punched his fist in the air. Someone slapped his back.

"Well, you lucky little son of a gun," One-Shot said through the noise, tossing two Franklins on the table. "You got hustle, Jingo Sparks. Next time I'm in town, we'll play a real game, legitimate. You won some money tonight. I'll get it back." Nodding at Gloria, he walked toward the door.

Gloria stood there, glaring, her eyes like lasers, trying to burn a hole in One-Shot's back.

After a moment, she turned around to the crowd, Jingo at the forefront. Her face softened. She walked to him and put her hand on his arm, but he brushed it away. She started to speak, but Jingo didn't listen.

One-Shot's words roared in his ears. The guy wanted to play him again. He'd said it in front of everyone. Jingo turned his back to Gloria, moved into the crowd, high fiving his admirers. Nothing—*nothing*—could beat this high.

Not even Gloria.

The Art of Making Pies

A fan on top of an old restaurant refrigerator thrummed, its metal blades shuttling humid August air through the diner kitchen. It blew an occasional sweep of coolness across Annie's forehead as she stood at the baking table. She raised her head to feel the breeze on her neck while staring idly at the fan's whirling blades. They seemed to imitate the daily circle of her life that took her from home to work, from work to home.

Six days a week she waitressed at Patsy's Place, her mother's diner in Yucca Valley. She also helped make Patsy's Famous Pies. It used to be fun. But the days just seemed to get longer and harder. She'd grown weary of the place with its stuffy kitchen, inadequate air conditioning, and hot ovens.

On the baking table, three empty pie shells stared up at her, ready to be filled. Twenty-four apples waited to be peeled. Lemon juice, flour, butter, brown and white sugars, plus Patsy's secret spices sat to the side, premeasured and ready. During the afternoon lull, Annie always made pies. She wanted her mother to use commercial pie filling, but Patsy always shook her head and said, "Fresh apples make the best-tasting pies."

The three pies would bake open-faced to become Patsy's famous Dutch Apple. Her mother claimed pie making was an art. Annie found no art in standing at a wooden table, its surface knife-scarred from years of pie making. She found no art in peeling, cutting, coring, slicing, and mixing. It was a monotonous, messy job. She pulled on a pair of clear-plastic food service gloves. Soon her hands would sweat inside them.

With careful turns of a paring knife, she peeled a Granny Smith apple. At the same time, turning in her mind, were ideas about starting over. She'd leave the diner, leave her troubled marriage, leave life as she knew it behind.

But the thought of uprooting her daughter always made her reconsider. Eight-year-old Mandy loved her Grandma Patsy. After school, she came to the diner, did her homework, and helped her grandma until Annie finished her shift. Annie enjoyed seeing them together. And her husband Del did have his sweet moments between the bad. If she did leave, she worried about making it alone. Being a single mother would be a challenge. Perhaps life wasn't that bad. She had a family. She had a home. She had work. *Oh, stop feeling sorry for yourself.*

Annie sighed and split the apple in two. She cored the halves and cut each of them into pie-sized crescents. Slice after slice after slice. The knife blade thumped on the table, adding new scars to the wooden surface.

Through the order window she saw Jake Abernathy and his cousin Ed Simmons (men she'd known all her life) talking with her mother. Patsy always said they were the best "uncles" her Annie could have. They sat at the counter on the same two stools every day to drink coffee, eat pie, and talk about "the news." Annie sighed. Her life just seemed to be coffee, pie, and "the blues."

She ran a sweaty forearm across her brow and reached for the next apple to peel, cut, and core. The white blouse Del told her to wear stuck to her back. Her jeans fit too tight. A stained apron tied around her middle added another layer of irritation. The uncomfortable clothing, her troublesome thoughts, the boring repetition of pie making—she felt like a marionette dangling from strings with no control.

She paused her work for a moment.

Del seemed to grow touchier every day. Maybe the word "moody" described him better. He called her a nag, said she was always bitching about something. Money, a nicer place to live, a new couch. She didn't know what to do. If she worked real hard at cleaning the house, making it neat and tidy, he didn't seem to notice; still called her a lousy housekeeper. If she cooked his favorite meatloaf, he said it tasted like cardboard. If she tried a new makeup or bought a pretty blouse, he said she was a lost cause and was spending too much money.

She went back to peeling and halving another apple, coring it, and cutting it. Slice, slice, slice. She sprinkled lemon juice on the pieces.

Del kept having "expenses." Some medical, some not—like poker. They struggled to afford a 1950s stucco house with its cheap rent and traffic noise, two bedrooms and one bath. A rusted cyclone fence surrounded the place and made it feel more like a prison than a home.

She was glad to have the monthly child support check for Mandy. It was hidden in a zippered compartment of her purse. She'd run over to the Wells Fargo on her break and cash it. Del told her to demand more money from an ex-husband who sometimes fell behind on the payments. "Take the S.O.B. back to court," he snarled. Annie felt lucky to collect the money she did.

She picked up the next apple and automatically peeled, halved, and cored as before. She began to cut. Slice, slice, slice. Each piece fell away from the knife.

Most of the time, with Del's constant carping, she felt anxious. When her nerves took over, food took over, too. She couldn't seem to stop gaining weight.

"You're gonna get fat like your mother. I didn't marry that," Del would complain.

His words cut deeper than any knife. One day during an argument, he'd slapped her face. She put her fingertips on her cheek, feeling the shock of it and the sting like it happened yesterday. It was the first but not the last time he struck her. A lump rose in her throat.

Annie dropped the knife. It clattered on the table. Her thoughts played like a TV rerun, always with the same ending. She glanced through the order window again into the diner's interior, her gaze shifting toward the front window.

To her surprise, she saw Del on the far street corner, about to cross the road to the eatery. A handsome shortstop for the Rancho Cucamonga Quakes when they married, his face now wore a permanent frown. His once athletic body had gone soft, a beer belly pushing against his belt. His big-league dreams ended when a motorcycle accident left him with a bad knee. He'd settled for a job managing Bowden's Hardware Store.

Her sixth sense told her something was up. Del should be at the store. She'd dropped him off at work this morning, plus he never came to the diner anymore. He and Patsy had stopped getting along.

At the sink, she filled a glass, took several deep swallows, then held the cold glass against her hot cheek. She half-listened to Patsy and the two men.

"Hey, Patsy, wanna sell me this apple pie recipe?" Jake laughed.

Patsy bantered back, "Planning on buying it with your good looks?" A spoon clanged on a coffee cup. Laughter erupted among the three.

Annie pulled off her apron and gloves, dropped them by the sink and walked into the diner. Del now stood on the sidewalk in front of the place. He saw her through the window and motioned for her to come out.

"Ma, Del needs to talk to me a sec," Annie said.

Patsy nodded in Del's direction. She replied, "I see him, signaling like a damn baseball coach. Doesn't he work today? Remember, we need those extra pies for the supper crowd."

"Why don't he come in, honey?" Ed asked.

Annie ignored the question. Grabbing a napkin from one of the tables, she wiped her face and stepped out onto the sidewalk.

She walked toward Del. "Something happen? Aren't you supposed to be at the hardware store?"

"Knock off the damn questions," Del snapped. He glanced in Patsy's direction.

Annie looked over her shoulder. Her mother stood behind the counter, watching through the diner window. She looked back at Del.

"What's the matter?" She smoothed her blouse, making sure it was tucked in.

"My damn knee," he whined. "Bowden let me leave early to go see the doc for a cortisone shot." His tone hardened. "I need some money."

"You know I don't have any," Annie answered.

"What about the child support check?"

"Not here yet," she lied.

"That bastard's late again?" he asked.

Annie nodded. She'd picked up the mail from their mailbox yesterday before Del could learn the check had arrived. He wouldn't start anything, not with Patsy watching, not with the two men acting a bit curious.

"You better not be lyin' to me," Del said, the threat in his voice unmistakable.

She glanced in her mother's direction, as did Del. Patsy seemed busy talking to the two men. Del grabbed Annie by the upper arm.

"I know you got some cash stashed somewhere," he muttered.

It made him mad that Patsy took money from her paycheck weekly, so they'd be sure to make the house rent. His fingers dug into her arm, adding bruises to the ones already there, bruises she had to cover to hide the damage.

"I've got a little." Her voice sank low in her throat. The resolve to stand up to him collapsed. Like her insides. Like always.

"That's more like it," he said and released his grip.

She reached inside her blouse, into her bra. His gaze followed her hand, eying her breasts. Out came three twenty-dollar bills. Grocery money.

"That it?"

She nodded.

With a quick look toward the diner, he snatched the bills from her hand and shoved them into his pocket. He grabbed her upper arm again. This time he pulled down on it with a quick, hard jerk. She felt pain in her shoulder and neck.

Annie winced. "You hurt me."

"Just a reminder," he said. With a disdainful look, he turned and limped back across the street.

She blinked the tears away, not wanting to cry; not now, not here. She took a deep breath. Patsy knew their marriage had problems, that Del had a big problem. Her mother tried to talk to her, but Annie always said they could work through their troubles by themselves. Her mother didn't know the half of it.

Annie watched Del make a quick turn onto First Street. The doctor had his office in a small medical building on Third Street. She should have known. Buck's Bar with its shady, backroom card game was on First.

She turned toward the diner to see her mother and the men looking. Annie mouthed, "I'm coming." What had they seen?

Patsy had survived on her own after her husband left early one day in his big truck—permanently. Annie wished she'd gotten the "toughness gene" in her DNA like her mother had. She opened the diner door.

Patsy started to speak, but Annie shook her head. Jake studied his newspaper. Ed reached for his glass of water. No words were spoken. But the air grew heavy with a knowing, a speculation, a curiosity. In the kitchen, out of sight, she rubbed her upper arm and neck. They ached, but her fear, humiliation, and sadness ached more.

After a moment, she took a deep breath and, puppet-like, went back to work. She disposed of the old gloves, put on new ones, tied her apron back on and finished prepping the Granny Smiths. In an extra-large stainless bowl, she mixed the apples and other ingredients with her hands. When the mixture was ready, she scooped several large portions into the first pie shell, folding the sides of the single crust inward to hold the contents. The oven needed to heat. She set the dial to 375 degrees.

Her thoughts also began to heat.

What would Del be like when he came home? If he didn't drink too much or if he won at cards, he might be the Del she married. But if he lost and had too many beers, there'd be a ruckus. Sometimes Sheriff Barnes shut the poker game down. Sometimes the man simply winked and told the boys to cool it. The game and the drinking always found a way to continue, any time of the day or night—as did the aftermath at home. Annie shuddered.

She'd seen the TV talk shows, read articles in magazines, and heard the gossip at Daisy's Beauty Shop about men who hit their wives. One day, while getting her hair cut, she'd confided in Daisy about Del's shouting, about the shoves and the slaps. Daisy said that men who do this get worse. Annie knew that was true. She knew Del *was* getting worse. Her Mandy had seen too much, heard too much. Daisy told her to be careful, that she should leave. Annie had seen a domestic abuse hotline number on a billboard.

After folding the crust on the last pie, she removed her gloves and dropped them in the trash. Suddenly craving food, she took a round tin from a shelf behind her and opened it. The scent of Patsy's oatmeal chocolate chip cookies floated into the kitchen. For a moment, the world felt good. She surveyed the contents, selected one, and closed the tin, placing it back on the shelf. She leaned against the table and bit into the homemade cookie, the largest one in the container she could find.

Instinct told her to get out of the marriage. Run. Leave. Do it. Now. She didn't like tiptoeing around, trying not to set Del off. She didn't like the sleepless nights, being afraid for herself and Mandy. She didn't like lying to her mother. But the old habits, the memories of good times, pulled on her. It was the only life she knew.

She took another bite of cookie, chewing on it and her feelings.

Was Del's behavior different today? No. It was typical of one of his ugly moods. Except this time, he'd bullied her in public. Her mother had looked worried. The men had worn solemn faces. She'd seen their looks, feeling them like knife cuts. She hated what she'd become. She seldom smiled or felt happy. Her body seemed to have lost a spine. Was her behavior different today? No.

The last swallow of cookie slid down her throat.

The oven beeped. She wiped her hands on a towel, placed the pies in the oven, and set the timer. Soon their satisfying smell would drift from the kitchen into the diner. Unlike the comforting aroma of baking pies and the sweet scent of cookies, her broodings were neither. She wondered about her backbone. Could it stiffen again?

She turned her back to the table, leaned against it. Despite her headache, a thought seemed to be forming. It began to take the shape of a decision. An impulsive decision. Maybe that was the best kind. No time for second guesses. She had to leave. A surge of excitement flared but stopped. She didn't even have a plan. She folded her arms. Or did she?

She had the car. She'd dropped Del off at work in the morning. He'd walked from the hardware store to the diner, to Buck's and would get a ride home after the card game with one of his buddies. The child support money would be enough to take Mandy and her to Phoenix. It would be enough to live on if they stayed with Patsy's sister, Aunt Bertie, until she scrounged a job. She'd call her mother from the road to explain and apologize for leaving without telling her ahead of time. It was better Patsy didn't know. That way, Del couldn't accuse her of being part of a scheme. She felt her mother would be glad but also sad for what had to be done. Annie would call her ex and give him the new address for the next support payment. The other waitresses at the diner could pick up the slack.

There wasn't much time. She had to act fast, use the rest of the evening to make her move before she started to doubt herself. Mandy would stay at the diner, have supper, and help Grandma Patsy in the kitchen like she loved to do. After Annie's shift, they'd go home, throw things in the car and leave. Mandy would be upset, but, hopefully, she too would understand. By the time Del arrived home in the early morning, they'd be on Interstate 10, well on their way to Phoenix. Maybe she'd found her own "toughness gene" after all.

Annie thought about another cookie but shook her head. If she stayed true to herself and didn't lose her nerve, Del wouldn't be able to hurt her anymore. She was a good waitress, and good ones always found work. An energy began to travel through her that she hadn't felt in a long time.

She looked around the kitchen, at the scarred baking table, at the commercial ovens. She couldn't call pie making an art. To her, it wasn't. But there was something to be said for the art of making a life, a new life.

A Brief Interruption

A soft *click* interrupted the evening stillness of Palma's small studio apartment. Glancing up, she listened, heard nothing more, and settled back on her Murphy bed. She resumed studying Arthur Miller's play *A View from the Bridge* in preparation for the literature class she taught at the community college. It met the next morning at ten.

Click. The sound intruded again. Puzzled, she slipped her pencil between the book's pages and set it aside. She noted the time on the bedside clock. A few minutes past eleven.

What was making that odd little sound?

Curious, she looked from the clock to the kitchen doorway, over to a closet door, past an alcove leading to the bathroom, and around to an easy chair sitting by a screened, six-foot high front window with the lower sash open. A slight breeze ruffled the window's sheer white curtains, reminding her of timid ghosts.

Her search proceeded past the window to a mirror hanging by the front door, then to the door itself. The doorknob suddenly turned to the left. *Click.* After a pause, it rotated back to the right. *Click.* Palma didn't move, coming to a stark realization. The only lock protecting against someone entering was a flimsy button in the center of the doorknob. The security chain hung free and the deadbolt hadn't been set. Involved in her work, she'd not yet locked up for the night.

Who was out there?

Heart racing, Palma quietly got up. A lighted pole lamp by the bed hung shadows on the ceiling, walls, and thrift store furniture, giving the room an eerie feeling that stirred her uneasiness. She took her bathrobe from the foot of the bed and slipped it on, covering her flimsy nightgown. With cat-like treads, she stepped to the center of the small room, transfixed on the doorknob. It again turned to the left. *Click.*

Palma waited for the knob to make a deliberate return to the right. Instead, it snapped back. In quick succession, the bushes outside her open window rustled. Only the screen separated her from whatever stirred outside. She was afraid to go near the door or the window.

She darted into the unlit kitchen, guided by light filtering in from the main room, her bathrobe flaring like a superhero cape. She needed a weapon. From a cupboard drawer, she pulled out a chef's knife. Gripping it in her right hand, her knuckles white, she quickly checked the back door lock, deadbolt and security chain. They were in place.

She slipped back into the main room. No white noise intruded from the street or neighbors. No bushes rustled. No doorknob turned. Life seemed becalmed. But not for Palma.

She stood in the middle of the room holding a knife, staring at the front door, afraid to close the window in case someone lurked just on the other side. Before a deep, tension-releasing breath could escape her lips, the knob turned again, this time back and forth with urgency. Her muscles and nerves went on high alert.

Newspaper stories flitted through her brain. "Los Feliz Area Robbery," "Los Feliz Peeping Tom," "Rape Reported in Los Feliz

Neighborhood." A 1969 *Los Angeles Times* headline about the Tate/La Bianca murders, instigated by Charles Manson, flashed into her mind. The murders had occurred a year prior, a few miles from her apartment in the trendy Los Feliz district she loved.

Palma's eyes darted to the telephone on her desk. She took three quick steps, placed the knife on the desk's surface, picked up the receiver, and dialed.

"Operator," came a woman's monotone.

Palma, her eyes on the door and window, whispered, "I need the police." Her hand shielded her mouth.

"One moment, please."

While she waited, Palma looked at the knife, remembering what an old boyfriend had taught her. Go for the gut, lunge the blade up. Don't raise your arm high in the air. An assailant can grab your arm and gain control of the weapon.

"Police Department," a voice barked in her ear. "Officer Lutz here."

"I need help," she murmured, again covering her mouth. "Someone's outside my door, trying to get in. I also hear noises in the shrubbery by my open front window." A crackling noise from the bushes made her jump.

"Your name?" the officer asked.

"Palma Sheffield."

"Address?"

"4204 Los Feliz Boulevard, apartment 4."

"Your telephone number?"

"Plaza 6452."

"Stay inside," the officer instructed. "A car is on its way."

"Please hurry." She hung up the receiver.

Time crawled while her thoughts raced. She wondered if she could stab or get away from someone. She recalled girlfriend conversations. Knee the attacker in the crotch. Go for the eyes. Bend back a finger. Don't freeze. Scream. She tied the belt on her robe, as if girding herself.

The doorknob rattled. Palma grabbed the knife. *Oh, God, hurry.* She ran her tongue across her dry lips, felt her stomach churn. In a few days she'd be celebrating her twenty-seventh birthday. Too much living lay ahead to be injured . . . or worse. Her heart sounded like rolling thunder in her ears. She waited by the desk, time seeming to stand still.

All at once, amber and red lights flashed into her apartment. Car doors slammed. A two-way radio crackled, and muffled male voices could be heard. The police. She hurried to the front window. A squad car and two policemen filled the driveway of her apartment building. After a moment, she heard an insistent knock on the front door.

"Police," an overloud male voice said.

Using her free hand, she turned on the outside light with a switch by the door.

"LAPD," the same voice repeated.

She unlocked the door and cracked it open to peer out.

"I'm Officer Jensen." Another man stood behind him. "My partner's Officer Henderson." The men waited.

Officer Jensen returned her look. Henderson glanced out into the night. She could see Jensen's badge highlighted beneath the porch light. At the top of the shield were the words "Police Department." Under it, "Los Angeles Police." Under that, the numbers "54928." She opened the door and stood back.

Jensen didn't enter but remained in the doorway. Henderson, the taller of the two, stood right behind him. Palma felt their scrutiny.

"Miss, put the knife down," Jensen said.

She looked at her right hand, as if surprised by what dangled from it. She dropped the knife on the easy chair.

The two officers walked in. They stood a moment, looking around the apartment. Henderson asked her what happened. Palma explained about the doorknob and the rustling bushes. The two officers stepped back outside. A commotion stirred in the shrubs by the window; a roaming flashlight beam danced in the shadows. She could hear indistinct conversation. The two officers re-entered her apartment.

Jensen walked over to the chair and picked up her weapon. "I assume this goes in the kitchen?"

"Yes," Palma said. "In there." She pointed to the darkened doorway. Jensen snapped on his flashlight and nodded, heading toward the kitchen. She heard the knife being placed on the counter and the officer's footsteps. Locks rattled and the back door opened. Jensen stepped outside.

Henderson smiled at her. "I need a little information."

She watched him take out a worn notebook and date the page. August 8, 1970.

"First name?" he asked.

"Palma."

He cocked his head, a questioning look on his face.

"P-a-l-m-a," she added, spelling the word.

"An unusual name," he observed.

"Yes, for the beautiful palm trees my parents saw on Sunset Boulevard. When they came to California. From Chicago." Palma stopped.

"Last name?"

"Sheffield."

"Tell me again what happened," Henderson said.

Palma recounted the event, the officer nodding, jotting down notes.

Jensen returned, strode past them, shaking his head, and continued to the squad car.

Henderson nodded at him, saying to Palma, "We found broken branches on the bushes and footprints in the damp dirt by your open window as well as fresh dirt on your front door mat. Nothing by the back door. I'm afraid whoever it was is gone. My partner is radioing in the information so other officers can be on alert. Maybe we'll get lucky."

Before leaving, the officers closed the front window, locked it, and checked the remaining windows in the kitchen and bathroom. They inspected the lights over the front and back doors and instructed Palma to keep them on every night, all night. They re-locked the back door. With security measures completed, the officers waited outside before leaving while she locked the front door. She secured the knob button, set the deadbolt and anchored the security chain. Palma heard car doors close and the squad car back out of the driveway.

She went to the kitchen, feeling grateful nothing serious had occurred, and put the knife, an unwelcome reminder of the night's events, back in the drawer. Still upset, she returned to the main room, removed her robe, picked up the telephone with its long cord—just in case—and, with it beside her, crawled back into bed. She wanted to close her eyes and drift into some sort of sleep, but she still had to finish reading Miller's *A View from the Bridge.* Her studying resumed, as did jotting notes in the margins.

Events in the play's final scene resonated closer to home than

Palma liked. She could visualize each character clearly: Eddie Carbone fighting with Marco; Eddie lunging at Marco with a knife; Marco gaining control of the knife and stabbing Eddie; Eddie dying in his wife's arms. She felt the trauma of the tragic event, more so after having held a knife in her own hand, intent on doing harm. She wondered what would have happened if she'd tried to use it, a weapon that could have been turned against her.

She closed the book, wanting, needing to sleep. As she tried to settle down, turning first one way, then the other, the phone rang. She stiffened and glanced at the clock—a little past one o'clock. Her nerves frayed, she decided not to answer. Then, she had second thoughts. Despite the lateness of the hour, the police could be doing a follow-up call or, and a slight smile crossed Palma's face, it could be her girlfriend Liz, who liked to call at any hour, after a bad day or a bad date, with stories to tell.

She reached for the phone. If the police had caught someone, she wanted to know. If it was Liz, Palma had quite a story to tell, too. She picked up the receiver.

"Hello."

No one replied.

"Hello? Who is this?"

Nothing.

"Who is this?" she repeated.

A male voice answered, "I'm watching you."

The Rule of L. Pennington Chalmers

L. Pennington "Penn" Chalmers strolled from the Beauregard Ballroom into the lobby of the exclusive Sutton Plaza Hotel in downtown Charleston. It teemed with fellow attorneys in town for the American Bar Association's annual three-day convention. Depending on what happened, Penn sometimes extended his stay at the event by a day or two. A kick-off cocktail party followed by keynote speaker The Honorable Thaddeus T. Rankin had been noteworthy, but the respected judge proved to be a little long-winded.

Penn's stomach grumbled. He decided to have a quiet meal by himself before retiring to his room for a good night's sleep. The days ahead could be long and busy with lawyerly meetings, the nights long and busy with other kinds of meetings. Anticipation churned in his gut, the same sensation he experienced when entering a courtroom.

A strange city promised adventure, one of the reasons he never missed the ABA's annual meeting. Intrigue sparked his libido, sharpened his instincts, and honed his courtroom acumen. However, his escapades were governed by a cardinal rule: Never pursue a woman at the convention hotel.

"Discretion is the better part of valor," Penn murmured. Tomorrow he'd explore.

Now, he needed dinner. Bella's Magnolia Bistro located in the hotel mezzanine advertised Charleston's finest eggplant Parmesan. On the way to the bistro, he stopped to chat with several colleagues, shake their hands, and promise to be in touch after the conference. He believed the networking garden should be cultivated.

Years of handshakes, mutual favors, plus a cunning shrewdness had earned him the respect of his peers. No one could deny that L. Pennington Chalmers knew how to negotiate behind closed doors and engage in hardball tactics in the courtroom. He played to win.

A large bronze clock above the concierge's desk announced 9:00 p.m. He entered the restaurant, spoke to the maître d', and waited to be seated. He heard someone shout his name. The loud voice caused patrons to look, seemingly annoyed at the disturbance. A heavy-set man waved him over to his booth. Eric Castelli.

Penn wanted to ignore the man but knew it wouldn't be politic to refuse, given their history. He liked to keep the waters calm. He thought of the old saying, "Don't burn your bridges." This jackass could be of value in the future. He walked toward the booth.

"Join me. I just sat down. My treat," Eric said.

"Why not? Good to see you." Penn settled into the booth, his quiet dinner now history.

Eric flagged a server, then drummed his fingers on the table, bongo-style. They waited only a moment before the waiter arrived.

"Sir?"

"How about an Absolut straight up," Eric said, "along with that famous lasagna."

The waiter looked at Penn. "And you, sir?"

"Ketel One on the rocks. I'll try your eggplant Parmesan."

The waiter jotted down their requests and on his way to the kitchen passed the drinks order to the bartender.

Eric Castelli had a record of being a hard man to trust. His trial tactics—his "gimmicks" in the courtroom—were legendary. Penn also sensed, from experience, that Eric envied the Chalmers' family connections and money.

"Well, Penn, haven't seen you for a while," Castelli said. "Those twin sons of yours must be at university by now."

"They are. How's the practice over in Memphis?"

"It's been better." Eric scratched his nose. "Your winning of that lawsuit against Rockwell Industries, one of my firm's biggest clients, cost them and us plenty."

The drinks arrived. Eric took two healthy swallows.

"Let's not visit that again," Penn requested as he laid his napkin in his lap. "We both know flawed construction caused six deaths plus serious injury to five others."

Eric signaled for another drink. "You could've just sued the company responsible for the steel framing."

"Doesn't work that way." Penn swirled his vodka, the ice clinking against the glass. "Go after the deep pockets, all the deep pockets. Law 101."

The waiter arrived with a small dish of antipasti, Eric's second drink and water for each.

Penn speared a large olive, chewing it slowly, recalling the case, a negligence trial after a disastrous accident. A section of a multi-level office complex had collapsed before completion. He'd won generous monetary awards for the victims and their families. Eric's firm received bad press after it appeared insensitive to the victims' needs.

Eric put his fork down, sweat glistening on his upper lip. "You also cost *me* big time. I had to pull in a few favors to even stay on at the firm."

"That's unfortunate. Nothing personal," Penn assured him. "I go into a courtroom to win."

Eric shrugged. The lighting, though subdued, played on his shiny forehead and bulbous nose, on his puffy face and hands. After a moment, the man picked up his clean coffee cup. He placed it upside down on the tablecloth. He then poured water from his glass into the empty saucer where it pooled.

Penn felt a gimmick in the offing. "What are you doing?"

Eric held up his hand. "Pay attention." He opened a cruet of olive oil sitting on the table and poured a drop into the water-filled saucer. It lingered a moment in a small dollop, then, unexpectedly, spread into tiny bubbles across the water's surface.

Seconds passed. Penn waited, annoyed. "Care to explain the hocus-pocus?"

Eric's face grew somber. "Watch yourself, Chalmers."

"Why?"

"Wait." Eric's eyes narrowed. He raised his head and looked upward. "Do you feel it, the humid, warm air settling around us?"

Penn wondered if he did feel a sudden change in the air or simply succumbed to the power of suggestion. He casually reached for a piece of garlic bread.

Eric put his hand on Penn's forearm. "Did you feel it, the heat?"

"I'm not much into sorcery." He removed Eric's hand.

"It's gone now. I know you felt it, Chalmers. I could tell by the quick, slight move of your head." Eric gave him a sly stare, his mouth becoming a thin line. "My Sicilian grandmother taught me this little ritual. When the oil spreads, it means someone has put a curse on you. It's called *malocchio*—the 'evil eye.'"

"Are you really trying to put a hex on me?"

"That's right, sport." Eric patted himself on the chest. "It's done, so watch out. Bad luck is coming your way."

"Your voodoo techniques must charm a judge."

Eric smirked. "Nothing like a little Italian legerdemain, Castelli style, to spice up the evening."

Before Penn could reply, the waiter arrived with two steaming dishes.

Eric pushed the plate of lasagna away. "You know, I believe I've lost my appetite." He finished his second vodka, tossed a rumpled napkin on the table, and said, "Thanks for the drinks." Unsteady on his feet, he shouldered past the waiter who looked questioningly after him.

"Just bring me the check," Penn said.

After a few bites of eggplant, he didn't feel like eating either, perhaps bothered by something more than Eric's cheap trick of leaving him with the bill. He paid the check and headed for the lobby, shaking off his unease with each step, deciding to leave superstition to the hacks.

Trying to jinx someone's luck with an Old-World curse was hardly a strategy taught in a law school or an MBA program. He had to laugh at Castelli. Penn had listened to his father's lessons well. "Son," he'd said, "if a man works hard, he makes his own opportunities, he finds his own luck."

Malocchio. He'd share this dinner story with friends back in Concord when he returned to his offices in New Hampshire. It would make for a few chortles over cigars and brandy. Maybe he'd even demonstrate Castelli's technique.

Penn walked across the lobby into the Pirate's Lounge. A brandy would settle him. He sat at the polished oak bar, pulled out his wallet and opened it. Margaret's picture, taken at the Rolling Greens Country Club near Concord, smiled back at him. After almost twenty-five years of marriage, her looks still turned heads—still turned his head, as did their sex. He removed a bill, closing the wallet gently.

"Sir?" The bartender waited.

"Your best brandy." He placed fifty dollars on the bar.

His thoughts returned to Eric Castelli. A curse? Bad luck? Rubbish. He was a winner, blessed with the Chalmers ability to come out on top.

An attractive woman sitting by herself at the end of the bar smiled at him. He nodded, sipping the twenty-year-old brandy, making no further eye contact, nevertheless pleased with himself. It paid to stay in shape. He worked out at the Concord Athletic Club regularly. Plus, Chalmers men kept a full head of hair to the end of their days. His dark brown hair showed streaks of gray at the temples. Margaret called the look "distinguished."

He sighed, wondering about his odd peccadillo, this need for a yearly fling. Was he reaffirming his manhood? Letting off steam from the constant pressure of work? He shook his head and sipped his drink. An answer eluded him. His thoughts wandered to the upcoming spree. Tomorrow night, away from the hotel, he'd play. With a final, satisfying sip of brandy, he allowed himself to slip into the vernacular. *Fuck you, Castelli.*

In the quiet lobby early the next morning, Penn chatted with the concierge. She placed a small map and brochure on the counter between them.

"After you finish your run through the park, Mr. Chalmers, do try Charleston's best cup of coffee." She tapped her finger on a red dot. "You'll find Miss Lucy's Latte in the heart of our historic district. Guaranteed to cure what ails you."

"*That* I can use," he replied.

Penn warmed up with a walk to Waterfront Park, the arched wrought iron entrance flanked on each side by large flowering magnolia trees, their scent heavy in the air. Several joggers passed by, the sound of their running shoes slapping the sidewalk. Slowly, he started moving. His feet felt heavy as he pushed to gain his stride. The Pineapple Fountain, featured on the front of the brochure, loomed on his right. Its fine spray cast mist on his face.

A brandy-induced sleep had worn off about 4 a.m., leaving him dozing until six. He'd thrown on his jogging clothes, still feeling a little anxious and restless. Why? About what? Eric Castelli's mumbo-jumbo? By a sore loser who'd lost a case? He took off at a good pace on the route suggested by the concierge.

A half hour later, Penn slowed his six-foot frame to a walk. A run always made him feel better. He patted his still firm stomach and abs. Not bad for a man of fifty, but he had to watch his weight and his intake of breakfast desserts. "Pastry pounds," he called them.

He crossed Front Street into the city's historic district.

The aroma of strong coffee drifted toward him. A sign in the shape of a cup and saucer hung over the sidewalk, announcing Miss Lucy's Latte. He entered, the jangle of a small bell above the door unnoticed in the morning bustle. Penn approached a young man behind the counter.

"Good morning," he said to the waiter. "I'd like a Kona coffee and that." He pointed to a bear claw in the bakery case.

"Yes, sir. Won't take long."

Penn surveyed Miss Lucy's. Sunshine-yellow walls. Lacy tieback curtains. The place had a homey feeling. On the walls hung paintings of stately mansions, works of art for sale by local artists. The homes were large wooden structures with grand columned porches, in sharp contrast to his brick, Tudor-style home in New Hampshire.

He thought of Margaret. What should he buy for her? After years of conferences with years of gifts, the process grew more difficult. A painting might please her. It would also make an impressive addition to their formal living room. He decided on the most expensive one. He'd arrange a purchase before he left Miss Lucy's.

Penn looked around for a place to sit. A family of four, toting cameras and water bottles, occupied a table cluttered with muffin wrappers. Three older women huddled together at another. One shook her head, one played with her napkin, one talked with emphatic gestures. He wondered what they would think of *malocchio*.

In a corner, he spotted several chintz-covered chairs with user-friendly sags. His pastry and coffee balanced in one hand, he managed to snag a *Charleston Gazette* lying on a nearby table with the other. He eased into one of the chairs. After a sip of dark Kona blend, he buried himself in the sports page. In the middle of reading an article on the New York Yankees, a rustling sound interrupted him. He looked up. A dark-haired woman slipped into the empty chair beside him.

"Hmmm," she said. "Disheveled hair. Slightly sweaty face. Reddened cheeks. I'd say you had a hard run. Haven't done mine yet. Need coffee to start my heart."

"This coffee'll do it." He liked what he saw—long shapely legs, slim waist, gracefully defined shoulders and upper arms, soft cleavage peeking from her tank top.

She put her elbow on the arm of the chair, her chin in her palm, seeming to study him. "Let's see." She peeked at the paper. "Ah, the sports page. You seem to have a little scowl. Did your team lose?"

"Actually, they won." He put the paper aside. "Did that scowl go away?"

She returned his smile. "Almost. You know, I come here every morning to begin the day. Shake my moods."

He smoothed his hair. "Good idea."

"I'm fourth-generation Charleston. Name's Emily Carmichael."

Penn did a quick calculation. "Ah, I'm Jack Anderson, from Los Angeles. Here on business for a few days."

"I'm an interior designer." She sat back, examining his ivy-league haircut, the blue and white jogging clothes. "I would guess you like traditional design, expensive traditional design."

"Well, I would say you're correct. Maybe I should fly you back with me to Los Angeles."

He thought a moment. "To redo my offices."

"That would be nice—to redo your offices."

He liked the way she smiled with her eyes, the tilt of her head, the soft Southern voice. She seemed to suggest that behind her playfulness waited a touch of mischief and adventure.

"Why don't we have dinner tonight," he asked, "to discuss

some ideas?"

"Oh yes, that would be nice. I have several ideas—for your office." She adjusted the shoulder strap of her tank top. "I believe a good designer should know her client, don't you?"

"I couldn't agree more."

Plans were made. Penn's pseudo "Jack Anderson" had met a successful, intelligent woman. Eric Castelli didn't know a thing. A man found his own opportunities, made his own luck.

When he returned to the hotel, Penn commented to the concierge that he felt much better after a cup of that famous coffee.

"By the way," he said, "I'm expecting a painting to be sent here from Miss Lucy's. Can you make arrangements with UPS for its delivery to my home address?"

"Of course, Mr. Chalmers."

"Amen," the congregation said in unison. Penn sighed, happy the Sunday church service had ended. He'd been back home in Clarkston Mills, New Hampshire, for a month following the whirlwind convention in Charleston. Since then, he'd taken on several new cases and, as CEO of the family businesses, overseen two recent lucrative transactions. Even though he'd had to hustle, it felt good to be home.

Margaret linked her arm in his as they left the family pew of Covenant Assembly Church.

The new pastor had delivered a rousing Sunday morning sermon, albeit a little heavy on the hellfire-damnation theme to suit Penn. However, protecting his soul for the hereafter *and* enhancing the Chalmers name did loom close to his heart. In his pocket nestled an envelope with a five-hundred-thousand-dollar check—and a promise of more—destined for the Meeting Hall Building Fund, thus assuring his legacy within the community. The name "Chalmers Hall" had a satisfying ring to it.

He made a point of greeting church members who could be counted on for checks, although not as large as his. As Margaret complimented a friend's dress or inquired into the health of a neighbor, they approached the heavy, hand-hewn doors of the old stone church. Penn inhaled, feeling his chest expand, making him stand a little taller than his six feet. His grandfather would have called such pride a sin. He didn't agree. A man had to make his own spotlight.

At the door, he stopped by a bronze plaque. He took a moment to enjoy it before leaving, although he knew the words by heart:

Covenant Assembly Church
Founded 1802 by First Deacon Moses Pennington Chalmers
National Historic Monument
Clarkston Mills, New Hampshire

What had his mother said? "Llewellyn, dear, you have become a pillar of your community, like all the Chalmers men before you." Pillar. He liked that. Yes.

His mother's use of his first name amused him. She refused to call him "Penn," and he refused to be called "Llewellyn," even though it was an ancestral name. As a young man, he railed against carrying the inevitable shortened name "Lew." "Penn" suited him. It was more unusual, more memorable.

He and Margaret walked down the worn stone steps into the late morning sun. The warmth on his face, coupled with a surge of well-being, promised a good day ahead. Nearby, a hand-piled stone fence surrounded a centuries-old cemetery, guarding gray headstones of the founders and descendants of Clarkston Mills—names like Chalmers, Pennington, Llewellyn, Spencer, and Clarkston. Penn felt pride in his roots, his hubris nurtured by the surroundings. They strolled through shade cast by tall elms on a well-tended lawn. His world and psyche felt in order.

Margaret stopped to chat with members of the Garden Society gathered by their award-winning rose garden. Penn regarded his wife; petite and blond, she balanced his aggressive, yet conservative, style with her more friendly, caring nature.

Upon completing Yale Law, he had asked her to marry him. Clients found her charming. She looked too young, too shapely to have adult twin sons, or for their twenty-fifth anniversary to be just days away.

Penn scanned the parishioners, spotting Joseph Lattimer. He strode toward the church elder.

"Beautiful morning, Joseph." They shook hands. "I have a little something to launch the building fund for Chalmers Hall." Penn removed the envelope from his pocket.

Elder Lattimer beamed. He slipped the envelope into his suit jacket's inside breast pocket, patting it. "As you know, we're planning a presentation ceremony at the church board meeting tomorrow with local press coverage. Of course, you'll be there?"

"You always do things well. I'll be there, as usual."

Penn took his leave, resumed his walk into the shade. He liked publicity, having his picture in the paper. *The Clarkston Mills Tribune* served all the nearby towns.

A slender woman, her hips swaying under a sheer yellow summer dress, walked toward him, probably a tourist out enjoying a bit of New England history.

"Well, hello," came a voice from beneath her wide-brimmed straw hat. "You are the last person I expected to see. Remember me?" She removed the hat, shaking out her long brown hair.

The slow, soothing Southern voice. The playful blue eyes. The trim athletic body. Oh, yes, he remembered all right. Last month. The convention in Charleston. Miss Lucy's Latte, gourmet meals, an evening on her friend's luxury yacht. He searched his brain for her name. What name had he used? Where had he said he lived? What the hell brought her to Clarkston Mills?

Penn cleared his throat. "Ah, hello." He commanded himself to think. "Emily, Miss Carmichael."

His glance darted over the crowd, most of whom he knew. Margaret, with her back to him, visited with Orinda Benson. Sightseers were not uncommon at the historic church. Safety lurked for a moment—a brief moment. He straightened his tie. Moisture collected under his arms.

Emily ran her hand through her hair. "Miss Carmichael? My, we are formal on a Sunday morning. Isn't it a gorgeous day?" She put her hand on her hip. "What are you doing here, Jack, so far from your office in Los Angeles?"

Penn rubbed his sweaty palms together. "Ah, some business in Concord. A little sight-seeing." Elder Lattimer cast a look in his direction. "What brings you here?"

"I'm staying with my sister over in nearby Gainesville. She told me about this historic church. I decided to visit it. Maybe she hopes a little religion will rub off on me." She smoothed her dress. "I thought you were going to call."

Mr. and Mrs. Cecil Perkins, generous contributors to the church, walked past on their way to the parking lot. They nodded at Penn.

Penn dropped his voice. "I've been very busy."

"Where are you staying, Jack?"

"Ah," Penn cleared his throat. "Over in Concord at the Hilton."

Emily jotted a number on a business card. "Well, I have to rush back to Gainesville, my nephew's surprise birthday party. It's not far. Do call me. Or I can call you at the hotel. I'm here for a few days." She walked away, turning once to wave.

Penn wiped his brow with his monogrammed handkerchief. He always had his fun at that convention. Did for years. No harm done. He was careful, told a few white lies. They were consenting adults. But how in hell did he find "fun" who had a sister in nearby Gainesville?

God Almighty.

He took his time walking across the lawn toward his wife. What if Emily Carmichael found out his true identity? He ran a finger inside his shirt collar. For a hundred-dollar shirt, it seemed tighter than usual. What if Margaret found out? His heart beat faster. What about his reputation? The family name? His sons?

Penn's gut seized. Early morning coffee churned the chocolate croissant in his stomach, causing a wave of nausea. He caught his breath.

All at once, he sensed Margaret's presence beside him.

"Penn, dear, are you ready for brunch at the country club with Pastor and Mrs. Milner?"

Thursday morning, Penn pulled into the parking lot of a run-down strip mall just east of the Concord city limits. He dodged two potholes and parked his rental, a Toyota Echo, next to a black Honda sedan with expensive spinner hubcaps. He refused to drive his Mercedes into this neighborhood. Too much chance of drawing attention and being recognized. Ed Keeler, an old law school friend, had given him the address, saying, "If anyone can help you, this guy can."

Neon signs announced the Uptown Quik-Mart, Sam's Pawn Shop, and Liberty Bail Bonds. From Mike's World Class Burgers, the smell of grilled meat wafted in the air. Then he saw it, black letters on a store window: Spizer Investigative Services.

Usually, business trips to the state capitol included brunch at the Athletic Club with a corporate client, followed by drinks with a few lawmakers; not an appointment in a sleazy, run-down mall. He didn't have a choice. Using his firm's private investigator to find out about Emily Carmichael would cause more problems. Out of the question.

He clenched his teeth, recalling the unexpected telephone call he'd received at the office yesterday. It kept him tossing most of the night.

"Hello, Jack. This is Emily Carmichael. Remember me? Or do you prefer I call you L. Pennington Chalmers?" The Southern voice had a granite edge. "What's the 'L' for? 'Loser'?"

What? "How did you get this number?"

"You're all over the newspaper. You told me you were divorced."

That damned article. "We're all adults here, Emily."

"I really liked you, your sincerity, your sensitivity. I don't date married men, you lying bastard. You're a first-class Yankee P-R-I-C-K." She delivered the spelling with staccato precision.

Penn's face flushed. No one talked to him like that. "Miss Carmichael, I think this conversation is over."

"No, Don Juan, not until *I* say so. Don't be surprised if your wife—what's her name? 'Margaret'?—gets a letter or a telephone call."

Penn gripped the receiver. "How did you find me?"

"I told you. A wonderful picture accompanied by a very newsy article in the *Clarkston Mills Tribune* along with the internet. Aren't you the lucky one?"

Penn slammed down the receiver, shaking his head, knowing the article and the picture's caption all too well. "Church Deacon and Prominent Businessman L. Pennington Chalmers Donates $500,000 to Covenant Assembly Church Building Fund." He thought it one of his best pictures until Emily's call. The article supplied her with plenty of information.

Immediately, he notified the telephone company to change his home number, telling Margaret he had a problem with an unhappy client. The mail also became a concern. Sarah, their housekeeper, always put it on the entry hall table. Margaret seldom bothered with it. Now he couldn't take any chances. Last evening, he told Sarah to put the mail in his study until further notice.

Penn stepped out of the car into the heat. He smoothed his jeans and tucked in his navy-striped golf shirt as he thought about Emily's threat. It could ruin him. The situation was just too close to home. At the entrance to the private investigator's office, he squared his shoulders, opened the door.

"Help you, hon?" A buxom woman behind a cheap walnut desk, her knitting interrupted, scrambled a blue pencil from her frizzy red hair while grabbing a scrap of paper.

"I'm looking for Jacob Spizer."

"You must be his 3:30." She pointed her pencil toward a closed door. "Just knock." She resumed knitting. A black cat, buried in her lap, poked its head over the edge of the desk. It leveled an unblinking stare at Penn.

Finger smudges dotted the computer, fax machine, telephone. Two fans on low speed ruffled the air, blowing the edges of papers stacked haphazardly atop a row of metal filing cabinets. Penn crossed the room and entered Spizer's office, closing the door behind him.

A small balding man looked up from a cluttered desk, an open file in front of him, a glazed doughnut in one hand. "Mister, I didn't hear a knock."

"I'm Penn Chalmers. I called yesterday. Said I'd be here at 3:30."

"Oh, you're the guy." Spizer flipped the file shut. "What can I do for you?" Reading glasses perched on the end of his slightly off-center nose—the shape a nose gets after being broken. Pieces of sugar glaze clung to his mustache.

Penn looked around the unkempt office, not answering.

"Relax, pal," the man said. "Everything is confidential. I got a reputation to protect, too." He gave Penn a sly look. With two quick bites, he finished the doughnut.

Penn began, "Look, Spizer, I don't know what you think you know. Don't presume—."

"Touchy, touchy." Spizer interrupted, brushing his hands together, still chewing. "Did I hit your last good nerve? Look, a guy dressed like you don't come to a guy dressed like me for corporate work. Price tags hang all over that so-called *casual* outfit." He studied Penn while unbuttoning the collar of his checked shirt and loosening his flowered tie. He wiped the sugar from his mustache.

Penn's eyes narrowed. "Let's just get this over with."

"Look, Chalmers, I've done my homework on you. One. You're

a hotshot lawyer from Clarkston Mills. Two. Your family owns the town. Three. Your buddy Congressman Keeler gave you my name. All you big shots manage to find me when you get your Johnson caught in your zipper."

Penn took a step toward the desk.

Spizer put up his hand. "Don't do anything you'll regret. Something else. My sources say that although you're good, you're not as good as your old man. Let's see. What did the guy say? 'You don't quite fill your old man's shorts.'"

Penn flinched. He'd been fighting his way out of his father's shadow all his life. He knew he measured up, well established at the helm of the family enterprises, stronger than ever.

Spizer smirked at him, drumming his fingernails on the desk. Penn caught himself. He'd been baited many times, knew the tactic well—stake your ground, muddy the waters, try to throw your opponent off balance. Penn said, "You have an interesting way of building rapport with your clients."

"Just so we understand each other."

"Never doubt my understanding, Spizer. Let's get on with it."

"You can call me Jake." He pointed to a wooden chair in front of the desk.

"All right, *Jake*." Penn brushed the chair seat with his hand before he sat. "I want you to find out all you can about a woman from Charleston by the name of Emily Carmichael." He explained the meeting, the fling, the telephone call. "I need something on her, fast."

Spizer nodded. "Okay. I can start with my sources. DMV. Social Security. Credit cards. Maybe a trip to Gainesville. Definitely a trip to Charleston. That'll be five-thousand dollars up front, plus expenses billed directly to you."

Penn raised his eyebrows.

"No retainer, no expenses? No work," Spizer said. "I don't do this for cheap."

"Half to begin, the rest when you deliver." Penn pulled out his checkbook.

Spizer nodded. "That'll work, for now."

"Don't try to con me." Penn stood. "I'm used to knowing the answers to questions before I ask them."

Spizer pushed back in his chair. "Yeah, right. You must have lost your mojo on this one."

"Just get me some answers."

Penn left the office, the sound of the private investigator's smug chuckle following him. He'd had enough of the green walls, cheap office furniture, and dirty vinyl floor. Penn usually liked to throw the last remark. Not today. He hoped he never saw the man face-to-face again.

"Bye, hon'," the receptionist said. She smiled, her coffee-stained teeth outlined by deep pink lipstick.

He hurried to his car, feeling sweat run down the small of his back. What troubled him? He played hardball all the time—telling a client what to do, being in control, having the power. Questions nagged. He wiped at perspiration.

How could he control an Emily Carmichael? Or a loose cannon like Spizer?

At that moment, he noticed the ego license plate on the black Honda still parked next to him.

"ISPYZER," he murmured. *God Almighty.*

Penn jumped in his car, vowed to never visit Spizer's office again, and pulled out of the crowded lot.

Three days later, via overnight delivery to his office, a large envelope arrived from J. Spizer, with the return address The French Quarter Inn, Charleston, South Carolina. Penn frowned. The French Quarter Inn. One of the most exclusive hotels in the city. Spizer had expensive taste when someone else paid the bill. Penn stuffed the envelope in his briefcase until he could deal with the contents in private, at home, in his study.

A busy day with a series of appointments, followed by dinner with a client, finally ended. At home he and Margaret had a late-night brandy together before she retired. He feigned having work to complete for a meeting the next day.

Behind the closed door of his study, the room quiet except for an heirloom grandfather clock in the corner striking midnight, Penn took the envelope from his briefcase, put it on the desk. He sat, moving the desk lamp closer. Part of him wanted to know what Spizer had found. Part of him didn't.

He removed the envelope's contents. What had Spizer learned that couldn't wait until he returned to Concord? The man had scrawled a message on hotel letterhead and paper-clipped it on top of several eight-by-ten photographs. Penn removed the clip, ready to set the letter aside to go straight to the pictures, like peeking ahead to the end of a good book. He paused. The ending might be one he didn't want to know.

Taking a deep breath, he slipped on his glasses and decided to be lawyerly instead. He'd look at each item in order, like he did with pieces of evidence, pre-trial. Let the evidence test theories, lead to conclusions. He began to read:

> Located Emily Carmichael. Piece of cake. She works at a place called The Cos Bar on King Street. Guess that's hip for Casbah. Near the hotel where you stayed. Expensive and exclusive cosmetics place. She lives with three roomies in a pricey apartment by the river.

Penn pursed his lips. Another pretty woman looking for a rich hook-up. He should have known. He continued reading.

> Her bank account shows a recent deposit of $25,000. She ain't no fancy decorator or fourth generation anything.

Money? Where had that much money come from? Penn slammed his palm on the desk. Eric Castelli. Castelli schemed the whole thing, a classic B-movie maneuver using the ploy of "another woman." A "chance" meeting for drinks, the *malocchio* hogwash, the curse of the evil eye. The guy's idea of revenge. His face feeling like hot lava, Penn looked at the letter again.

> You'll find something interesting about that deposit. The check was drawn on a bank in Clarkston Mills. Follow the money.
> Later,
> Spizer

A bank in Clarkston Mills? Castelli didn't practice law in New Hampshire. He worked in Memphis. What the hell? He grunted. Follow the money? To where? To whom?

> P.S. You'll figure it out.
> J.S.

What did that mean? Penn pushed his chair back, massaging his temples. Selecting a decanter from a nearby side table, he poured vintage bourbon into a Waterford glass and took a slow sip. He removed the paperclip, slid the letter aside.

First photo. Emily behind the counter at The Cos Bar. The ultimate chic cosmetic saleswoman. Coiffed, trim, stunning. Next, Emily at a pool with several people. Then, a close-up of Emily in her bikini. Penn's eyes lingered on each picture, as he sipped his drink, remembering.

So far, the pictures were a waste of time. They didn't connect with anything, especially a bank in Clarkston Mills.

Then a picture of Emily entering the Lake Charles Country Club, Charleston's most posh, followed by another of Emily at a table by herself with a full wine glass, looking at her watch. She had to be waiting for someone.

One picture remained. Penn made a bet with himself. If Spizer's pictures were leading him anywhere, if someone showed up to meet her, it would be Castelli. It would be easy for old Eric to set up an account in Clarkston Mills to try to throw him off. He slipped the picture of Emily aside only to stare at the final photo.

Penn's mouth dropped open. "God Almighty."

Across the table from Emily sat, not Eric Castelli, but his wife, Margaret.

He reached for his drink, knocking it over. He grabbed for the glass, liquor spreading like fingers onto business papers, bills, mail, turning the desktop's fine leather into a wet, dark surface. He yanked the letter and pictures out of the way, all the while fumbling in his pocket for a handkerchief. With a dab here, a swipe there, he stilled the mayhem on the desktop. He couldn't still the fireworks in his brain.

He sat back, slowly removing his glasses. Only the ticking of the clock in counterpoint with his uneven breathing broke the silence. He poured another drink.

Penn stared in disbelief at the picture of the two women. He stood, took a few steps, kicked a hassock aside and slouched into his leather recliner. Lines furrowed his forehead. How did the two even know each other? How did Emily get to Margaret? When?

What could he possibly say to his wife? Just dinner? Drinks? No, Emily would have told her more than that had happened.

Tell her he walked into a set-up? Eric Castelli, still angry over the Rockwell case, had set the events in motion. Had gotten him drunk. One thing led to another.

Admit to a meaningless fling for a surge of excitement? Like a drink he enjoyed, then put down. Empty, done, over with.

Everything sounded hollow. Logic usually worked when he had a problem to solve, but not tonight. He could find no logic in what he'd done.

A strange feeling spun inside him. It tapped at his conscience. As much as he tried to deny it, the letters for what he felt spelled but one word: G-U-I-L-T. And about what? Being caught? Perhaps; no one likes to be caught. For the first time, he was forced to acknowledge what truly touched him with deep remorse. He loved Margaret. He had never intended to hurt her.

Closing his eyes, he rubbed them, surprised at the moisture slipping from beneath his lashes. Would Margaret forgive him?

At fifteen, he'd stolen a hundred-dollar bill from his mother's purse to play the big shot with friends. His mother discovered the theft. When his father confronted him, he responded with typical teenage attitude: "I took it because I could."

Had he "played around" because he could? Because he knew Margaret would always be there, life going on as before?

What would be her response? Tears? Anger? *Divorce?* Everything he'd worked for all his life could disappear in a moment. Family, business, reputation.

The facts confronted him. When had he become so full of himself as to jeopardize everything he valued? He put his head in his hands, vowing never to stray again, never to play his childish game. He hoped to convince Margaret, rebuild her trust. How could he have been foolish enough to think life could be divided into compartments, one not affecting the other?

Tomorrow would be their twenty-fifth wedding anniversary. He and Margaret were joining fifty friends at the club for a dinner party he had arranged. His temples throbbed. The clock chimed its hourly preamble to announce 2:00 a.m.

As the hour struck, the study door opened. Margaret stepped into the room. A long black negligee brushed the carpet as she came toward him. She glanced at Penn, at the messy desk. Her eyes settled on the telltale picture in his lap. She nodded, as if confirming something to herself. Then she returned his gaze.

"Margaret," he whispered.

She untied her robe. It fell open, revealing the soft, translucent gown that enfolded her trim figure. She ran her hands down the sides of her body—breasts, waist, hips—her eyes on his face.

Penn rose.

"Don't try to touch me." Her voice pierced the air between them, delivering her anger like a lance to the stomach. "Don't bother. Sit down."

Her eyes returned to the photo. "I know you so well. You were very preoccupied this evening. Then up so late. I knew you must have learned something." She took a deep breath. "Remember the trips I made to Pittsburgh to visit my sister? To go shopping? To help decorate her new townhouse? To celebrate her promotion?"

Penn nodded. "You didn't go to Pittsburgh."

"No, dearest, I didn't. They were trips to Charleston. After all these years, did you think I didn't know? I'm sure you thought you were careful. The smell of different perfumes on your shirts caught my attention long ago. I've worn Chanel No. 5 for years, an established, distinctive scent. It's not trendy enough for the under-thirty-five crowd. I just kept my peace. I didn't plan to throw away my life or my place in the community."

Margaret's voice cracked. Taking a deep breath, she continued to hold her demeanor together. "Last year I found a condom in a bright blue wrapper. The broken stitching of your sports coat pocket allowed it to slip between the fabric and lining."

Penn winced. He started to respond. Margaret shook her head as she re-tied her dressing gown. Her calmness surprised him.

"Did you think all of this didn't hurt?" She sat on the leather hassock. "That you only had to come home, bring a fancy gift? Continue like nothing had happened? But I had to make very, very sure. I believe you call it 'gathering evidence.'" She played with the tie on her negligee. "So I came up with a plan. I scouted Emily myself at The Cos Bar. She was able to take a little vacation while the conference was in Charleston and I hired her, my own private investigator. Sisters under the skin. A willing participant for the right price. My little treat for you."

"Emily means nothing to me," Penn protested.

"Oh, please," Margaret answered, rolling her eyes. "I did enjoy how Emily played you at the church. How the picture in the paper fueled her delicious phone call. She did have to scramble early to meet you at Miss Lucy's, but thanks to her great surveillance and moxie, she accomplished everything I asked." Margaret laughed softly. "She may have discovered a new career."

"What if she'd missed me?" Penn asked.

"Oh, we had that covered. I would have called you to buy a special face cream available only at The Cos Bar, at their finest cosmetics counter."

Penn leaned forward. "Now I suppose she's blackmailing you. Next she'll try me."

"No, Penn, dear," Margaret said, "*I* am blackmailing *you*. You will pay for my silence." She put her hand up to stop his reply. "You are going to reward Emily handsomely each year at this time—a salary, if you will. We'll decide on the amount. You will never be allowed to forget our agreement. If anything happens to her or me, my lawyer—yes, I have my own—has a sealed letter of instructions to inform our puritanical church, our conservative New England investors, your political friends and your clients, as well as the newspapers. If the situation warrants, the police. Of course, our sons, of whom you are so proud, will suffer the most. I believe you would call that 'collateral damage.'"

"What!" Penn was stunned. "My God, Margaret, I would never . . . "

"Well, I hope not. You'd better listen. I'm now in control. Emily is assured a life of luxury. For all outward appearances, our life will be quite normal. No divorce, no scandal. Your reputation, your business, your political ambitions will remain intact, as will our family honor, and the respect of your sons."

Penn looked at his wife in disbelief. Each word bludgeoned him. How could this be the woman he thought he knew? "I want to explain," he said quietly.

Margaret waited, her face expressionless.

"It happens—*happened*—once a year at the ABA conference. It never meant anything. I never had further contact with the women. It had nothing to do with you. Simply an elixir, something that fueled me, my ego, my drive."

"I didn't realize you were that shallow."

"I come home to you. I always have. My life is with you. It will never happen again. I want you to know how sorry I am. This is something we can work out. Margaret, I love you."

In a cold voice, Margaret replied, "It's already 'worked out.'"

Penn's face flushed. "I'm not going to pay Emily or anyone else." He set his jaw, thinking of how Emily had played him, the irony of one liar conning the other. "She's been paid for her so-called job already. Why dredge this unpleasantness up each year? I've given you my word."

"You've had your fun once a year, now I will have mine once a year. If you fight me, I'll see that the scandal puts L. Pennington Chalmers, Esquire, wealthy New Hampshire playboy, on the front page of every major newspaper, every major magazine. I know how you love publicity." Sarcasm hung on each word. "You're a reasonable, savvy businessman who weighs his choices. Who considers the consequences—although I can't say you did in this instance. You will pay for the decades of deceit I've lived through. Rest assured, I will derive great pleasure from my scheme. You will never be allowed to forget."

"Margaret, please."

"This is *my* moment, Penn." Margaret rose, standing over him, tying the satin ribbon on her robe. "As for sex, I will be your only partner, or the consequences will be dire. I know you still find me desirable—if I ever decide to be your partner again."

She strode toward the door and turned. "You know, I've given your interesting code of behavior a name. I call it 'The Rule of L. Pennington Chalmers.' In its spirit, we shall go on as usual, pretending the betrayal of trust and of love never happened—as you have so arrogantly done in the past."

Penn flinched.

She waved a dismissive hand. "Happy Anniversary, darling. I hope you like making your yearly gift. I'm looking forward to our anniversary party tomorrow evening." She let herself out of the study with a soft click of the door.

Penn leaned back in the chair. The community and business awards on the study wall hovered around him, made meaningless by the single photograph dangling from his hand.

For the first time that evening he noticed something different about the room. The oil painting of an English hunting scene no longer hung above the fireplace. A new painting had taken its place—a stately plantation home located outside of Charleston. Margaret must have found the painting hidden in the guest room closet—the anniversary present he'd bought at Miss Lucy's.

He spotted a small note tucked in the corner of the large gesso frame. Too curious not to look, he opened it.

Dearest husband,

May this picture always be a reminder of my yearly gift . . . to you.

—Margaret

The Phone Call

The kitchen lurched. Its vinyl floor began to undulate underfoot like small swells on a sea. Jillian fell against the kitchen counter. Pots and pans banged a discordant sound on an overhead rack. The silverware drawer thudded open just as a cereal box toppled to the floor. She gripped the countertop's edge in a rush of fear. *Earthquake.*

Behind clenched eyes, Jillian saw her body slip beneath a pile of rubble, her hands reach upward from the darkness, grasp at the air. She heard voices. Her boyfriend's whispered promises. Her mother's admonitions. The warnings of friends. Their words gave way to her pleas for the earthquake to end. Trembling, she cried out. Her body suddenly felt hot, her bathrobe too warm.

A final jolt.

The quake stopped. She opened her eyes, stepping away from the counter. Her palms felt sweaty, her mouth dry, her throat taut. Trying to settle her nerves, she took a deep breath and loosened the belt on her robe.

On the counter, her favorite cup had toppled on its side, pooled in coffee. Jillian wiped away the spill, discarding the soiled paper towel in the trash container kept under the sink, and refilled her cup from the coffeemaker. A warm, lingering swallow of the dark liquid soothed her, but each unfamiliar sound she heard made her tense, made her fearful of an aftershock. She closed the silverware drawer.

The open box of Kellogg's Corn Flakes stared up at the ceiling, its contents scattered on the vinyl. She settled her cup on the counter. No longer hungry, flakes crunching beneath her feet, she picked up the box and returned it to the cupboard. With a dustpan and hand broom from under the sink, she swept up the flakes and threw them in the trash. She put the utensils back in place.

A bit calmer, she checked her cell phone on the counter, still plugged in. It indicated a 92 percent charge. She brushed her fingers along the edge of its glittery gold case—a new purchase from Target.

A car door banged. A woman laughed. Footsteps moved across the floor overhead. Someone thumped down the exterior stairs. Jillian checked her watch. Sunday mornings were usually quiet in the ten-unit building, but not today. At 7:05 a.m., people in the high desert town of Yucca Valley had been roused from their leisure.

Her neighbor would say it was only a little shaker, that she shouldn't be so concerned, so dramatic. But an earthquake never seemed little to Jillian. Someday it might be "the big one." She'd never be California-blasé about earth moving under her. Not now. Not ever.

She rolled her shoulders, rotating her neck from side to side to loosen tense muscles, and walked into her cramped dining room. Above the table, the light fixture still swayed in slow motion. She steadied it with her hand. In the china cabinet, an antique Nippon vase her grandmother had given her leaned against four stacked pasta bowls. She placed it upright, happy to find no chips or breaks.

A large, rectangular wall mirror she'd hung a week ago to make the room appear bigger caught her reflection. Lines feathered from the edges of her brown eyes. Beneath them, puffy morning pouches. She fluffed her short blond hair with ringless fingers and pinched her cheeks. A splash of color soon appeared. Her hand strayed to her chin, slid slowly down her neck to rest on her chest, feeling a yet rapid heartbeat. She straightened the mirror.

Mindful of ten extra pounds, Jillian studied herself, noting the need for a hair appointment. Dark roots cried for attention. For a moment longer, she pondered her appearance, but her life, the reality of it, took over. Time, she knew, wore a magician's cape. Seconds stretched to a lifetime. Years shrank, only to disappear.

It seemed just yesterday she'd turned eighteen and gotten a job at the Mojave Diner. She brushed her hand down her arm, shaking her head. It hadn't been her plan to be waiting tables at the same diner fifteen years later. It just happened. Because she let it.

Steady customers called her by name.

"Mornin', Jillie. Gimme a cup of java, strong."

"Hey, Jillie, how about one of those banana nut muffins?"

To admit life had become routine, unfulfilled, and dull unnerved her. Suddenly, the passage of years circled around her, a tarnished necklace strung with beads of regret. She backed away from the mirror, hating the thoughts that paraded in her head, and escaped to the living room.

A small stained-glass image of the fertility god Kokopelli dangled in the front window above her tan faux-suede couch, catching the sun. She sat and tucked her legs beneath her, trying to push away the Sunday morning blues. Her gaze wandered about the room. Baskets collected at the swap meet hung on the far wall. Two colorful ceramic lizards from Mexico adorned the coffee table.

A desert painting of a solitary Joshua tree, its arms reaching skyward with a range of purple mountains in the background, leaned against the wall, waiting to be hung. She'd just bought it on sale at Hanson's Furniture Mart—somehow drawn to it, wondering if the Joshua tree ever felt as alone as it looked. Alone like her.

Perhaps she wasn't using the right word. She closed her eyes, feeling her neck flush. The real word was "lonely." That's how she felt all week until Friday. By Sunday morning, the blue funk settled in. Again.

She opened her eyes, only to notice something she hadn't seen when she'd first entered the room, something small, something white near her foot. Its brightness stood out on the muted colors of the southwest area rug. "Oh, no," she murmured. It wasn't lint or a scrap of paper, but a tiny porcelain arm. She glanced at the lamp table. A music box with a blue-gowned figurine on top had fallen to the floor, its pieces scattered.

Sighing, she took the solitary arm in her fingers. On hands and knees, she gathered the headless torso, the other arm. She picked up the severed head with its demure eyes, serene face, its red lips frozen in a half-smile. The mahogany pedestal, porcelain legs jutting from it like unwanted prostheses, lay nearby.

Why was a birthday gift from her boyfriend Ray the only thing to break? Why not the sun-catcher from the swap meet? Or a lizard from Tijuana? She placed the pieces on the coffee table in front of the couch. The breaks appeared clean, not splintery. Although the figurine would never be the same, she might be able to put it back together.

She went to the kitchen, gathered a dishcloth, a dishtowel and, from her catch-all drawer, a small plastic bottle of glue. Settled again on the couch, she attached the head to the torso, then the arms, using her fingers to wipe away seeping glue. She wiped her hands on the cloth and propped the mended figurine against the towel, rumpled in such a way as to support the newly glued pieces. While she waited for her handiwork to dry, she took the round pedestal in hand, reached beneath it, and turned the silver key three times, hoping it would play.

Soon the soft tinkling sound of "The Tennessee Waltz" kindled memories. In a soft voice she sang along with the old 1950s favorite, watching the torso-less legs turn in a circle.

"I was dancin' with my darlin' . . ."

With great care, she glued the mended body to the legs, wishing her fragmented life could be made whole so easily. As before, she wiped away the extra glue and, leaning back into the couch, waited for the figure to dry. After a half hour, she turned the key again.

The figurine circled around on the mahogany pedestal, reminding Jillian of herself, reminding her of Ray. If a soulmate truly existed, she knew she'd found hers the moment he'd introduced himself at the diner on her second day of work and asked her to go dancing.

She wound the music box once more.

They danced every Friday night at the Yucaipa Community Hall, forty miles away. They could do the jitterbug, twist, disco, salsa, cha-cha, western, the tango, even the waltz. Both were surprised the waltz became their specialty. It felt so smooth, so elegant as they moved with Hollywood style across the polished wood floor, the skirt of her blue chiffon dress swirling about her legs, the other dancers clapping at their grace. "Just like *Dancing with the Stars*," friends said. She and Ray had done it all, for fifteen years.

Before the music faded, she twisted the key again to hold on to the mood.

The picture in her mind remained. She tapped her fingers to the rhythm. *One, two, three, one, two, three.*

An unwanted feeling came over her. The image began to darken like neglected silver plate, tarnished by years, by unfulfilled pledges. She beat the table harder. *ONE, two, three. ONE, two, three. ONE, TWO, THREE.*

Without warning, she seized the music box in her hand, tightening her hold, the muscles of her chest constricting. Lost dreams flashed like roadside warnings, colliding with hurt feelings, with broken commitments. Anger began to build from deep inside her, each tremor rising stronger than the last, until she hurled the keepsake across the room, shattering it against the far wall. Porcelain pieces scattered onto the floor. The wooden base landed with a thud. It split, spewing Medusa-like metal coils.

The air grew quiet except for the cry that escaped from her throat.

She hurried across the room, dropping to her knees before an array of broken porcelain, twisted metal, and splintered wood scattered at the base of a now damaged wall. Tears burned her eyes as she gathered the remains. Nothing could be done with them now. Her steps heavy, she walked to the kitchen and opened the cupboard door beneath the sink to drop the remnants in the trash. The door closed with a click. She leaned against the counter. After a moment, her sobs filled the room. She stayed there, hugging herself, until her weeping subsided, until she felt she could move.

Her steps pensive, she walked to the bedroom closet and removed her blue chiffon dress, a talisman of the past fifteen years, replaced on occasion to keep in style. She held the hanger, letting the dress dangle in front of her before she tossed it on the bed. Slowly, she straightened the fabric, arranged the folds of the skirt. Each stroke became a gentle caress. Her hand stopped. She stepped back with a faint sigh.

She'd take the dress to the cleaners tomorrow to be ready for Friday's dancing. She loved how the fabric felt against her body, how it shook with the cha-cha, how it billowed with the waltz. Blue was Ray's favorite color.

She returned to the kitchen, unplugged the cell phone from its charger, and clicked it on. She sat at the small café table by the kitchen window, examining her nails, pushing back the cuticles on each finger, the phone in front of her. It was almost 11:00 a.m. Soon it would ring, Ray's regular Sunday morning call. He'd be at home, his wife at church.

V

A Steady Presence

"I began to relax, knowing I would have missed my free-spirited, engaging friend."

—Mallory Hudson
"The Art Connoisseur"

The Art Connoisseur

A uniformed security guard stepped from a brick kiosk at the estate's entry, peered into the car and asked our names. After checking a guest list secured to his clipboard, he pushed a button and electric, wrought-iron gates whirred open. Ahead lay a winding, tree-lined drive.

We drove onto lush, manicured grounds, the gates trundling closed behind us. In the distance, above the treetops, rose the gables of a Tudor mansion, our invitation-only destination, courtesy of the owner of a valuable art collection.

My friend Britt recounted the important artwork we'd see at the soiree. Mondrian, Warhol, and Picasso, among others. The art excited me. I also wondered about the connoisseurs and collectors. Would they be as exciting as the art? Would we make important connections?

We drove until a tiered fountain came into view, surrounded by a lighted pool filled with water lilies, their petals closed, waiting for morning. Slowly, we continued around the fountain toward a valet who stopped us in front of the home's entrance, a lighted arch with a dark oak door beneath. To the side of the entry, I noted a massive chimney extending beyond the gabled roofline of the grand home, tall windows on each side catching the waning sunlight of a balmy June evening. The valet opened my driver-side door. Another valet materialized to open the passenger side.

Britt wriggled around to unhook her seatbelt, peering at the impressive building, rolling yard, large oaks, and massive shrubbery. "Seems an odd place to hang a modern contemporary art collection."

"Reminds me of Edgar Allan Poe," I said as the valet gave me a claim check.

We stepped from the car into a gentle offshore breeze cooling Los Angeles and the wealthy enclave of Los Feliz. One of the valets drove my white Audi toward a grass-covered parking area. The other directed a new arrival.

I took a moment to smooth the skirt of my black cocktail dress (purchased for the event) while Britt adjusted the jacket of her dark green cocktail suit. We stepped carefully along a flagstone walkway in our high heels toward the entrance.

Brit and I had met at the Los Angeles County Museum of Art two years before. I stood viewing Georgia O'Keefe's *Black Iris III* when the woman next to me introduced herself as Britt Wilson, Special Exhibit Curator for LACMA. I was about to launch a gallery in Laguna Beach, a lifelong dream, and I invited her to its opening. A friendship developed.

"How did you know about this soiree?" I asked as we stood at the front door.

"Christine Hoffman. She's on the LACMA Board of Directors," Britt replied, raising the heavy brass knocker to give three short raps on the oak door. "Time to network."

The door opened to reveal a slender forty-something woman standing in the grand entry. To her left stretched a massive drawing room with a vaulted, beamed ceiling and walnut wainscoting. In contrast to the medieval feel of the home, contemporary paintings lined the walls. Voices of well-dressed men and women, animated with champagne, hummed amidst the otherwise minimalist décor of high-tech industrial design furniture. I felt the incongruous energy of old-world architecture and modern art collide. My expectations grew.

"I'm so glad you could come, Britt," the woman said. She turned to me. "And you are?"

"Mallory Hudson," I replied.

"I'm Christine Hoffman. Do come in."

Her sweeping gesture jangled silver and cloisonné bracelets on her slender wrist. A gray sheath clung to her sylphlike body, the line broken by an arresting Picasso scarf in reds and blacks draped about her shoulders. Her long dark hair, parted in the middle, partially masked large silver ear hoops. She seemed ethereal and graceful, like a haute-couture model.

As we entered, she clasped my hand in both of hers, looking me up and down. "Again, welcome." Her brown eyes met mine, lingering uncomfortably. I looked away. "Please take time to enjoy." Christine stepped between Britt and me and put her arms around each of our waists to guide us into the crowd. She ran her hand down over my hip where it dallied and slid lower. I moved away. "Our host will be with us in a few moments," Christine said.

I watched her weave back to the door to welcome more guests, wondering what *that* was all about. I started to say something to my friend, but she had already begun to mingle. I followed, with Britt making introductions. Soon, a server, clad in black and white, approached with a silver tray holding flutes of champagne. Another server offered finger food of shrimp-topped cucumber slices. With a drink in one hand and an hors d'oeuvre in the other, we surveyed the crowd.

"Tell me about Christine," I said.

"She experiments with oil painting . . . and other things." Britt sipped her champagne. "Her passion, though, is being part of the art world and the artists."

I nodded, swallowed my hors d'oeuvre, and looked out through the bevel-paned French doors onto a garden and large swimming pool surrounded by flagstone decking. Roses and English ivy bloomed around the pedestals of weathered statuary. In the foreground, I recognized a sculpture called *Bird Girl*, one of only three cast and made famous by the book cover of *Midnight in the Garden of Good and Evil.*

I sipped my champagne. "Christine looks familiar. I think I just saw her at a gallery opening in Santa Monica featuring avant-garde and performance art."

My attention wandered to a tall, wiry man in a gray suit, white shirt and striped tie. He stood talking to a shorter man dressed in jeans, a sport coat, and a blue shirt open at the neck. A black beret completed his ensemble. I smiled to myself, noting conservative business meets liberal art. Near them a waterfall cascaded into the pool.

I turned to Britt. "Who are those men? Do you know?"

"The tall one is Christine's husband, Lucas." Britt paused. "The other is a lover, Robert Stein."

"Of Christine's husband?" I raised my eyebrows. "Is Lucas gay?"

Britt shook her head. "No, I mean *Christine's* lover."

Before I could respond, we heard a tinkling sound. We moved back inside. Christine, holding a small silver bell, stood beside a large Jackson Pollock canvas splashed with magenta, red, yellow, and black on a white background, the colors seemingly a study in surprises—like her.

"Welcome, everyone," she said. "We are indeed fortunate that Robert Stein has opened one of his homes to share a portion of his marvelous collection."

Christine continued her opening remarks, her gaze settling on me several times. I looked away and noticed the two men from the pool area entering the drawing room. Lucas, with a flute of champagne, made his way to the back of the room where he stood surveying the guests. The shorter man walked to Christine. She linked her arm through his.

"Ladies and gentlemen, may I introduce our host and collector extraordinaire, Mr. Robert Stein." They kissed each other on both cheeks, European style. The guests clapped.

Christine stepped aside, giving Stein the limelight. I noticed she gazed at me from time to time. Lucas also glanced at me, looking away quickly. I wondered if this was how a newcomer was welcomed, sized up, and vetted. After Stein's remarks, Britt and I wandered through more of the collection and then back into the garden.

"How do you know Christine?" I asked.

"From the museum."

"I know she's your friend, Britt, but she makes me uncomfortable."

Britt watched Christine chatting with a gray-haired dowager. "She can do that, an interesting but unpredictable person. Quirky. Bizarre." A pause. "Bisexual."

I glanced at Christine. "How do you know she's bisexual or that Stein is her lover?"

"A pattern. She often 'falls in love' with an artist and his or her art, or the collector and his or her collection. As for Stein, they were seen last weekend at the Chateau Marmont on Sunset."

I cocked my head. "What about Lucas?"

"He seems to move among the lovers of both sexes with ease."

During July, I accompanied Britt to other salon exhibits Christine arranged. Among them, a visit to an artist's loft in an old chocolate factory in Santa Monica, the opening of a Charles Burchfield exhibit at the San Diego Art Museum, and an artist's reception at the Laguna Art Museum.

Even though she sometimes could be "unsettling," I no longer found Christine off-putting. Her private life was her business. Intellectually, she intrigued me; her conversation was stimulating, her knowledge of art exquisite. Whether at an art opening or over a casual coffee, I enjoyed her questioning nature, our in-depth discussions.

"Mallory," she would ask, "What is wisdom? Do you have wisdom?" On another occasion, she said, "I believe in reincarnation. What would you like to be in your next life?" And once, "I wonder why Freida Kahlo stayed with Diego Rivera. What do you think, Mallory?"

One afternoon, chatting in the LACMA café, and because I thought we knew each other well enough, I asked, "You seem to enjoy close friendships with many artists and collectors. Does Lucas ever become jealous?"

She put aside the demitasse spoon with which she had stirred her coffee and gave me a coy look. "Ah, that's for me to know and you to wonder . . . or find out. I *am* available, you know."

"I'm not trying to pry. Just, well, curious." I ignored her inference—or perhaps invitation.

"Well, my dear," she said, "my relationship with Lucas is my business, but I am open to adventure." Her hand covered mine. She drew it toward her.

I pulled away. "Not what I do, Christine."

On an afternoon in early August while visiting galleries along Rodeo Drive in Beverly Hills, I ran into Christine. She invited me for sushi at the trendy Urasawa Restaurant. Our conversation drifted to a recent art theft in a nearby gallery. In the news report, the owner stated he should have had a gun on the premises. I mentioned I was thinking about buying a gun to keep in my gallery and perhaps becoming licensed to carry.

"Oh, no." Christine dropped her chopsticks, shaking her head. "I abhor guns."

Her intense tone prodded me. "Why?" I asked.

"All that gallery owner has to do is hire a good security company. Do you realize how dangerous guns are? Think of the accidental shootings. Think of what can happen if the gun gets into the wrong hands."

"Of course. In the wrong hands . . ."

I was cut off by Christine's next words: "Mallory, my brother was a promising artist who kept a revolver in his home. On a normal Saturday afternoon, while he was engrossed in his work, his young son found that revolver in a box in the master closet. The little boy played with his new toy and shot himself."

"I'm so sorry." I swallowed, biting at my lower lip.

"It was a double tragedy. The boy was dead, and my brother never painted again, preferring the bottle to a paintbrush." Christine folded her hands, staring at her food. When she looked up, she said, "I wish you would reconsider the idea of owning a gun, let alone carrying one."

"I hear you. A gun can be dangerous, but I'm a woman alone with an art gallery housing valuable work."

Christine brushed her hair back from her flawless face. "How wonderful," she said, her scorn not to be missed. "You realize, of course, your ultimate target is in the shape of a human being."

"I have faith in my judgment."

"What about the bad judgment of another?" Christine's fingers tightened on her cup. "Guns are the mark of a decaying culture, Mallory. A culture must have its dreams, and dreams are portrayed by artists, not guns."

"Sometimes we have to dream with our eyes open."

Christine's eyes narrowed. "What would I have to do to convince you?"

After a moment, I replied, "I'd say we have an honest difference of opinion."

Christine studied me. "The smart gallery owners I know are well-insured and have an alarm system to protect the art in their care."

Ouch! Before I could respond, she pushed away from the table, threw her napkin on her plate, and walked rapidly away through the crowded restaurant toward the door.

I saw her at several art events after that. She was cordial but distant.

On a Saturday morning in late August, Christine called. "I know you haven't heard from me in a while. Let's let bygones be bygones. Just drop everything. I'm picking you up in less than an hour. Wear jeans."

"But . . ."

"Less than an hour," she commanded and hung up, making me wonder about this sudden change in demeanor. Had she discovered a new artist she wanted me to see and couldn't contain herself? I also knew this quixotic behavior to be vintage Christine.

Soon we were twisting through Malibu Canyon. Christine's leather-gloved hands gripped the wheel of her red Carrera convertible as she pushed the speedometer past eighty.

"Slow down," I yelled. The wind pummeled us.

"Oh, Mallory!" she shouted. "Enjoy the freedom. Take a risk!"

"Slow down!" I screamed.

Christine's face became solemn, like a child slapped on the hand. The car slowed. "Can't you ever step out of the box?"

"The way you're driving, we'll end up *in* a box!" I complained.

We arrived at windswept Zuma Beach, parking in a crowded lot between a camper and a Volkswagen bug. She opened the Carrera's trunk, grabbed a small wicker picnic hamper, and tossed me a Moroccan throw.

She closed the trunk and said, "Picnic time. Let's enjoy the day."

A breeze whipped at us from the west. Waves hammered onto the sand with surfers in black bodysuits waiting in the roiling brownish-green water to catch a ride. My body felt cool. We trudged over sandy hills and found a sheltered spot among the dunes. Here, protected from the wind, the sun felt warm on my skin.

I spread the colorful blanket and weighted the corners with sand. Christine pulled a bottle of Groth Chardonnay, Danish cheese, Lavosh flatbread, and red grapes from the basket. Next came a corkscrew, two stemmed crystal glasses wrapped in small tea towels, and several books of poetry.

She set out the crystal, uncorked the wine with expert precision, and poured it, inhaling the aroma. "Happy end of summer, Mallory, and . . . Happy Birthday." She extended a glass to me. I took it.

Surprised, I said, "How did you know?"

Christine laughed. "Britt told me. I believe a person's 'birth day' should be celebrated. Happy forty-fifth." She raised her glass in toast. I tapped it with mine and let the smooth chardonnay warm my throat.

We took turns reading Margaret Atwood, Maya Angelou, and Sylvia Plath, passing the books between us and sipping wine. After Christine read from a Robert Pinksy collection, she closed the book, lay back on the blanket and took my hand, drawing me to her.

I pulled away. "Christine. I thought we were clear about *that*."

"Don't you ever feel like exploring your sexuality? It's called 'risk,' Mallory." She reached for me again.

I pushed her hand away. "I do enjoy our friendship. Please don't spoil it."

She laughed softly and became quiet. The voices of children down along the beach reached our ears. Christine looked toward the sound, unable to mask the hurt in her eyes. We sat in silence. Then, as if to clear her feelings, she shook her head. By mutual unspoken decision, we gathered the remains of the picnic and placed them back in the basket. I shook sand from the throw, folded it and draped it over my arm. Lastly, she handed me my signature large purse, the one that made people wonder if I carried all my belongings with me.

"Did you ever do it, buy a gun?" she asked.

I nodded, taking the purse.

"Is it in there?"

"Yes," I said. The sound of the sea rumbled in the distance along with her displeasure.

"Mallory, what am I going to do with you—to convince you about guns?"

"What am I going to do with you?"

She smiled. "Point well taken."

We trudged to the car, Christine back to her old self. "Oh, well, 'nothing ventured,' as the old saying goes. I hope I didn't offend you."

"I felt a little betrayed for a moment."

"It won't happen again."

I wondered which she was talking about. A birthday celebration, a gun purchase . . . or something else.

Several days later, I called Britt and told her about Christine's advances.

"Typical Christine," was her wry reply. "She usually makes a move sooner or later . . . if you've been chosen."

I was stunned. "You knew what might happen, and you didn't warn me?" Anger edged my voice. "What do you mean, 'if you've been chosen'? It happened to you?"

"Yes. Look, Mallory. I *am* sorry. She's discreet and selective when it comes to her women companions. I didn't know if she'd approach you or not, and I didn't want to color your opinion of her. I have a professional relationship to maintain. Don't forget, she's on the LACMA board, plus she is a valuable patron to emerging and established artists, as well as gallery owners such as yourself. She knows her art."

Frowning, I didn't reply.

"Mallory?" she asked. "Are you there?"

"Yes."

"Am I forgiven?"

After a beat, I replied, "Yes."

I didn't see Britt for a month, until she invited me to an exhibit preview at LACMA of Allan Tenney's work, a prominent American southwest artist. We attended a cocktail reception for him in the museum's Art of the Americas Building the next evening. I was familiar with Tenney's paintings, especially one depicting Nevada's wild horses called *Racing from the Dark*. His use of light and color caught the strength of his subject and their majesty.

As Britt and I dawdled through the exhibit, Christine appeared on the arm of the man I knew to be the featured artist.

"Mallory, Britt, so nice to see you," Christine said. "May I present Allan Tenney?"

Britt and I shook his hand.

"Your work is striking, as is your use of color," I said.

"You are too kind. Thank you." Tenney nodded, with a slight smile.

The artist was Christine's height and stocky. She stood in a model's stance, wearing silver flats, willowy against him.

"I'm a gallery owner in Laguna Beach," I said, "and would be honored if you'd consider showing one of your paintings there."

"Perhaps we can talk in the next several weeks." He handed me a card.

Christine cast me a look I hadn't seen before. Territorial? Jealous?

After a few more pleasantries, we moved on. I turned to Britt.

"Another?" I indicated Christine and Tenney.

Britt nodded as Lucas entered the gallery, hanging back, watching Christine and her companion.

"I don't understand their marriage. It goes beyond any 'open arrangement' I've encountered." I looked at Britt for an explanation.

She merely shook her head. "It's been like this for the ten years I've known them."

Early in the morning, four days later, Britt called. "I have terrible news. Allan Tenney was struck and killed in a pedestrian crosswalk in Santa Monica last night. Hit and run. Story's on the front page of the *Los Angeles Times*."

"I know, I know. I just read the article. A terrible loss. What will happen to the exhibit? Will it shut down?"

"For one day—out of respect. Interest is going to skyrocket," Britt continued. "His work will increase in value. Everyone, sadly, will profit from his death."

Before I could speak, she added, "Mallory, I'm not sure Christine knows. She often sleeps late. If I'm correct about their relationship, this will be a horrible shock. I'd go over but I'm on my way to a directors' lunch meeting. I've left Lucas a voice message. I think he's on a business trip. Would you call her?"

"Of course."

Christine's phone rang and rang. I was about to hang up when I heard her breathless voice.

"Hello?" She sounded weepy.

I paused. "You know."

A soft reply. "Yes."

I couldn't ignore the pain in her voice. "Would you like me to come over?"

"Please."

Taking the interstate north from Laguna Beach, I made good time to Bel Air. The road into Beverly Glen twisted through hills, becoming narrower, jammed with parked vehicles along the road's edge. Purple flowered jacarandas trailed over fences. Oleander and bougainvillea bushes crowded beside each other to give an air of privacy to homes squeezed side-by-side on hillside lots.

I pulled up the steep drive and parked beside her Porsche. I knocked several times on the door of the mid-century modern home, peering through the door's glass but unable to see anyone. After a brief wait, I tried the door to find it unlocked. I opened it, calling, "Christine, it's me, Mallory."

I found her sitting in black silk pajamas on a white couch, her eyes red and puffy, her hair disheveled. She fondled a gold brocade clasp on her Mandarin-collared pajama top.

Her despair hung in the air. I paused beneath the archway to the sunken living room. "Christine, I'm so sorry." Quickly, I stepped in, dropped my wrap and purse in a chair, and went to her, taking her hand. Her sobbing increased.

"Allan and I planned to run away to the New York art scene when the exhibit ended." She wiped at her cheek. "I've searched my whole life for him."

"I had no idea." I paused. "Does Lucas know?"

She shook her head. "This time was different. Allan and I were painted by the same brush." She lay back, closing her eyes.

"Can I get you something?"

"Yes, please, in the master bath or maybe on a nightstand. A prescription vial of Valium."

I didn't see or smell liquor. She held an open bottle of Perrier. I replied, "I'll get it for you."

I went upstairs to the master bedroom and looked on the bedside tables, each topped with a scented candle, an incense holder, and a decorator lamp. I opened the nightstand drawers, encountering a box of colorful condoms, lotions, oils, and sex toys. I found no Valium in either the bedroom or the bathroom.

I entered a walk-in wardrobe, the size of a large bedroom, containing Christine's clothing, handbags, and shoes along one side. On the other hung Lucas's clothing. Two shelves completed the wall, holding high tech equipment—a music system, video apparatus, wires and speakers linked discreetly into the bedroom. The lower shelves held rows of labeled video boxes, CDs, and DVDs. A leather chair commanded the middle of the room with a side table holding several remote controls and a laptop computer.

Surprised by the voyeur setup I'd blundered into, I turned to leave, and then noticed a prescription bottle sitting on a built-in chest of drawers. Valium. Beside the chest was a closed door. I opened it to find the dressing room had its own entry from the main hall. I left quickly through it, having no desire to retrace my steps. I'd seen enough.

When I returned to the living room, Christine took a Valium with a swallow of Perrier. I covered her with a cashmere throw and sat on the floor beside the couch, listening to plans she'd made with Allan. Slowly, the stressed look on her face softened and she nodded into sleep. I moved to sit in what I recognized as a Stickley-designed lounge chair. Copies of *Artnews* lay on the lamp table beside it.

Time passed. A light knocking on the door interrupted my reading and Britt joined me. We talked in low tones about Christine's affairs and Lucas's steady presence. I told her about our friend's plans to run away with Allan, about what I'd discovered upstairs.

"I'm not surprised at anything," she said. "I did think she might run off some day, but I always felt it would be just a fling. Perhaps this with Allan was real."

"Does she love Lucas?"

"In her way. It seems an odd, but comfortable, relationship for each of them. He's a patient man, a steady presence. He seems almost proud of her allure. That she comes home to him." Britt glanced at Christine. "I finally reached Lucas on his cell. He's on business in San Francisco."

Christine stirred, murmuring, "So sweet of you both to come." She sat up, rubbing her forehead, tidying her hair. "I'm feeling calmer. A little groggy." A long sigh escaped her lips. "I think I'd prefer to be alone now. Would you mind?"

We took our leave, but not before formulating a plan. Britt would call her the next morning and I would visit again the next afternoon.

The following morning my phone rang at 11:30. It was Britt. "I can't reach anyone at Christine's."

"Maybe she's in the shower or the garden," I replied.

"I've been trying since 8:30 this morning."

"I'll go right over."

I grabbed my car keys and purse, double-checking I had money in my wallet. Somehow the purse felt different. I hadn't noticed in the confusion of the previous day. I unzipped the center compartment. My new twenty-two-ounce handgun, a Walther CCP pistol, was gone. My breath caught in my throat. Had Christine taken it?

After breaking every speed limit, I arrived at Christine's house and ran up the steps to find the door unlocked. I rushed in, calling her name, and found her sitting on the couch, dressed in black slacks, a white silk blouse, her favorite Picasso scarf draped about her neck. She held my handgun. I froze. If I moved too fast, she might take her life.

"Please put the gun down," I said in a quiet voice. "You don't want to do this."

She looked up. "I did . . . earlier." She paused. "But I thought about my life. About Allan. Wondering if I really would have left. Or if I had, would I have stayed with him? Wondering about art and its gifts. About Lucas who knows and loves me, who understands me."

"When did you take my gun?"

"Yesterday, after you went to get the Valium."

"Please give it to me."

"It would have been so easy, don't you see?" Christine extended the handgun to me, the safety still on, the magazine in place.

I slipped it into my purse and sat beside her. She lay back into the cushions, the back of her hand on her forehead. Tension in the room ebbed like a slow, receding tide. I began to relax, knowing I would have missed my free-spirited, engaging friend.

Rupert and the Methodists

When my daughter Beth-Ann, youngest of six and always a handful, gave birth to her own child, little Lila, she said God double-cheated her . . . He let her boyfriend run off *and* He cursed her with a baby.

She sulked around our doublewide, sayin' she hated the desert, the Coachella Valley and the dusty old town of Desert Palms. I said it was a darn sight more excitin' than the four-corner-stop in Iowa where I grew up. She'd just shake her head, sayin' she wanted to run off, live by the ocean and be free.

Only sixteen, she was. Let her pretty little self get all frumpy and . . . the thing that made me so real sad? She didn't want nothin' to do with the child.

"Diaper's all shitty and stinky," she'd say, holdin' her nose.

"Hush up," I'd say.

I dragged Beth-Ann to the Desert Methodist Church every chance I got. Prayed for God to touch her. One Sunday He whispered to me, *"Addy, it's the baby blues."* But even with huggin' her when she cried, holdin' my tongue when she sassed, and tryin' to show her how to care for little Lila, nothin' changed. I wondered if maybe the devil himself was in her.

My ideas had about run out and, much as Pastor Moore talked to Beth-Ann and prayed, we didn't seem to be gettin' nowhere. Then I thought of a longtime friend of my late husband Henry, a man by the name of Rupert Arenas. To see him, I just had to drive up Highway 74 to Route 371 to the Cahuilla Reservation, his family Cahuilla and all. He reminded me of a Dakota Sioux friend Henry and me had back when we lived in Iowa. Both knew special tribal ways.

So I called Rupert. He said to come on out. Beth-Ann stamped her foot, said she wouldn't go. But we went—after I said her daddy would want her to be happy and she sure wasn't happy now. She whined all the way there.

That day travelin' from Desert Palms to Anza is one I'm not gonna forget anytime soon. Good thing we left little Lila with my neighbor who knew what was goin' on. My old four-door Honda overheated goin' up the mountain, and Beth-Ann's anger steamed right along with it. Had to pull to the side of the road, give the car a chance to cool down. Good thing I had a big plastic jug of water with me to add to the radiator so we could get underway again. But Beth-Ann sure didn't cool down.

Seemed like forever before we got to Rupert's place and turned off the paved road. A sandy cloud trailed us all the way up to the house. Dust come in the open windows, got in my eyes and Beth-Ann's throat, makin' her cough. Sweat slid down between my bosoms and settled in the rolls circlin' my middle.

Rupert waved, peerin' at us from under a black Stetson, his brown skin lined, lookin' all leathery. He still had his crooked, friendly grin, but the blue and brown plaid shirt looked tighter over his middle than I remembered. A faded red bandana hung around his neck along with a small leather pouch that looked new.

"Hi, Addy, Beth-Ann," he said, leanin' in my open window. "Park over there." He pointed to a spot between a rusted oil barrel and a round, dome-shaped hut all covered in palm fronds and brush. Way back, Rupert's family used to live in that out-buildin', but now he lived in a small stucco house next door, all neat and tidy.

I drove over to the parkin' place, opened my car door and got out. Beth-Ann sat, her seatbelt buckled around her. I leaned in and said, "Let's get out, Beth-Ann." I heard a sigh.

Now, she'd known Rupert since she was a baby, sometimes even callin' him Uncle. And she'd been here before with me and her father when she was younger. This foot draggin' was gettin' on my nerves.

"Get out, Beth-Ann." She didn't move.

I said it again, louder. "Get. Out."

I heard a real heavy sigh and then a snap-click. Took her sweet old time openin' her door, pullin' herself from the car, and comin' over to us.

"Beth-Ann, I hear you got troubles," Rupert said. He waited.

The girl narrowed her eyes at me, lips clamped tight.

"Rupert's talkin' to you, Beth-Ann," I said.

She scuffed her foot in the sand.

Rupert just nodded and said, "Follow me," as he led us to the out-buildin'. I nudged Beth-Ann ahead of me. We bent over to get through the low doorway, Rupert followin'. The place had that brushy, earthy smell and tule mats on the floor like I remembered from when I was here with my Henry, when he first got sick with the cancer. Rupert sure eased his way.

"Come, sit with me here, Beth-Ann." Rupert gestured with his hand. She turned away.

I started to say somethin', but he shook his head. "It's okay, Addy."

He sat cross-legged in the middle of the hut, puttin' his Stetson on the floor beside him and pushin' loose strands of gray hair behind his ears that come loose from his thick ponytail.

"Sit with me, Beth-Ann," he said again. He patted the space in front of him.

My girl wouldn't move. I can still see her standin' there, lookin' at the doorway. About then, I readied myself in case she tried to run out. But, takin' her sweet old time again, she sat cross-legged in front of him.

"Addy," Rupert said, "please sit over there." He pointed to an old stool off to the side. Guess he remembered about people like me. If we set on the floor, we have trouble gettin' up.

Rupert skooched forward a little closer to my daughter and extended his hands, palms up. "May I hold your hands?" he asked. Beth-Ann hesitated. Then, like in slow motion, she set her hands in his. He held them, smilin'. In a kind voice, he said, "Beth-Ann, I'm going to pray. You won't understand what I'm saying. My language is old, as are my people's ways. But everything you hear me say or see me do is for you."

He bowed his head, eyes closed, and said nothin', his breathin' deep and steady. Beth-Ann glanced over at me, her angry scowl replaced by a wonderin' look. Minutes passed without a sound. Beth-Ann kept her eyes on Rupert. I watched my girl.

Rupert raised his chin. He began to chant. Low, high, soft, then a bit louder, back to soft again. His chant made everythin' seem like the world had stopped its ruckus and we could hear ourselves. His voice grew soft and the chantin' faded away. Slowly, he began to speak his prayers. Beth-Ann closed her eyes. I did, too. His deep, gentle voice filled the hut, bringin' a feelin' of peace and calm, clearin' the bad air we brought in with us.

When he stopped, everythin' was quiet. I took a peek. They sat with their hands still joined, eyes still closed until Rupert took his hands from hers. Beth-Ann opened her eyes, watchin'. He brought his palms together, then parted them, fingers spread like petals openin' on a flower, and lowered them to his knees. I heaved a quiet sigh.

More minutes passed without a sound until Rupert opened his eyes. Movin' slow, he untied the bandana from around his neck and spread it in front of Beth-Ann, smoothin' out the wrinkles. He took the pouch off and set it on the bandana.

"Beth-Ann," he said, his voice low. "Sadness and hurt are with you right now but they are only visiting. If you no longer make them comfortable, they'll leave."

She inhaled quick, turned her head away.

"Beth-Ann, I have some things I want you to see," he said.

She turned back.

Reachin' into the pouch, he removed two tiny vials and three fat pumpkin seeds and set them on the bandana. Last, he pulled out a miniature toy horse, one front hoof raised. Looked to be made of white plastic. He laid it on its side next to the seeds.

Takin' one of the vials between his thumb and forefinger, he held it up. "Earth," he murmured, shakin' the vial. Loose dirt moved back and forth. He set it down. He took the other vial and tipped it from side to side, the clear liquid in it shiftin' one way, then the other. "Water," he whispered. Last, he touched each seed with his index finger. Again, in a whispery voice, he said, "Food."

Beth-Ann watched his ev'ry move.

After a pause, he said, "They give us life."

Everythin' real quiet.

I thought he'd forgotten the little horse, but he set it up. It fell on its side. He set it up again. It wobbled but stayed steady on the tule mat. "Life is precious, Beth-Ann," Rupert said, his voice gentle. "We must be strong. Even though we wobble and fall, we get up again. I want you to get up again. For your life . . . for your baby's life."

Everythin' still real quiet.

He picked up each item, put them back in the small leather bag, and cinched the tie tight. "I collected what's inside especially for you. They're your spirit guides. Keep them close. Remember each of their blessings. Earth. Water. Food." He paused. "Life." Takin' her hand, he set the pouch in her palm.

Beth-Ann glanced at it, dropped it on the bandana and stood. She hurried toward the doorway but stopped. She turned. I could see tears in her eyes. She rushed back to quick grab up the pouch. With it clutched in her hand, she run out.

"Addy," Rupert said, "Be patient. Your daughter has much to think about. She will be in my prayers. Come back whenever you want."

After I thanked Rupert for his kindness, me and Beth-Ann drove home, her fiddlin' with the strings on the pouch. I tried talkin' but she just looked out the window.

With all the happenings on that trip, I didn't see no difference in Beth-Ann. She kept to herself even more. At night, I still heard her cryin'. If I tried to talk to her, she'd say, "Stop dragging me to church and trying to take me out to Rupert's again. Just leave me alone." I didn't see the pouch either and thought she'd tossed it in the garbage.

But one day I noticed somethin' new on her bedroom dresser.

On it set a tiny wooden cross she'd been given at Sunday school way back when she was confirmed. Next to it was Rupert's pouch. Next to the pouch stood the white plastic horse, tall and steady with its front hoof raised.

Even with all that, I still didn't see no change. I kept prayin' every night and at church every Sunday. I called Rupert again. He said, "Just be patient, Addy, just be patient."

I started makin' an old-fashioned quilt in the fan pattern for Lila. I worked on it to take my mind off things, usin' all my fabric scraps from years of sewin'. I wanted to make somethin' Lila'd have to remember me by. I also took more than my fair share of aspirin. Some days my patience, instead of bein' fat like me, got wore pretty thin.

One day, Beth-Ann hung near while I tended Lila. I just minded what I was doin', pretendin' I didn't notice her. I didn't want no arguments or be accused of tryin' to ruin her life or some such. Out of the blue, she said, "Mama, I want to hold Lila." Oh, my stars! I thought my heart would stop. I gathered the child up and set that beautiful baby in my daughter's arms. I almost burst, I felt so happy!

She started sayin' more about her baby an' less about the daddy, things like, "Look, Mama, Lila drank all her bottle." "Look, Mama, Lila's smiling at me. Aren't her dimples cute?" My daughter's eyes started lookin' clear as a desert sky, her clothes all neat, her long brown hair combed and shiny. My heart filled with hope.

To this day, I thank God and Pastor Moore and Rupert for showin' Beth-Ann and me the way. You know how sometimes you have t' keep talkin' to different folks about the same thing until you finally get it? The girl had to figure things out on her own, in her own time and I had to let her. Dealin' with hurt and anger and guilt and bein' betrayed . . . *plus* a baby—that's a lot for anybody, let alone a sixteen-year-old. The whole thing almost wore me out, too.

I kept up my prayin' and added a new one. I guess I should tell you about it. I prayed all the sadness and hurt leavin' Beth-Ann would dump down on the boy who'd run off and make *him* downright miserable. But God? He caught on to what I was doin' real fast. He shook me by the shoulders and whispered, "Forgive him, Addy. Forgive him."

I told God I'm tryin', but it don't come easy.

The Gourmet Divas

My friend Krista opened her green eyes wide, then narrowed them to conspiratorial slits. She dropped her fork. It clanked onto her appetizer plate, an artichoke heart slipping from its tines. From our booth in the piano bar of Malibu's Islander Restaurant, she stared at something or someone behind me.

"What's happening?" I offered a questioning look and poked my fork into a jumbo shrimp, sautéed in olive oil and garlic.

With a toss of her red hair, she leaned toward me. I sensed I was about to receive a secondhand epiphany. I rested my fork with the impaled shrimp on my plate.

"The fellow at the far end of the bar. With the blond."

I turned, only to have Krista grab my arm.

"Don't look now, Kate." She leaned across the table. "It's Rick Morrison and that *is not* his wife Nancy. Whoever she is, they're wrapped around each other."

I glanced at Krista and again turned toward the crowded bar for a quick peek, spotting the couple. "The world's full of cheaters." I returned to my shrimp, adding, "She's younger than he is. Who is he?"

"My sister's next-door neighbor." Angry scowl lines formed between Krista's eyes.

Before I could reply, Loren and Jenna returned from "the loo," our name for the ladies' room, courtesy of Jenna's trip to England last year.

Loren settled her Rubenesque figure into the booth beside me. "Okay, what's up?" She had a Sherlock Holmesian sixth sense, able to glean a piece of gossip from fifty yards. She peered at Krista's still indignant face.

Jenna gathered her beige dress around her and slipped into the booth by Krista. "Talk, ladies, talk," she commanded.

We all leaned in. Krista proceeded to enlighten us about Mr. Rick Morrison, evidently an Olympic Gold Medalist in the "player" department. This was par conversation. The four of us often met at a chichi restaurant to tell all, see all, and give unasked-for advice.

"I met him at my sister's house parties," Krista confided. "The Lothario hit on me at one of them. Can you believe it? His wife was in the next room."

We nodded knowingly, each having experienced husband problems and unpleasant divorces. We became acquainted at a women's support group, soon going out to dinner together, and naming our foursome The Gourmet Divorcees. That name evolved into The Gourmet Divas. Better to be a diva than a discard.

Based on our memories of the opposite sex, we peered with varying degrees of subtlety at said Olympian Rick and his lady friend with the blond tresses. They now seemed to be in serious conversation.

"Hey, gals," Jenna whispered. "Do we have to be so obvious?"

"The jerk probably thinks he's 'G. S.'" Krista sneered.

Jenna's eyebrows arched. "He's what?"

Krista surveyed our faces. "G.S.—Geographically Safe. You know, far enough away from his home turf, no chance of being seen."

We all nodded a collective, "Ah, 'G.S.'" We paused, each thinking of appropriate remarks. Krista and Jenna sipped Mai Tais. Loren clinked the ice in her Manhattan. I needed to slow down on my dirty vodka martini.

Loren broke the silence. "I declare the lowlife guilty. Krista, give his wife my card. Maybe I can represent her in what could be a nasty divorce."

"Give her my card, too," Jenna added. "Just in case the house has to be sold in the settlement. The real estate market is hot."

"Not if I can help it." Loren put her hand up like a stop sign. "I'll make sure she gets the house."

"Well, I'd like to psychoanalyze Don Juan. I think I'll give him *my* card." Krista dug in her purse, all of us regarding her with disbelief. "Just kidding, Divas."

Rick Morrison, whether we knew him or not, didn't have a chance. He was convicted of all the sins since Adam.

"Do you think his wife knows?" I glanced at the couple again.

Krista bobbed her head up and down, a cunning smile on her face. "If she hasn't figured it out, she will after my sister tells her."

"How about this." I adjusted an earring, silver bracelets jangling on my arm. "I'll sketch the scumbag and we can throw darts at him."

"Here, here." Krista raised her glass.

"By the way," Loren fingered the chain on her necklace. "Have you noticed all the trophy wives in this place? Younger things on older arms?"

"And trophy mistresses," Krista added, stretching her petite frame for a better look.

Trying to seem casual, we scanned the patrons again.

Jenna shook her head. "You know what? I'm not passing judgment. There's always two sides to a story, male and female."

"Ah, St. Theresa has spoken." Krista gave Jenna a smirk.

Loren, the bloodhound, surveyed the room. "Well, whatever."

Just then, the maître d' arrived to escort us into The Aloha Room. Our table, draped with a cream-colored cloth, had a small glass vase in its center containing a single red anthurium surrounded by greens. He gave us each a menu and removed a "Reserved" placard.

Seated at our window table overlooking the Pacific, we watched waves break to Mother Nature's rhythm. Rattan furniture and wallpaper with large tropical leaves set against a black background added to the atmosphere.

I opened the conversation: "A gorgeous room, a gorgeous night. No offense, Divas, but I wish I were here with, oh, say, James Bond." I placed my napkin in my lap and picked up the dinner menu.

Krista looked at me. "Craving the thrill of a sexy adventure?"

"In your dreams," Loren added.

I sighed as we prepared to order dinner in honor of Jenna's fortieth birthday.

"This place makes me miss Hawaii." Loren gazed at the breaking surf.

"You know, I've never been. Let's plan a trip," I said, hastily adding, "Don't look now. Here come Rick and Not-Nancy." I studied my menu, unable to avoid taking peeks at the couple. Morrison had his head down, his arm around Not-Nancy, acting like the intense conversation we witnessed in the bar had not ended.

We studied the entrées as the maître d' escorted the couple toward the reserved table next to ours. I wouldn't be able to see much.

Rick and I were back-to-back. Krista, sitting across from me, promised an in-depth report during dinner.

"Let's have a bottle of wine or two. I've earned this fortieth birthday." Jenna tapped her glass. "I've had a hard day showing property to people with big ideas and no money."

We decided on a light Sauvignon blanc to mellow out the hard liquor. Our bottle soon arrived with a basket of assorted crusty breads and seasoned butters.

"Aw, the 'lovers' are drinking red wine and still seem to be having serious conversation," Krista reported in a low voice, chomping on a piece of rosemary bread.

Jenna and Loren, their peripheral vision active, verified the data, nodded in agreement. I slipped a black-fringed shawl from my shoulders and turned, draping it over the back of my chair. I couldn't see much.

Turning to my friends, I semi-whispered, "Wonder what they're talking about so intently." Our table grew quiet, but we couldn't overhear a word. Damn, why couldn't they speak louder?

I smoothed the skirt of my black dress and reached for my wine glass. In mid-swallow, I suddenly heard a loud female voice. Krista pointed and sputtered. Jenna and Loren scooted their chairs back from the table. Something wet hit my shoulder and neck. It dripped into my cleavage. I turned just as a second onslaught of red wine rained down.

The blond stood, grasping their wine bottle, hurling its red contents at Morrison, who ducked and weaved from side to side. She slammed the empty bottle on the table and grabbed the breadbasket. Crusty missiles sailed through the air, hitting the man's face, landing on his shoulders, and on the floor. As I turned away, pieces of bread struck my back, my head, my lap. The recipient of collateral damage, I hunched over, grabbing my dinner napkin.

"Oh, great," Loren said, as a piece of bread landed in her wine.

I squirmed out of my chair. On the couple's table, empty wine glasses lay overturned. The blond threw the breadbasket to the floor. Morrison hauled himself to his feet. Red drops dripped from his hair, onto his face and his power-blue suit.

The blond stepped in close to Rick's face. "Make a choice. Me or Nancy," she hissed through clenched teeth. She turned, a whirlwind of indignation, and flounced from the Aloha Room.

Morrison glowered with cavalier indignation, B movie style. He dabbed at the wine on his face and suit and brushed away pieces of bread. Squaring his shoulders, he threw his napkin on the table.

"Sorry," he murmured to everyone within range, casting a furtive look to the immediate tables near him. "Relationships are . . ." He stopped in midsentence as his gaze swept our table. For a moment, his eyes lingered on Krista. No question if he recognized her. She shot him a look of disdain, equally recognizable. He hurried after the exiting tornado.

"What a loser." Krista wore a satisfied sneer. "He knows I know. Sleep on that, Tricky Rick."

Still a bit startled, we watched him disappear around the corner. I brushed away a solitary drop of red wine slipping from my ear lobe to my neck. We stood, straightening our dresses, mine new and stained with red wine, all wiping and blotting where needed, while the wait staff quickly tidied up. The diners returned to their meals, the evening's spectacle over. We ordered another bottle of wine to help us settle back into the moment.

"Well, didn't know the evening included dinner *and* a show." I smoothed the napkin in my lap.

Jenna asked Krista, "Are you really going to tell your sister?"

I thought a moment and said, "I would. Hopefully, your sister will tell his wife. The woman should know. Then she can do what she will."

"I wouldn't get involved." Loren shook her head and looked at Krista. "It's really none of your business."

Krista chose not to reply. But from the look on her face, we knew her answer. Conversation paused as the painful subject hung in the air.

Blame wore many hats, without offering easy answers. I sipped my wine, alone for the moment with my own thoughts on love, marriage, and divorce. How quickly buried feelings could parade from the past into the now. I looked around the table at my friends, thankful for their love and support, thankful for the evening together. And thankful for life . . . that goes on.

VI

It Settled on Our Eyelashes Like Tears

"In his mind, he heard the soft click of a door opening between them, one closed for too long."

—Dr. Chesley Manning
"The Affair"

CREEK SONGS

Summer of 2010—Palm Springs, California

August in the desert. I hide inside, watch Netflix, explore the house—closets, cupboards, mysteries inside boxes. The air conditioner runs day and night. The humidity soars. I wait for the weather to break, for October's start of "The Season," for it again to be the fabled Palm Springs of vacation brochures enticing tourists and snowbirds to spend winter in the sun.

An open cardboard box sits on the floor before me with *Miscellaneous* scrawled on its side. Inside is a collection of theater playbills, souvenir cocktail napkins and matchbooks, colorful postcards, a stack of old letters bound with a rubber band, and two photograph albums.

I relax at the kitchen table, looking through one of the albums, pausing at a picture of a rambling 1920s clapboard house, once the summer home of a wealthy Buffalo businessman. It dominated an acre of land on Maple Road in Dodd's Corners, New York.

My parents bought the place years after the summer colony heyday. Remnants of grandeur remained—a carriage house garage, a white picket fence, a brick walk to the sprawling front porch. In a side yard sat a gazebo surrounded by rose and peony bushes. The backyard sloped to Ellicott Creek, where a small boathouse nestled on its bank.

Wide and gentle, the creek always drew me to its side, to the slow-moving waters with giant weeping willows along its edge. Turtles slipped into the brownish-blue current. Robins, frogs, and crickets sang on its airwaves.

As a teenager, I sat beneath those willows, watching the lazy creek. Questions and mysteries filled my head. Was I pretty? Would the boy in biology class notice me? Why did my best friend stop speaking to me? Adolescent anxieties mingled with expectant wonder. It was a special place—to think and discover, to sort out problems, to ponder my existence.

On its meander to the mighty Niagara River, the lazy creek offered peaceful days along its banks. Its occasional ominous moments of flooding or drought hinted of life's perils. I heard its songs, growing curious about what lay beyond, knowing naught of fate or chance or life.

December 1944—Dodd's Corners, New York

I clumped along, trying to ice skate, hating my bulky blue snowsuit. I wanted flesh-colored tights and a short skirt like the famous ice skater Sonia Henie. I had a Sonia Henie doll that I loved. The blond pigtailed likeness wore a white skating outfit trimmed with red ribbons. On her feet tiny white ice skates sparkled.

My father skated ahead with graceful strides, hands clasped behind him, long blades on his black skates glinting in the daylight. A 1930s-style tweed cap with a soft crown, pork pie flat, shaded his eyes. A dark plaid jacket warmed him.

Suddenly, I stopped—a crack in the ice—right in front of me. *Step on a crack, break your mother's back.* I *never* stepped on a crack.

Why would I *skate* over one?

The crack snaked across the ice like a huge python I'd seen in *National Geographic Magazine*. Why did Father bring me to Ellicott Creek Park? Why not skate closer to home—the creek flowed behind our house and when it was this cold, it froze. He glided back and forth, away from the dam forming the pond, away from the crack—and me. My breath formed a misty cloud of dread.

Turning, he called, "Come on, Carolyn."

"There's a big crack here."

"What?" he asked.

"There's a great big crack here," I called back. My voice—high-pitched, thin.

"It's okay. Just skate over it. I want to show you something."

Three skaters glided by me—over the perceived chasm. Nothing happened to them. I wasn't convinced. I couldn't move. Father motioned me forward. Did he really have something to show me or was it a trick—a trick to make me go over the crack? Stiff-legged, I pushed myself closer. The blades on my new white figure skates cut tiny gashes in the ice. My mouth felt dry.

I peeked into the crack in the thick, thick ice, quickly looking away. Miss O'Dell, my favorite teacher, had just taught my third-grade class about dinosaurs. "During the Ice Age, glaciers crept across the earth, perhaps the reason dinosaurs became extinct," she'd said. Could dinosaurs and glaciers be sneaking *this* close? What if a dinosaur survived beneath the icy surface, ready to pull me deep into the freezing cold water? I couldn't breathe.

"Let's go, Carolyn." Father's voice sounded crisper.

Time with my father was precious. For a whole Saturday afternoon

I had all his attention. I had to show him I wasn't afraid, or he'd think I was a big baby. I put the toe of my right skate behind me. The blade's jagged teeth snagged the ice. My heart was beating faster. I squeezed my eyes shut, tight. I pushed off, launched on one leg.

"Good," Father called. "Push your legs to go faster. Pump the air with your arms."

I felt a bump. *The crack!* Push! Push! One leg, then the other. *Skate! Skate!* I didn't know I could go so fast. *Skate! Skate!* I opened my eyes, glanced quickly behind. I saw no monster, no monster at all—only a stupid, sissy crack.

I pumped and pushed. Father waited. Taking my hand, he skated beside me—not fast or scary, just comfortable—showing me how to match my strides to his. We skated in a figure eight and then continued up the creek.

Push, glide. Push, glide. I watched as my wobbly ankles began to wobble less.

Father put out a hand to stop me. "This is what I wanted you to see."

"Oh, I didn't know . . ."

Father interrupted me. "Shhh."

Before us hung Ellicott Creek Falls. Frozen—majestic—a silent wall of cascading aqua blue ice draped with snow. Not a sound, only our breathing, everything held motionless in time. Father squeezed my hand as snow fell gently around us. It settled on our eyelashes, like tears.

December 1953—Dodd's Corners, New York

Her name was Ruby—Ruby Litchfield—a hard, old bitch, with kinky, blood-red hair and blotchy, wrinkled skin, courtesy of a private stash of gin. I nicknamed her Ruby-Red-Eye. She wasn't going to be happy. I was late.

On that snow-covered Saturday morning in December, I had to be at Ruby's Restaurant, *her* restaurant, at 8:00 a.m. I worked there on weekends during my senior year of high school to save money for college.

Tourists stopped at Ruby's, rain or shine, snow or hail, on the way to see Niagara Falls. The restaurant had a prime location on Ellicott Creek at Maple Road and Niagara Boulevard. After heaping breakfasts of eggs, pancakes, and hot coffee, tourists left big tips. It was a good place to work.

"Get up, Carolyn." Mother's voice pierced a hazy dream about sunny Florida. My friends and I hoped to go in a few months, at Easter break.

I glanced at the clock. 5:30 a.m. *Groan.* I played on the girls' basketball team for Central High School. Friday night we'd been at a tournament until late.

"The weather's not good," Mother warned. "You'll have to drive slow, and you're going to need the extra time. Get up."

I plodded downstairs, buttoning a clean restaurant uniform—my mother always made sure one was washed, starched and ironed.

My father greeted me. "When you're almost ready to go, I'll get your car warmed up."

The garage, near the road, had a short driveway. I knew he'd have it shoveled before I was set to leave. The county snowplow had cleared our road earlier.

I stifled a yawn, wishing for my warm bed. My mother watched the clock.

"You should give yourself an hour," she said.

"An hour?" I fussed. "It isn't *that* far."

"You never know in this weather."

I left at 7:00 a.m. Although I hated to admit it, my parents were right. Driving was slow. On the way, I saw Bobby Gordon shoveling his driveway. I stopped to tell him we'd won the tournament. Patty Nieman, out with her dog, stopped me to talk about Janet Wilson's party that night; did I know if Jack Vannier was invited? She giggled at the thought. I hoped Ron Peterson would be there.

I waved goodbye. The countryside around Ellicott Creek looked like an old-fashioned Currier and Ives Christmas card—missing only a horse-drawn sleigh. Snow hung on the pines. Maples and oaks resembled artist Charles Burchfield's leafless trees. Ice crust drifted downstream. The road followed the creek all the way to the restaurant.

A glance at my watch told me to get going. I tapped the accelerator. I could go a little faster. I tapped it again. Yes, I could go a little faster still.

As I rounded a bend, I caught up with an Erie County garbage truck looming large in front of me. I followed, impatient, until suddenly, it stopped. I slammed the brakes. My yellow Studebaker sedan skidded on the icy surface. The brakes didn't do any good.

What do I do? I can't remember—turn into a skid? Out of a skid?

I pumped the brakes. They wouldn't grab. I was going too fast. My gloved hands gripped the wheel. To my right—a ditch. In front—the garbage truck. To the left—Ellicott Creek—close to the road, no guard rails. It was too late.

The car slid toward the creek. My adrenalin pounded. *Jump!* I grabbed the door handle. *Jump! Jump!* I took a deep breath.

Bang! The car lurched to a stop.

Slowly, I focused. My car was still on the road, facing the opposite direction. The trash truck's red lights blinked *behind* me. I could see them through the back window.

"You okay?" A man in coveralls motioned to lower the window. "You hit my truck. Spun you around. Good thing I was here, or you'd be in the creek. You hurt?"

"I don't think so."

The man explained, "You've got a few dents. Better slow down. Cinder truck hasn't been through yet."

He gave me a stubby pencil. We exchanged insurance information.

"Headed home?" he asked.

"No, on my way to work." I was shaken, but not hurt. I'd rather face Ruby-Red-Eye than my parents. I drove the car in the direction it was facing until I spotted a shoveled driveway. I turned around and cried all the way to the restaurant, parking where no one could see the fender damage or the crease in the side. I went into the restroom and threw cold water on my face. As I stepped out, wiping my hands, a voice scratched my eardrums.

"You're late," Mrs. Litchfield announced, loud enough for everyone to hear. "You high school kids are all alike. Do you want to work or just have fun? You can run the dishwasher until we get the lunch crowd. An hour late again and you're through."

I wanted to tell her I hadn't been having fun. I rinsed dirty dishes and loaded the heavy-duty commercial dishwasher. As I worked in the kitchen, my learning curve worked, too—on my character, about being on time, responsibility, judgment, driving too fast.

Ruby-Red-Eye walked by to make sure I was doing my penance.

April 1956—Dodd's Corners, New York

The flat-bottomed motorboat bobbed in the chop. I was scared. Glenn, our neighbor, edged the boat closer to our back door. Taking a deep breath, I opened the storm door and stepped into the water, praying my boots were tall enough. Ellicott Creek had flooded. Water surrounded our house.

"Here, Carolyn, toss me your things." Glenn extended his large hands.

My books were stuffed in an old briefcase. I prayed my report on the Brahmaputra River wouldn't land in the water, along with an expensive English lit book and precious cram notes. I took a last look at the case and tossed. Glenn caught it like a football.

"Okay, Carolyn, wade to me. When you're close, give me your hand. The water's shallow here. Just the wind making us bounce."

With baby steps, I inched toward the boat. Glenn helped me on board. He revved the motor, and we pulled away into the swollen creek waters. My parents waved from the dining room window. If anyone could help transport their daughter to Elmwood College, it was their friend Glenn.

I didn't want to go. I'd voiced my resistance the previous night. "Why do I have to take a motorboat to the Greyhound bus stop, take the Greyhound into the city, then catch a city bus? It isn't safe and it'll take forever."

Father shook his head. "The creek has crested. You'll be safe, just inconvenienced. You'll leave early."

"I'm doing all right. I could miss—"

"Carolyn, you can't miss important tests—flood or no flood." Case closed.

Education had the highest priority. No excuses. Unable to finish high school, my parents made sure my older sister and I did, that we were there every day. I was a sophomore in college, a commuter student, and the rule still applied, more so than ever. It didn't matter that the spring flood of 1956 broke all records; that an ordinarily peaceful Ellicott Creek had gobbled up the countryside.

Small whitecaps sloshed against the boat. Giant weeping willows trailed branches on the water, their trunks inundated. Only the roof of our boathouse was visible. Our neighbor's house built on lower ground sat in water rising above the first-floor windowsills. Glenn had been there several days before and taken Mr. and Mrs. Hampton to their daughter's home.

"What time's the bus?" He guided the boat into our front yard where Maple Road lay under water.

"In about twenty minutes!" I shouted. Usually, I *drove* into downtown Buffalo to the college. Today I was in a boat dressed like Nanook of the North.

"Hang on!" Glenn hollered.

The motor roared as we bounced through the water, past treetops, partly submerged telephone poles, rooftops cursed by being on low ground, or houses on newly made islands. People in motorboats and canoes waved as they surveyed damage, helped neighbors. I hung on, feeling the wind burn my cheeks, glad I'd worn jeans and a warm, waterproof jacket.

The boat slapped through the small waves. Mist sprayed my face. Overcast weather made everything shades of black, gray, gray-brown and dull white. I saw myself an unwilling participant in an Ansel Adams photograph.

Suddenly, the motor choked, gasped, and stopped.

"What the hell?" Glenn yelled as he pulled the rope starter to prime the small engine. It gasped again. He inspected the motor. "Goddammit. Sheared a cotter pin."

"What?" I asked. Whatever it was, it was about to save me from a trek to college via boat and bus.

"Broke a cotter pin! How much time we got?"

"About ten minutes. It's okay if we don't make it."

"We're going to make it. Your dad told me you've got tests today. You're not missing them on my watch!"

Glenn tipped the motor out of the water, cursing under his breath. He grabbed two oars from the boat floor, slipped them in the rings and heaved. A World War II Navy man, he was no stranger to rowing. "Hang on, mate!"

I wanted to say, "Let's go home," but something stopped me. The veins on Glenn's forehead bulged. His huge hands gripped the oars and pulled. He gritted his teeth. Glenn could have said, "No, I have concerns of my own," when my father asked him if he could get me to the highway. He didn't. When the motor failed, he could have turned around. He didn't.

My family held WWII veterans in high regard—their sense of duty, their effort, their sacrifice. During the war, my parents picked up hitchhiking GIs, bought war bonds, used ration stamps, consoled a friend after his son was killed in the battle for Europe.

I realized I respected Gene's commitment, this time not to his country but to his neighbor.

We neared Highway 80, its course on higher ground. I could see the Greyhound bus approaching.

"This is as close as I can get!" Glenn shouted. "Grab your gear."

Glenn stood up in the boat, waving his long arms at the bus driver.

Scrambling over the side, I shouted, "Thank you."

"Run, kid. You're launched."

The driver slowed the bus as I waded out of the water. I hoisted myself up the steps to be greeted by a smiling driver and clapping passengers. Through the window, I saw Glenn in the bobbing boat, still waving. I waved back.

July 1958—Dodd's Corners, New York

Paul rounded the bend, paddling a blue canoe. A shock of hair fell across his forehead. Sunglasses shielded his eyes.

In my mind, I heard my friend Allyson's words: "He has a glass eye."

"He lost his eye in a car accident," I answered. "That doesn't make him any less handsome."

"If something happens to his good eye, you'll be married to a blind man. Do you know what that would be like? How would he be able to work?"

When Paul saw me, he lifted the paddle from the water and waved it. He guided the canoe into our boathouse, easing it up beside the dock.

"Hi," Paul greeted me. "Give me your hand. I'll steady you in."

We glided along Ellicott Creek on a lazy Fourth of July afternoon, bound for a girlfriend's barbecue farther upstream, ready to celebrate. We'd graduated from Elmwood College in June.

Paul and I met as freshmen. Slender, tall, with thick dark hair and long graceful fingers, he'd graduated with a degree in education, like me. On the weekends, he played sax in Hal Leonard's Orchestra, a local Buffalo group.

"Who's going to be there?" He grinned his crooked smile.

"Most of my sorority," I answered.

"How about your friend Allyson? I don't think she likes me."

"Oh, that's *her* problem. Besides, she's gone to Pittsburgh to see her aunt." I'd never tell him the things she'd said—that sometimes I thought about the things she'd said.

"Great. Let's have a good time. We've earned it."

We pulled beside the dock. Elvis Presley's "Jailhouse Rock" blared on the hi-fi. Smoke wafted from the barbecue, bringing the scent of grilled hot dogs to the air. Tables bulged with dishes of baked beans, coleslaw, and potato chips.

"Man, I'm hungry." Paul rubbed his stomach.

He took two Carling Black Label beers from the drinks bucket and uncapped them. We drank with our friends, talking about college memories, about our futures. Later in the evening Paul and I danced—close. I hadn't had many boyfriends, but I felt sure I loved him. He occupied my every thought. Time always passed slowly until the next moment we could be together. My parents, however, expressed taciturn advice: "You should wait."

Hand in hand, we walked beside the creek to an old wooden bench. The evening wrapped its sounds around us—the rustle of trees, friends' laughter, voices from across the water.

He leaned forward, elbows on his knees, staring into the darkness. "Are you going?"

"I don't know." We sat in silence. I missed my older sister who, after graduating from nursing school, got married and moved to California. My cousin and I thought we might drive to the west coast to see her later in July.

Again, Allyson's words were in my head: "What will you do if something happens to his eye?"

"What could happen?" I'd asked.

"He lost one eye in a car crash. Maybe he'll lose the other. Strange things happen. Illness, disease, another accident. I wouldn't marry him if I were you."

"Oh, shut up, Allyson."

Paul's voice interrupted my thoughts. "Don't go. I want us to be together this summer, all summer—before we start teaching in the fall—and get married."

"It'll only be for a week or two. There's so much . . ." I didn't finish.

"Yeah, I know. There's so much we haven't done. But we'll do it together—find an apartment, travel, get a dog. We can go to California for our honeymoon." He took my hand. "I don't want you to go."

"You've already been hired to teach at a high school in Buffalo and I have a job interview at the new Dodd's Corner junior high," I said. "I'm almost certain I'll get it. They really need teachers. Then we'll both be set."

"When's the interview?"

"Mid-August."

"It's just a visit, right?"

"Just a visit; a graduation reward."

He kissed me.

My cousin and I drove to California. I called Paul every night from a motel while on the road. I called him every day from my sister's. He told me he missed me; told me to have a good time; he'd see me soon.

He asked if my sister was going to be my maid-of-honor.

But the freedom, the ocean, the palm trees—it all began to cast a spell over my first time away from home. One week turned into three.

Every day became an adventure. I met a weightlifter at Muscle Beach. He wanted to be an actor. I met a girl named Helen at a party. I didn't know she would become a lifelong friend. I happened upon the current Miss Maryland in a Westwood Village coffee shop near UCLA. She arranged a blind date with her boyfriend's buddy, saying, "You have to have one date with a California boy."

Was I being unfaithful? No, no one would know. But guilt whispered to me the entire evening.

On a whim, I investigated employment with the Los Angeles City School District. I learned teachers earned a higher salary than back in Dodd's Corners. I interviewed and was offered a teaching position in a second grade. The assignment would begin second semester when the current teacher left to be married.

Paul and I argued through a long, expensive call as I explained. I wanted to stay and have a chance to earn more money. I wanted him to visit me at Christmas. "No," he said. "I'll be busy teaching and playing music, saving money—for us."

We decided I'd stay, take temp work through December, fly home for Christmas and return to California to start the teaching job in Los Angeles in January, just for the semester.

When I returned for the holiday, he was the same, welcoming me, regarding this California thing as just a whim that would end in June. I wasn't the same, but not ready to admit it to myself, nor acknowledge how much being back in familiar surroundings felt stifling to me. When I flew home again at Easter break, I knew it was over.

My horizon had broadened, grown fuller. Paul seemed a little more distant. Our calls and letters tapered until they became nonexistent.

I stayed in California, Paul in western New York. Life went on.

February 1977 – Laguna Beach, California

My fourteen-year marriage to Lee ended in divorce. Even though friends were supportive, and I was now dating, I felt lonely—scared, even. One evening I thought of Paul, ironically seeking the familiar from which I'd fled so many years before. I called him. For some reason I'd saved his number. Paul's mother answered, still at the same house after all these years. She said she'd let him know. He no longer lived in Buffalo but had moved to East Haberville.

I waited for his call, but never received one. Several weeks later a letter arrived. Paul was surprised to hear from me.

> I've thought of you often through the years. I'm now a professor at the University of Buffalo. I married Allyson Newman and have two fine sons. You used to know her. You were in the same sorority.

I expected he might be married. But to Allyson? She hadn't been in my thoughts for years. I read the sentences again, then crumpled the envelope in my fist, feeling betrayed. Was this how she'd always felt? Had she been that two-faced? Or had she simply grown up, guided by her destiny? I threw the letter on the table, tears on my cheeks. After several deep breaths, I continued reading.

> Recently, I drove by your parents' old home out on Maple Road. Do you remember the Fourth of July party? That night by the creek? For a long time, I wished you'd never gone to California. For a long time, I didn't marry.

Yes, I remembered the evening by Ellicott Creek. I wondered what my life would have been, had I stayed, had I married him.

June 1997—Dodd's Corners, New York

"Why are you taking pictures of my house? Do you work for the county?" The loud, angry voice belonged to a short, heavy-set woman in a faded housedress. She tromped across an overgrown front yard studded with fir and maple trees.

"I used to live here." I held the camera at my side. "I'm visiting from California."

"Well, I don't want any pictures taken of my house. I'm in a boundary dispute with the town." The woman reached the road's edge where I stood.

"As I said, I used to live here."

I hardly recognized my old home on Ellicott Creek. Hammers pounded in a tract of houses under construction next door. I could see the boathouse was gone. The once undeveloped land across the creek now housed the north campus of the University of Buffalo.

"You used to live here? What's your name?"

"Carolyn Siddall—my maiden name."

"Oh, you're the Siddall's daughter? I bought the house from them."

Before I could reply, she added, "What'd they do with their grand piano? I wanted to buy it. They wouldn't sell."

"They gave it to me."

"Well, lucky you."

I had hoped to be asked into the yard or invited into the house. That wasn't going to happen. Ordinarily, I would have apologized for taking pictures without first going to the door. But not now. Not to her. Just before I got into my rental car, I snapped another quick photo. The woman whirled on her heel and walked back in the yard.

I drove away, denied one last walk down the sloping backyard to the creek bank where, beneath the weeping willows, I could have watched my creek idle by once more, rekindling lost years and lost choices.

Summer of 2010—Palm Springs, California

I close the album, deep in thought. Images of my parents; Ruby's Restaurant; our neighbor, Gene; my first love, Paul; the family home; Dodd's Corners—all of these are assembled in my heart. They'll always be a part of me, flowing through my memory like Ellicott Creek flowed past my home, singing its song to the young life unfolding by its side.

The creek—with its spring floods, summer ennui, autumn storms and winter ice—didn't exist just as a setting for my teenaged life. It created unforgettable experiences—sometimes ominous, sometimes harsh, sometimes gentle—that shaped me as a person. And like the creek, my life's journey has continued through its own seasons, its own settings, all singing *my* song . . . writing *my* story.

I sit for several minutes, absorbing my thoughts. The room is still. With a sigh, I push away from the table, and step past the clutter of stalled cleaning to peek at the thermometer mounted outside on the kitchen window frame. An image of a little girl skating across cold, thick ice nudges me as I read the temperature: 115 degrees.

THE AFFAIR

Chet turned his head away from the sound of a familiar voice. In the middle of an afternoon nap, he resettled himself in his leather recliner.

"Wake up," the voice insisted. "There's a gal at the front door who wants to see you."

He opened one eye. His son, Joe, stood framed in the study doorway. "Tell her I'm busy. Come back tomorrow after lunch. Former students drop by all the time."

Joe shook his head. "Doesn't look like a survivor from a Literary Criticism class to me. She's waiting on the front porch."

"Oh, all right," Chet muttered. "Talk to her while I get moving."

Joe beckoned at him to hurry. "I'll tell her you'll be there in a few minutes."

Resigned to his nap being over, Chet yawned and stretched his arms. A push on the recliner button brought him to an upright position, enabling him to ease out of the chair. Standing, hands on his hips, he leaned from side to side, the stiffness in his torso from the morning's golf game already evident. With a sigh, he slipped his feet into worn loafers, designated by wife Emily as his house shoes. He glanced about the room.

Paneled in dark mahogany, the study had lost its aura of contentment, of permanence. Items he and Emily had spent a lifetime collecting—books of literature, treasured Native American baskets, lithographs by Navajo artist R. C. Gorman—now seemed irrelevant.

"What am I going to do?" His voice cracked. A sadness settled around his shoulders like a magician's cape he wanted to pull off but couldn't. Nor could he escape the family pictures hanging on the wall. Graduations. Weddings. Births. Grandchildren smiling back at him. Images of his oldest son Joe, younger son Brandon, daughter Kristen.

Of the three, Kristen gave him ongoing problems. Tension between them grew from the time she entered middle school. She always did the opposite of what he advised, including her marriage to Adam. Now she faced the man's upcoming trial.

Anger flashed unannounced—intense as red-hot embers.

Damn it, damn you, Emily. You'd know what to do, what to say. Why did you leave me?

A picture on his desk sent a sharp spike of guilt through his thoughts.

Oh, Em, forgive me.

His eyes lingered on the image of their forty-fifth wedding anniversary.

I was so lucky to have found you.

He absently straightened a stack of dog-eared professional journals next to the picture. He ran his fingers across his closed laptop, wondering when he'd get back to his writing—*if* he'd get back to it. His nameplate, Dr. Chesley Manning, stared back at him. University degrees, along with academic awards, filled another wall. All seemed like ancient artifacts, at best.

Before the cancer took you so quickly, Em, you told me to continue to write, to live, to love. Do you know how hard it is without you?

A loud voice from the kitchen penetrated the study. "Hey, Dad," Joe hollered, "the gal waiting on the porch? She's growing older by the minute."

"I'm on my way, I'm on my way."

Chet paused by a black-and-white framed photo. A pretty coed held the hand of a grinning young man in a Stanford sweater. His eyes moistened. Melancholy still arrived without warning any time of the day or night.

"I wish you were here beside me now," he whispered, pulling a handkerchief from his pocket. "This past year has been hell."

On his way to the kitchen, he wiped his eyes, shoved the hanky back into his pocket. At the sink, he filled a glass with cold water, felt a punch on his shoulder. Joe stood beside him, grinning.

"That gal is a ten, Pops. What have you been up to?" His son smiled the impish smile capable of melting his mother's heart from the time he was two. Now forty, his grin still worked. Chet saw it several times a month when Joe stopped by.

"Son, you're a real piece of work." Chet took a quick swallow of water.

He tucked at his shirt and smoothed his hair on the way to the front door. Through the glass he saw a tall, shapely blond dressed in magenta capris, complimented by a too-tight white sweater. He opened the door slowly.

"Dr. Manning?"

Chet nodded, struck by the resemblance. "Anyone ever tell you how much you look like Marilyn Monroe?"

She laughed. "All the time. This is for you." And then her smoky voice rendered the familiar birthday song. Before he could move, the blond leaned forward to kiss his cheek. "Happy birthday," she whispered.

Chet stepped back. Her eyes radiated kindness. He also saw a tad of mischief.

"Have a great day!" The blond clicked her way down the porch steps in high-heeled sling-back shoes toward a pink van parked at the curb. It was then Chet noticed the vehicle's signage, Affairs-Are-Us.

With a shake of his head, he closed the door. Only in southern California, he thought. Suddenly aware of a commotion behind him, he turned to see adults and children hustle from the backyard through open French doors into the living room.

Oh, hell, what's this?

Caught off-guard, managing a smile, he stepped into the room. Someone released balloons. Confetti swirled into the air. Children, grandchildren. Relatives, neighbors, friends. All talked at once.

"Surprise!"

"Happy Birthday!"

"Many more!"

"Happy seventieth, Dad!" Joe shouted, patting him on the back.

"Happy birthday, you old codger." Ed Clark, a fellow professor and best friend, came through the crowd to shake his hand. "It's about time we got together for a beer. And I'm counting on you to write an introduction for that textbook I'm just finishing."

Chet nodded. "I'll give you a shout-out soon."

"Looking forward to it." Ed moved on into the room. Brandon stepped in.

"Hey, Dad," his son said as he slipped an arm around Chet's shoulders. "Welcome to the bash everyone's waited for. Happy birthday. It's the big seven-oh."

His strapping son filled the space beside him. "You know, big guy," Chet said, "I planned to let this birthday just slide on by."

"Not a chance, Pops." Brandon winked as he stepped away in the direction of the buffet. "All your kids are here. Look around."

There they were. Joe and his wife, Melissa. Their sons, Tyler and Carter. Kristen, alone. Brandon, his wife Annette. Their twin daughters, Meg and Beth. Chet remembered the last time his family had gathered; it was at Emily's funeral. He now understood why Joe insisted on a golf game together earlier in the day, insisted he rest after the game, why the gal waited at the door as he jostled himself awake.

"Hi, Grandpa." Tyler appeared in front of him. "Happy birthday."

Em, he looks just like his father. I wish you were here to share this.

"Hi, Tyler. How about the two of us get some punch?" Chet suggested. On their way to the buffet table, he was surprised to see his younger brother, Lawton, in from the east coast, accompanied by his wife, Yvonne. They nodded from across the room. It always took little brother a while to warm up to him.

Chet and his grandson enjoyed a cup of punch together, but Tyler soon drifted away to explore the sandwich tray. Alone for a moment, a smile fixed on his face, Chet casually observed his children, thinking about each one in turn.

Joe stood by the fireplace, talking to a neighbor.

You probably planned this affair, Joe. A damn fine businessman, but a real heller as a kid. "Borrowing the car" without permission. You destroyed Dave Hampton's mailbox and landed in Betty Altman's prize-winning rose garden. Cost me a few dollars.

Joe nodded at him. A line from *All Quiet on the Western Front* ran through Chet's mind, something about revenge being black pudding. *Your time will come. Wait till your boys can drive.* Chet returned the nod, chuckling to himself.

Brandon, the football player, the college coach, now filled his plate at the buffet table.

Took you a while, son, to discover girls, but when you did, you made up for lost time. Won't be too long before your girls attract the boys. Wouldn't be surprised if you make tackle dummies out of the young Don Juans.

Brandon waved at Chet, pointed to his plate, heaped with food. "How about it, Dad. Want me to get you some chow?"

"Not just yet."

Kristen stood in conversation with Melissa. It appeared serious. Kristen, the budding journalist. The difficult one.

Em, you always said Kristen and I didn't get along because she was too much like me. Headstrong. Opinionated. "Just listen to her, Chet. Don't judge," you'd say. I tried, but then Adam came on the scene. Stock market whiz kid, big money, high times. Womanizer.

With a slight shake of his head, Chet momentarily reflected on life's uncharted and unpredictable nature. He thought of himself, of his family and friends. How the results of choices revealed themselves more fully over time. How understanding or acceptance or disapproval or denial grew as the years passed. He took a deep breath and exhaled, somewhat at peace, somewhat unsettled. He also had to acknowledge the unbearable in life. He'd lost Emily.

He sighed again and reached for a cracker from the cheese tray. A rustling occurred beside him. Lawton and his wife, Yvonne, a non-stop talker, edged into his space. The woman insisted on fixing a sandwich and chips for him like the one she'd fixed for Lawton.

He and his brother stepped aside, exchanging small talk about his brother's real estate company. The conversation lulled as Lawton chewed on a potato chip. He then asked, "By the way, whatever happened to that second book of yours, Chet?"

"I'm giving it a rest at the moment."

"It's been resting for a while, so I hear. Pity. You'll probably never get back to it now."

Lawton picked up another chip from his plate, took a bite. "So what does a Professor Emeritus do with his time?"

"Today, I played golf."

"Must be nice to have the time and the money. This boy still has to work. No retirement for me anytime soon."

Chet ignored the barbs as Yvonne returned.

"Oh, Lawton, please," she said and shook her head at her husband. She gave Chet a plated ham sandwich, chips on the side.

"You know, dear brother-in-law," she remarked, "I have this idea for a story . . ."

Many words later, Chet's ham sandwich gone and Yvonne immersed in relaying her plot, daughter-in-law Annette slipped her arm through his.

"Excuse us, Aunt Yvonne, Uncle Lawton. We need Dad for a moment." She took Chet's paper plate from his hand and replaced it with a long, serrated knife, the handle tied with a blue ribbon. "Let's cut the cake. It's your favorite, German chocolate."

Out of Yvonne's range, he murmured, "Thank you, my dear, for saving me." He squeezed her hand.

Annette dropped his plate in one of the cardboard trash

containers placed about the room and led him to a table holding a large sheet cake. "Once we sing 'Happy Birthday,' just make the first cut. We'll do the rest."

After the singing, cheers went up. Grandchildren rushed the cake. Chet stepped out of their way.

We did well, Em. You're not here, but you are here. I see you in our children, our grandchildren.

He tensed. His daughter walked toward him, steps deliberate, her jaw set. She looked like her mother, only taller, more assertive. They hadn't spoken for a year.

"Happy birthday." Kristen looked up at him and asked, "How are you?"

"Some days are better than others. Thanks for coming," he said. Seconds of silence seemed more like long, tense minutes. He needed to fill them. "So, have you settled everything? With Adam?"

Why the hell did I ask that?

Kristen's body stiffened, her tone hard as she replied, "The divorce has been over for months, Dad."

More awkward moments. They stood before each other, yet miles apart.

"I know you never liked him," she finally said. "Well, he's gone now." She projected a hint of attitude.

Chet cleared his throat, wishing past words could be taken back. He didn't respond.

His daughter's tone softened. "I loved him." She put her head down. "He's been arrested for embezzlement. I didn't know what he was doing or about the secret accounts."

"Joe told me today, on the golf course." The news had made Chet angry. He'd invested a few thousand with Adam, at the time a new broker on the way up. Unless Adam pled out, Kristen could very well be involved in an investigation, followed by a trial. Now he realized Joe had wanted to diffuse a possible scene between them, to give him time to adjust.

Chet cleared his throat. "He crossed the line."

Stop, don't say another word.

He watched Kristen smooth her dress, square her shoulders. Each waited for the other to speak.

His daughter took a deep breath. "You were right, Daddy."

Careful, Chet.

"Honey, let's not say any more."

"Thank you for not saying, 'I told you so.'"

"The past is past." Chet put his arms out, waiting. Kristen hesitated, then stepped close, leaning into him. He embraced his little girl. It had been a long time. "Endings, no matter the circumstances, are bittersweet."

"Sometimes I feel so lonely." Kristen stepped back and looked up at him. "Excuse me, Daddy. I didn't mean to go there, especially on your birthday."

"It's all right." Chet took her hand. "I've come to learn a little about loneliness, about anger. They're emotional thunder, rumbling in the background. The storm may pass, or it can crash into you."

"I guess it's like that song about raining on your parade." Kristen tried to smile.

"You know, I'm always here," Chet said. "The days ahead might get a little rough."

His daughter placed her other hand on his. "I guess we have the same challenges. The loneliness, the sadness, the anger."

"Yes." He paused. "But I think we'll find our way."

In his mind, he heard the soft click of a door opening between them, one closed for too long. He also saw another door, one Emily urged him to unlatch. He could feel her pushing him, ever so gently, giving him permission to open it, to live.

Inner Canyons

We make our way down into the canyon, alone on the trail, the air hushed—almost eerie. Faint sounds—a human voice, the shuffle of hooves—break through the stillness. Soon, a ranch hand on a buckskin horse rides into view, urging his train of pack mules up the footpath, their bodies swaying in disjointed rhythm. To make room, Danny and I press our backs against the inside wall of the South Kaibab Trail, knowing the other side of the narrow path drops into one of the lesser ravines of the Grand Canyon. Sweat collects under my arms, on my forehead. I push harder into the stony dirt behind me until I resemble a modern petroglyph. I'm scared. I don't want to be the reason someone falls over the edge.

The man nods, tapping the brim of a black hat protecting his weathered, unconcerned face. The five mules snub us. They breathe heavily, blink, bob their heads, pass close enough for us to count their eyelashes. It's hard to ignore their fetidness or the gritty dust settling in my mouth and nose. Linked together by a loose rope, they carry bags of refuse from facilities down by the Colorado River. I was told mules have the right of way. I'm a believer.

We brush ourselves off, continuing down the steep seven-mile trail, a late August sun hot on our skin. The canyon's mesas and buttes unfold before us, a labyrinth of pinks, browns, and orangey reds, painted with shadow and hinting of mystery. My awe mixes with apprehension, but Danny reminds me, "You have to experience this place, not just stand on the rim like a voyeur."

A two-week trip to southern California after graduation from college has turned into three months. After a summer of fun supported by part-time jobs, reality smacks me. The party's over. I must go to work. Real work. The big question is where? Do I want to begin my teaching career back east or on the west coast? Do I want to return to my hometown city of Buffalo in western New York State or stay in Los Angeles?

Rather than deal with the conundrum, or admit September is just days away, I'm in the Grand Canyon with Danny. We've dated all summer, after meeting in Venice Beach at a volleyball game. He's English, from Barbados, a recent UCLA grad with a degree in business and the promise of a job in his uncle's L.A.-based insurance company. His future is secure. My future isn't.

Stay or leave? I carry this question with me as we continue down the trail. Gradually, I slip into the rhythm of the trek, letting curiosity overcome both my current problem and the uneasiness I felt at the Kaibab trailhead. We pass layer upon layer of limestone, sandstone, and shale. Surreal sculptures appear, chiseled by wind, by driving rain, by ice. We see hidden gorges and gaping crevices, each bend in the path revealing a new formation. Danny tells me the canyon sits on a floor of metamorphic bedrock. It supports the canyon, preserves its stories.

I think of my bedrock, my heritage of strong, solid people from England, Germany, and France who were farmers, commercial fishermen, factory workers and entrepreneurs. Who had left family and hometowns in Europe. Who worked hard to establish themselves in a new land different from their own. I know their narratives; now I wonder about mine. I sense that my own stories, old and new, are piling onto each other and pressing into me, trying to shape me.

Compared to my conservative, back-east upbringing, southern California life is freer, the social scene more fluid. It's a great place to see and be seen. I'm wide-eyed at the beaches, the clubs, the convertibles. Tanned, blond and outgoing people play volleyball or swim or surf. They seem to balance work with fun.

Just when I think I'm fitting into my new environment, feeling a little comfortable, a little more relaxed, something happens. The new friend . . . isn't. They move or want to borrow money or have other issues. The quiet apartment complex by day explodes into annoying neighbors with blaring televisions at night. The urban neighborhood bustles with excitement, only to deliver disinterest and the message, "You have to find your own way." Even with the crowd around me, I feel alone.

Despite the negatives, I like what I see. In Los Angeles, I walk along busy Vermont Avenue, with its boutiques and ethnic restaurants, with the lure of pizza and deli. I hear the rhythmic cadence of different languages and the blare of music emanating from a small club. It's a place far from small-town Main Street and small-town viewpoints. What I don't like is feeling lost, losing my identity. Full of fears and anxieties, I become a speck on a canvas of bustling humanity. I had the same feelings as a lowly seventh grader attending my first day at Amherst Central High, a big suburban school containing grades seven through twelve. I wondered if anyone would notice me or want me to be a friend. I was a microscopic ant then like

I am now, descending into the canyon.

We make our way, passing ponderosa pine, pinion pine, oak, desert scrub. Farther down, dead tree trunks, surrounded by sun-scalded vegetation, stretch gnarled limbs toward us. There's little shade. Solitary lizards scurry from rock to rock. A sudden flurry startles us as a colony of bats soars from a crevice, their fragile wings cupping the air, filling the sky; their black eyes assessing us. Unlike them, my own wings falter, my own eyes peer into the future, then look away. When I look ahead, I feel a sense of vertigo, of jumping from the trail into unknown space.

Switchback after switchback of downhill bracing pushes my toes into the tips of my boots. My calf muscles ache. Even with my discomfort, a mantle of prehistoric time wraps around me, welcoming me onto this sacred land. I feel the presence of a people who lived here for thousands of years, leaving arrowheads, stone tools, grinding stones, and petroglyphs for others to find. I imagine families who played, loved, worked, and cried. Who quarreled, faced challenges, and died. Who sought guidance from gods, shamans, their elders, or nature. I place my fingertips on the rough wall, trace the edge of a thick layer of small stones set in fine gravel, sandier than the layer upon which it rests. Fragments tumble down onto the path like lives tumbling through time. I grow quiet, thoughtful.

I wonder about the ancient people I feel around me. *The young people. Did any of them ever want to leave the fold? To what consequence or punishment or sacrifice? If I leave my roots, what will I lose? What will I gain?*

And then disjointed pieces of my life tumble down: doll clothes my mother made for my favorite doll; my father's work-soiled hands;

a new bicycle; a bedroom set for my twelfth birthday; a sometime-boyfriend back home, Danny close by. So many thoughts.

Only the scuffing of our hiking shoes on the trail's surface breaks the calm. We adjust our backpacks. I wipe my forehead, swat at flies, scratch a bite on my arm. I think about a 2,600-mile trip to California, about an Arizona hike taking me a mile deep into the earth. I wonder what the hell I'm doing. Deep down, I know: *I'm doing what my mother taught me.*

I remember my mother sharing her hurts, her frustrations. She was a daddy's girl whose father died young. She watched her mother dote on a little brother. Her era and limited means took away the chance to complete an education, have a career, or travel. From the time I was little, she sent me into the world with the admonition *to not be like her.*

The role my mother knew was that of wife and mother. She'd only completed tenth grade. She'd say, "You're going to college." I'd nod. She'd add, "Did you hear me?" It never occurred to me not to go.

When I turned sixteen, she took me to the Social Security Administration for working papers. She said, "You want to be able to earn your own money." That sounded good to me. For a long time, my mother didn't learn to drive; however, she supported the purchase of my first car, bought with my own savings when I was seventeen. That car also brought me freedom. My mother created opportunities for me, possibilities far greater than hers.

But she judged me by *her* experiences, *her* world, the only one she knew. I juggled this confusing "stay-go" message, trying to maneuver myself through the long, dangling apron strings. When I stayed within reach, she'd push me away. When I pulled away, she'd guilt me close. Many words—her words.

"Don't be like me," she'd say as she counted the money she'd saved so carefully to buy material to make my school clothes.

"Why are you late?" was the question she'd ask when I came home from school after basketball practice or band rehearsal, suspicious of after-school activities.

"Where have you been?" was queried when I came in from a friend's house. My mother worked hard all her life. She had little time for socializing. She told me friends would waste my time. These questions made me feel I was doing something bad or wrong.

"You're too independent," she said when I expressed a viewpoint or opinion—about a person or incident—different from hers. I lived at home, but my world broadened as I went to college in downtown Buffalo during the day and worked as a grocery checker three nights a week and on the weekends.

Our resentment toward each other built up. Our communication broke down. All I heard was, "Don't be like me."

Her words fade from my thoughts as we continue along the trail, drinking bottled water to keep hydrated, eating raisins or nuts to maintain our energy. We check for blisters, notice a hawk flying overhead. We talk about finally being out of college, starting our careers, the heat. Danny wants to talk about us, but I back away from the subject.

I wonder if the west coast is the right fit. I'm used to ice skating, skiing, swimming in Lakes Erie and Ontario, lying under a huge weeping willow by Ellicott Creek, hearing the thunder of Niagara Falls. I'm used to an old, industrial city where nothing is too far away. Los Angeles and the adjacent San Fernando Valley spread for miles.

The distance between places is difficult to navigate. The physical and emotional aloofness between people is more difficult. It's hard to break in. I've tried to find a center, a neighborhood, a tribe. In a sprawling, unfamiliar city I fight being alone—being *lonely.*

Danny likes me; I like him. But deep down, I know he's been a crutch to lean on. I'm not proud of this. I wonder if he senses it. I hope not. It's not my intention to hurt him. He's a good person. I just want to find my own legs without a crutch.

At last, we round a jutting rock formation. Before us, the clear azure water of Bright Angel Creek tumbles into the muddy Colorado. The Kaibab Suspension Bridge leads us across the river where we walk a well-worn path, knee-high grasses whooshing against our legs, cottonwood branches brushing our shoulders.

Quickly, we claim a space in the campground, run to Bright Angel Creek, sink into its coldness. Danny splashes water on me, his laughter echoing from the canyon walls. My long legs take me downstream away from him, but he catches up, hugs me. "You've made it to the bottom. You're halfway there," he says.

Yes, I've made it to the bottom. Will I find my way up and out of my dilemma?

After supper, darkness closes around us, except for neon-bright stars. We slip into our sleeping bags on the ground beside each other. Danny puts his arm across me, falls asleep. I catnap. Something rustles down by my toes, bumping along the foot of my sleeping bag. I grab my flashlight in time to illuminate the backside of a skunk waddling off into the darkness. Danny laughs when I move my sleeping bag up on a picnic table. Soon he does the same. Then he's asleep. Again.

I'm very much awake now, not because of the skunk. I lie beneath an ageless sky in an ancient gorge, feeling unsettled, out of place. Homesick one minute, wanting to stay out west the next. This is a grand life choice. I want to get it right. If I stay, I'll have to scramble. Substitute teach, waitress, job hunt. Decide about Danny. If I go home, I'm promised a position in a new junior high. There's also my on-again/off-again boyfriend Paul, a sax player with a local group on the weekends, English teacher by weekday. I miss the clubs where he plays, the music, our closeness, him. I run my fingers through my hair, try to fall asleep.

I'm restless. With each roll left or right, I'm afraid I'll fall off the table. My back hurts from the unforgiving board; even my mind aches. *If I stay, what if I can't support myself? I'll eat peanut butter by the case before asking my parents for money. If I did bring myself to ask, I know it would never be a gift, but a loan with strings. I'm not interested in being laughed at or admonished or hearing an "I told you so."*

Daylight arrives too soon. Already, coffee brews in a nearby campsite. We dig in our packs for pre-made food and begin our hike out via the nine-mile Bright Angel Trail. We pass tourists, swaying on mules, on their way down to Phantom Ranch. They look excited, energetic. I've exhausted myself, peeking under veneers, prying into fears, scraping and peeling away layers of myself. I realize an ageless canyon has embraced me in its stillness, lured me to think, to listen, to discover.

The image of enjoying a cold beer at the El Tovar Hotel in Grand Canyon Village pops into my head. I try to keep that picture, only to have it kaleidoscope away, replaced by mirrors, colors, and patterns of home. Of friends, family, a job. Of monotony, closed thinking, an easy rut.

Of being my mother. The last time I talked to her, she said, "Staying is up to you, but remember, you have a job waiting in a new junior high not far from your home. And you don't have a job in California. And you'd better think about that. And what about Paul?"

Just what was I going to do? My mother felt, I'm sure, the best place for her imperfect daughter was at home, with the familiar. She sensed that the independent woman she had shaped so wittingly and unwittingly might fly. My father added to my inner conflict. He'd often told me I could be or do anything I wanted—so long as it was legal. What *was* going to be my decision?

When Danny and I reach the trailhead, we turn to look out on the panorama, on the great spectacle of space, of color, of shadow. I'm more awed than when we began, but I'm no longer scared. I see new possibilities, new opportunities, new adventures.

And I know.

I'll choose my mother's mantra to not be like her. The mantra that built a chasm between us. I feel sad she perhaps doesn't realize what she's created. But I know her spoken and unspoken lessons give me the strength to stay in California, to enter a new world on my own.

And I thank her.

The Modeling Period

The story behind the solitary brick structure sitting at the end of a tree-lined sidewalk wasn't complicated. The boxy, two-story building with a covered front porch used to be a school, one of the town's few. Every weekday morning, an iron bell could be heard clanging high in its cupola. Kids ran through the neighborhood to the school door, racing to be on time. But as the community grew, the town fathers decided to build a bigger, more modern facility. Instead of a hand-rung bell, students now moved to an electric one. The old school sat vacant, its bell idle.

The town council eventually found a tenant for the old place. The bell began to ring again, only this time it called kids to Sunday school, including my friends and me. We'd scurry along the walk, then scramble up its cement steps, smooth and concave as sea stone, the result of decades of feet. We'd pull open a heavy oak door and slip into a back pew, just in time for the day's Bible reading. The structure had become Ascension Lutheran Church. It would function as such for many years until a bigger church was built. As I mentioned, the building's life story wasn't complicated; however, the place did help complicate *my* life story.

One morning I didn't hurry with my friends to Sunday school. Instead, I walked with my mother to church. Summer sunlight played on the patent leather of my new shoes. My new white dotted-swiss dress swished against my legs. I was eight. I felt like a princess. At the time, I didn't know how soon my grandness would disappear or how soon the familiar walk beneath the trees would become long and lonely.

We climbed the church steps. At the top of the stairs was a commemorative stone plaque cemented into the brick wall:

School District No. 18
Snyder, New York 1900

It was now 1944 and many years since the school's construction. I'd been asked to sing a solo, my very first, at the eleven-o'clock church service. We arrived an hour early for a practice run-through of the hymn "Beautiful Savior."

My music teacher, Mrs. Lew, from whom I took piano and occasional voice lessons, had worked with me on the hymn, showing me where to breathe, how to pronounce words, how to sustain notes, how to link phrases. In her home studio, she accompanied me on a Hammond organ instead of her baby grand to simulate the church environment. I wasn't worried. I'd played in many piano recitals and knew what it was like to be in front of an audience.

We walked up the center aisle toward the altar where the organist, Mrs. Rush, waited. My mother sat in an oak pew to listen. I smoothed the skirt of my dress, its bodice decorated with hand-embroidered daisies, all made by my mother for this important day. Mrs. Rush pointed to where I should stand, just left of the pulpit. My patent leather shoes squeaked as I walked in the quiet of the empty church. The sound seemed extra loud. A solemn feeling settled over me.

It's strange writing about being in a church or singing "Beautiful Savior." In my early twenties, I stopped believing the biblical dogma or attending services, even though my parents had dutifully sent me to Sunday school and celebrated my confirmation. Looking back on the day of my solo, I felt abandoned by any savior or higher power whatsoever.

Mrs. Rush played the last few measures of the hymn as an introduction, then struck the opening chord which was my cue. I took a breath. Out came my clear soprano voice. A few phrases into the hymn, something went wrong. Very wrong.

My voice began to quaver. It grew breathy. I rubbed sweaty palms on my dress, trying to control the strange sound. I couldn't. I struggled to breathe; my heart ready to jump from my chest. I tried to swallow. A gulp lodged in my throat. My voice wouldn't come out at all.

Mrs. Rush realized her soloist was no longer singing and stopped playing. I could feel my mother's stare. The organist looked from me, to my mother, and back to me. We tried again. The quivering breathiness sounded worse. I stopped. Tears slid down my cheeks as the two women talked, their voices a jumble. All I could hear was a ringing in my ears, all I could feel was the trembling of my insides, all I could see were church pews filled with people, looking at me, waiting for me to sing.

Sing? I couldn't.

Did standing alone in the heavy presence of an almost empty church frighten me? Was it my mother looking at me, her face expressionless? Perhaps it was being confronted by the unexpected. Whatever the forces at work in my head, I couldn't sing. Mrs. Rush murmured, "Maybe another time." My mother and I escaped well before the service began.

Conservative and reserved, my parents weren't subject to bouts of loud laughter or deep emotional demonstrations or long conversations about feelings and life. Today's parenting is filled with phone calls, texts, emails, all ending with the words, "Love you." But on this particular day, no one said "Love you" or "It's okay" or "You can do it." My mother chose to express her feelings—whether disappointment or sympathy or anger, I couldn't tell—with silence, meaning there would be no discussion of what happened. Any demonstrations of empathy, if she had them, escaped me. I felt sad, guilty—even foolish.

A word blazed like a neon sign in my mind. F-A-I-L-U-R-E. Its letters flashed behind my eyes as we trudged down the unending sidewalk. I'd failed to please my mother. I feared her displeasure. I feared I'd lost her approval. That neon sign with its accompanying feelings became baggage I was destined to carry for a long time.

My mother walked ahead of me.

One of two daughters, with a span of eleven years between us, I was overly protected by a stern, insecure mother, loved but held at arm's length by an older sister with her own life to lead and, except for the receipt of reconditioned bicycles, acknowledged absently by my father. Or at least, that's how it felt at the time. I struggled, constantly seeking validation, never being sure I had it, no matter how hard I tried. Rebellion lurked in the not-too-distant future and would surface in a few years.

I still have the church bulletin announcing my solo. Of course, it never happened. I was ambushed by stage fright. I could control the chords on a keyboard, but I couldn't control my vocal cords. I was just plain scared.

It's natural for the body to react to an unfamiliar or different situation with excitement or fear. Either reaction causes the body to secrete adrenaline, a hormone that initiates the fight or flight response. An adrenaline rush into the blood stream can cause shaking, trembling, stomach pain, vomiting, shortness of breath. A person may or may not be able to overcome the symptoms.

I was the latter. Mercifully, I didn't vomit, but I did flee.

Thinking back, I realize now that an undertone of fear lingered in my home, the result of three circumstances: the spread of polio, The Great Depression, and World War II. These events shaped the values, behavior, and family dynamics of my young world.

Sociologist Morris Massey states that we go through three stages of values formation: the Imprint Period from birth to age seven; the Modeling Period from eight to thirteen; and the Socialization Period from ages fourteen to twenty-one. About the Modeling Period, he writes:

> At age eight you begin to notice that there are people outside yourself and through to age 13 you start to look at the goings on in the world. You notice the behavior of friends and family and you start to model them.
>
> At this point, you start to develop heroes. Your major values about life are picked up between the ages of eight and 13. Your values will be based on where you were and what was happening in the world around you.

The last sentence of each of these paragraphs about the modeling of behavior and the development of values made me think. National fears affected personal fears. My parents—primarily my mother, who was the most present—showed me their fears consciously and unconsciously.

Linked to a national fearfulness at the time was polio. Dr. Jonas Salk had not yet made his discovery. I felt the reach of this disease daily. I couldn't be in crowds. I couldn't go to public pools or the beach. During this time, President Franklin Roosevelt succumbed to polio after an afternoon of swimming. I couldn't even go to the movies. Pictures of an iron lung helping a polio victim breathe appeared in the newspaper. A big, cumbersome machine, it scared me.

The National Foundation for Infantile Paralysis was officially incorporated on January 3, 1938, with the first March of Dimes radio appeal occurring shortly after that. I remember the March of Dimes campaigns in the schools in the 1940s. We placed dimes in coin-sized inserts on our own individual cards. When the card was filled, we gave it to our teacher and received another. Polio was a dreaded disease, spreading fear. Thankfully, today's parents don't have that worry.

On a wider stage, my parents had lived through the Great Depression. For their 1923 wedding present, my parents had been given a thousand dollars by my father's father, a prosperous farmer and cattle drover in Ontario, Canada. They invested that sum, a considerable amount at the time, in the stock market. Of course, they lost it along with its earnings when the market crashed. My parents, like many Americans, struggled, left with a fear of being without the necessities of life.

One way my mother economized was to make my sister's clothes, my clothes, and her own. She was a skilled seamstress and specialized in Vogue patterns. I did not have a store-bought dress until I was twenty-two.

My dad was a saver, too—nails, screws, nuts, bolts. He had little jars for everything. He reconditioned bicycles, sold them on the side.

We ate all the food on our plates, saved bottles, and didn't waste paper. Once having gone without, my parents were fearful it might happen again.

The country recovered from the Depression, only to be thrust into new fears with World War II. It raged in Europe against Germany, in the Far East against Japan. My last name was Schneider. It was softened to Snider. The name change was too subtle. Kids in the neighborhood called me Hitler. I now realize my closed middle class community offered up pieces of prejudice about heritage and religion daily. Distrust of someone or something different was common.

My family listened to Walter Winchell every Sunday night. His program always began with, "Good evening, Mr. and Mrs. America and all the ships at sea!" He then reported the progress of the war. It came closer to us when my sister's boyfriend enlisted in the air force. We worried about him. Servicemen hitchhiked along the highways. My father always gave them rides.

War became a favorite game of the neighborhood kids. One day we set up a military hospital in Bobby Zimdahl's garage. The "beds" were our wooden wagons, lined up across the two-car space. We pretended to be injured soldiers brought in by our buddies. Pilots who had been shot down were rescued. Nurses applied bandages. Doctors operated. We role-played with emotion, with a sense of urgency. If someone's parents called for them to come home and they were an injured soldier, they either recovered quickly or "died" before they left.

One day, a huge plane flew over the neighborhood at a low altitude. The color of it showed it was military. One of the older boys said it was a troop transport plane. I had no idea. I only knew the end had come. I ran home terrified that real war was about to break out in our neighborhood. My mother had to calm me.

A playmate's uncle came home from the service after being in a German prisoner-of-war camp. I saw him a few days after he arrived. He looked at me with sad and vacant eyes.

A boy from the neighborhood, while at the movies to see *The Courage of Lassie*, had seen a newsreel about the concentration camps. The boy described everything he saw, everything the announcer said. It filled me with fear.

My father received a phone call that changed the look on his face and the tone of his voice. I knew from his expression it was bad news. Sunday afternoon we took a ride to Mr. George's house, our coal deliveryman. He had a son serving in the army who had been killed in France and now a gold star hung in their window. My parents and I paid our respects. Even at my young age, I felt their loss, felt my own alarm. Today, when I hear saber rattling by world leaders, I experience the same dread.

In my home, my parents modeled fear, based on their own experiences within the circumstances of the day. They modeled other behaviors, the result of that fear. They saved. They worked hard. They kept going in the face of distress. They showed a strong will.

It shouldn't have been a surprise that fear grabbed me on the day of that ill-fated solo. By then, I had a few fears in my repertoire. Today, someone would offer strategies to cope. They'd tell me to breathe deeply or offer me water or say something funny to shift my focus. Someone would tell me to visualize being successful or say, "Focus on a friend in the audience." I'm fairly sure someone would have encouraged me. I'm absolutely certain a hug would have been part of the talk. I wish *someone* had talked to me or hugged me or reassured me. Could I have been coddled, prodded, and encouraged back into singing? I don't know. I do wish I'd gotten "back on the horse" instead of giving in to the fear.

Not singing, it turned out, was not all right with my mother. She set her jaw and we walked the endless distance home in silence, the loss of my mother's approval growing heavier around me with each step. Was she embarrassed? Had she hoped for a mother's satisfaction of having her daughter sing in church?

I dragged the memory into adulthood, although being in front of an audience remained a part of my young adult life. I played first oboe in the town's symphony orchestra, substituted for the church organist, played in piano recitals. I could use my hands, but not my voice, to make music. Had the strictness and fears surrounding me as a child literally taken away my voice? I was shy, afraid to speak up. I could not sing in public. The memory remained raw, holding my voice hostage, until I finally was able to free it. Later.

In my early thirties, I became interested in local community theater and joined a group called The Rancho Community Players. Playing a character on stage didn't seem to be a problem. It wasn't really me who talked; it was "someone else." I liked the feeling of family that developed during a production. We encouraged each other. We had each others' backs when someone dropped a line or missed a cue. We gave hugs. I had a sense of belonging.

After a few productions in which I proved myself, one of my friends also in the theatre group suggested I try out for the musical *Once Upon a Mattress,* a show made famous by Carol Burnett, and based on the fairytale "The Princess and the Pea." The audition was for the role of Queen Aggravain, a nonstop talker. It would be a speaking role. I'd be delivering dialogue—a great deal of it. I assessed the information. There didn't seem to be a problem until my friend added, "Oh, and the queen only has one big song."

Wait a minute. *Big song? Song? Sing?*

The old memory steamrollered in. However, I was assured the queen didn't really have to sing. Her song could be spoken in time with the music. Well, I thought, that might be doable. The lyrics of her song "Sensitivity" did have a certain irony. The words bemoaned her sensitive soul, stomach, hands and feet, and the exquisite agony of it all. The suffering the queen sang about resonated, beginning with my eight-year-old self so many years before. There was no doubt I felt sensitive to the whole idea of singing . . . in public.

After I survived the audition, I had the role of Queen Aggravain, plus the dread of that single "song" lingering in my head. The lead role, the princess, would be played by a sought-after singer who was on her way up: Toni Tenille. My already jittery nerves reached new heights. She proved to be a generous actor. Rehearsals were like going to music school. I watched her scenes, her dedication, her discipline, her physical warm-ups, her vocal warm-ups.

I learned. I survived the show. I didn't freeze. I proved my chops by winning the local newspaper critic's "Best Supporting Actor" award. Had I beaten the odds?

Not really. I hadn't sung.

The thought plagued me. How long was I going to play the wuss? I knew to scale this giant wall, I had to push myself. Try again. Or forget about it. But the idea of singing in public—really singing—just wouldn't leave me alone.

Again through my little theater group, I heard about an upcoming production of *Gypsy.* This time the part would be the lead, the role of Madam Rose. The role, if it became mine, would involve a major singing part. With auditions several months away, I found a good vocal teacher.

I confided to my new coach about the long-ago meltdown, about how I worried it would repeat itself. He told me to practice, to eat properly, get my rest, and exercise. We worked hard, but we also found time to laugh during the sessions. For fun he had me sing Rose's songs in different vocal styles—country, ballad, rock.

One of my character's songs, called "Rose's Turn," spoke to me, especially the lyrics about "lettin' loose" and "havin' the stuff." A week after auditions, the director announced the cast. I would play Madam Rose, mother of the famous stripper Gypsy Rose Lee. My vocal work evidently made the cut—but would it play out in front of a live audience?

Irony didn't escape me. On stage I was a driving, fearless, determined woman—first a despotic, domineering queen, then a pushy stage mother. However, offstage I was a fearful adult unable to sing in public with a long-standing history holding me back. Madam Rose and I now faced the "wuss challenge" head-on. This was the "make or break" moment.

Opening night, the lights came up on the South Coast Lyric Light Opera's production of *Gypsy.* Rose's opening appearance came not on the stage, but from out in the audience. As I slipped into the reserved seat, I watched the first scene unfold. My heart pounded. I heard my coach's final words repeat in my head: "Be alert. You're well-rehearsed. You'll handle the surprises."

On cue, I hurried down the aisle toward the stage, saying my lines. I could see the audience turn in their seats, sensed their eyes on me, heard their whispers. I hit my first song spot on.

Madam Rose was alive and well. I remember standing in the wings before each of my scenes, my heart ready to stop, but when I walked into the lights, the voice was there. I'd hurled a huge stone at my Goliath. I wasn't destined to be a Toni Tennille or an Ethel Merman. I was destined to overcome a childhood incident that had left a heavy scar. My mother saw me in *Once Upon a Mattress*, not in *Gypsy*. She said she liked the show.

I sometimes wonder if I ever atoned for that long-ago day of failing to sing in church, of not being able to control my fear. Did my anxiety stem from being unable to sing or from losing my mother's approval? I'd wanted both desperately. Did I do those two musicals for her or for me? It's a muddle. One thing I do know: I did them. I survived. It felt good.

I continued with little theater work, but I never performed in another musical.

Many years later, sitting in my office in southern California, I think about that old schoolhouse with a certain nostalgia, even though there was a time I never wanted to set foot in the place again.

On a whim, I google Ascension Lutheran Church. Soon I'm on the phone with a church secretary in my old hometown of Snyder, New York. I ask questions she can't answer. She does know the congregation of Ascension Lutheran built a new church and the old school building had been torn down. I feel a pang of loss. She suggests I call the local library, which happens to be built on the former schoolhouse property. I make the call, talk to the librarian.

I tell him I'm trying to locate information on an old brick school that had once been my childhood church. I learn of a book written by a local historian that might have information. He says he'll scan any material he finds and email it to me.

Ten minutes later, I hold three pages from *A History of the Town of Amherst, New York, 1818–1965,* written by Sue Miller Young. Among the pages is a photograph of School No. 18 taken in 1923. It appears as I remember, except the maple trees on either side of that long walk aren't as grand as they had become by 1944 when I walked slowly beneath them on that fateful day.

I remember the stone steps, porch, and cupola. The photo comes to life. In my mind, I see an eight-year-old girl walking alone. She runs up the church steps, hurries across the porch, opens the oak door. She walks down the aisle to take her place next to the pulpit, so happy in her new white dress and patent leather shoes. She smiles. Suddenly, the smile dissolves into tears.

I rush to her side.

"It's all right; don't be scared," I murmur. "This won't be the only time you're afraid, or things go wrong, or your world seems to fall apart or people you love fall short. You have a pretty voice. You can do it."

I wrap her in a hug and say, "Circumstances shape you in ways you cannot know or understand."

And then the scene fades from my mind.

I sit there, my head filling with thoughts. *Things change,* I muse. The old schoolhouse became a church and the church made room for a library. From our experiences and childhood traumas, we change, too. It's up to us, the quality of the change. Will we emerge stronger? Weaker? I have developed values that serve me well. I value work and perseverance. I value the ability to pace myself for the long haul. I value the ability to face my fears.

I had good models.

Endnotes

The Modeling Period

1. Information on Sociologist Morris Massey from: http://www.trevor.help/part-2-series-on-values/
2. Information on The National Foundation for Infantile Paralysis from: http://www.marchofdimes.org